Just Like Her Mother

BOOKS BY JULIA ROBERTS

My Mother's Secret
The Woman on the Beach
The Dilemma
My Daughter's Lies

THE LIBERTY SANDS TRILOGY
Life's a Beach and Then...
If He Really Loved Me...
It's Never Too Late to Say...

Christmas at Carol's
Carol's Singing

Alice in Theatreland
Time for a Short Story

One Hundred Lengths of the Pool

As J.G. Roberts
THE DETECTIVE RACHEL HART SERIES
1. *Little Girl Missing*
2. *What He Did*
3. *Why She Died*

Just Like Her Mother

JULIA ROBERTS

bookouture

Published by Bookouture in 2025

An imprint of Storyfire Ltd.
Carmelite House
50 Victoria Embankment
London EC4Y 0DZ

www.bookouture.com

The authorised representative in the EEA is Hachette Ireland
8 Castlecourt Centre
Dublin 15 D15 XTP3
Ireland
(email: info@hbgi.ie)

Copyright © Julia Roberts, 2025

Julia Roberts has asserted her right to be identified as the author of this work.

All rights reserved. No part of this publication may be reproduced, stored in any retrieval system, or transmitted, in any form or by any means, electronic, mechanical, photocopying, recording or otherwise, without the prior written permission of the publishers.

ISBN: 978-1-83618-693-9
eBook ISBN: 978-1-83618-692-2

This book is a work of fiction. Names, characters, businesses, organizations, places and events other than those clearly in the public domain, are either the product of the author's imagination or are used fictitiously. Any resemblance to actual persons, living or dead, events or locales is entirely coincidental.

*Dedicated to the memory of
Josephine Roberts, 13 August 1926 – 30 January 2025
and
Audrey Maxwell 6 March 1934 – 16 October 2022*

We are all orphans in the end.

PROLOGUE
THURSDAY 16 NOVEMBER 2023

We're clearly not going to be home by 8.30 a.m., the time I'd optimistically suggested in the message I'd posted in our WhatsApp Drummond family group chat, even after arriving on our overnight flight and collecting our luggage at Gatwick Airport in record quick time.

The traffic on the M25 is snaking ahead into the distance as far as the eye can see, with red lights flashing intermittently as drivers apply their brakes after moving a few yards. Stuck as we are in virtually stationary traffic, now might have been the perfect moment to tell my husband the truth, but the tail lights flashing seem to be warning me not to, not yet at least. I'm reluctant to spoil the memory of our fortnight in Barbados, but I'm also aware that my normally even-tempered husband is becoming increasingly agitated.

From the corner of my eye, I'm conscious of Stuart's leg moving: small, swift movements resembling vibrations, almost imperceptible, and only ever with his left leg. Whenever I notice it I'm transported back to my childhood tap dancing classes and the nerve tap that I found so difficult to execute. Tap was never my strong point; in fact, I'm not a natural dancer at all, although I can still throw a few moves on a night out despite my advancing years.

I allow myself a small smile, aware that 'advancing years' is more from Stuart's mum, Eva's, vocabulary than mine. It will be strange arriving home from holiday to an empty house, instead of being greeted by the smell of freshly brewed coffee and Eva's animated face eager to hear all about our latest escapades in far-flung destinations that she had no desire to visit herself.

My eyes flick back to my husband's leg. The motion seems more exaggerated now, suggesting his stress levels are mounting. Our Ford Kuga has barely moved in the past ten minutes and is unlikely to any time soon. The three lanes of vehicles ahead of us bear more than a passing resemblance to the long-stay car park which we vacated around twenty minutes previously.

'I know I'm doing it,' Stuart says.

He's obviously noticed my glance. He places his hand on his thigh to try and control the involuntary movement.

'It's hardly surprising I'm getting annoyed,' he adds, gesturing to the road ahead with his free hand.

I nod in agreement. My husband usually has a very mild temperament, but certain situations stress him out, traffic jams being one of them. Maybe if I'd let him drive it would have delayed his growing irritation. He'd offered, but he looked absolutely shattered after the overnight flight from the Caribbean, and as he's twelve years older than me, I thought the safer option would be for me to take the wheel. I can't be certain, but I think he may have dozed off for a couple of minutes when we were motoring freely on the M23, but he stirred the moment our pace slowed.

'I mean,' he continues, 'what is the point of setting the damn satnav if it doesn't alert you to heavy traffic? We know where we live, we've been there over ten years, we just needed it to direct us to the fastest route with the least amount of traffic. You're flaming useless,' he adds, directing his comment to the screen which is now showing a thick red line indicating very heavy traffic for as far as the eye can see.

'Imagine if it answered you back,' I say, trying to lighten the mood. There's no point telling him that I've just spotted flashing blue lights in the rear-view mirror. He'll find out soon enough when the wailing sirens come within earshot.

'I'm pretty sure it won't be long before these machines do exactly that, what with artificial intelligence and the like. I hope we don't live to regret programming them to be cleverer than us,' he grumbles, sounding exactly like Victor Meldrew from the comedy series *One Foot in the Grave*. When he does eventually become aware of the emergency vehicles, I'm half expecting him to say, 'I don't believe it!'

'You really are starting to sound like a grumpy old man. You should hear yourself.' I laugh, noticing that the distraction of our conversation has at least paused the nervous leg twitch.

'I don't know why you think it's so funny. In the future there probably won't be any need for humans at all. Take those flipping self-service checkouts in Smith's,' Stuart says, losing the initials W and H as he always does when talking about the high street retailer. 'All I wanted was a couple of books to read on the beach. What a flipping palaver! What is the point of having two assistants on standby helping old fossils like me to do the self-service thingy when they could just be behind the counter ringing up the transaction on the till? It probably cost them a fortune to install the machines, which they could have given to people in wages and kept more human beings in employment. It's utter madness! There's something to be said for spending your entire life on the Isle of Skye, like my mum. At least they know that people are more important than machines.'

When Stuart and I first got together, nearly thirty-seven years ago, he'd taken me to meet his parents on the Isle of Skye. We'd only been dating for about three months, and Eva had insisted that we slept in separate rooms, despite Stuart's protestations. I didn't mind that much. Nothing intimate would have happened between us because it wouldn't have felt right in my boyfriend's parents' home. The room I was allocated, one of the seven bedrooms in the house, was tastefully decorated in a cornflower blue, not dissimilar to the colour of Eva's eyes, and had a view over the fields all the way down to the sea. It felt like I was staying in a boutique hotel but without the price tag.

Stuart's mum was probably hoping that I was a passing fancy because she made it abundantly clear that she was desperate for her son to return home after his flirtation with life in the south of England. I suppose she thought that if things became serious between the two of us, there was no way I was going to up sticks and move to the Inner Hebrides. She was right. Beautiful as it is, there is no suitable employment for a would-be actress on the island.

Two years later, she couldn't hide her disappointment when we rang to give her the joyful news that we were engaged, particularly as her only other child, Mari, had moved to Canada when she was eighteen and hadn't returned home for a visit since. Things between us improved slightly when I agreed to get married at Dunvegan Castle, even though it meant all mine and Stuart's friends having to travel such a huge distance. To be honest, it suited me. I've never been a fan of inviting extended family that you haven't seen for years, or casual acquaintances and work colleagues, to the most important day of your life. Better still, the setting was idyllic. That was the first tiny step towards what eventually became a lovely relationship.

'Bloody hell,' Stuart exclaims, bringing me out of my reverie. 'Three police cars and a tow truck by the look of things. We're going to be here for hours.'

'At least there isn't an ambulance,' I say reproachfully, 'which hopefully means it's just a broken-down vehicle rather than an accident.'

My husband crosses his arms over his chest and huffs. His leg has started up again.

It takes us almost an hour to get past the incident.

Stuart and I had kept ourselves entertained while stuck in the queueing traffic by reliving favourite bits from our holiday. It was supposed to have started six weeks ago as it was to celebrate our pearl wedding anniversary. Our honeymoon had been in Barbados, and although the hotel we'd originally stayed in had been knocked down to make way for a luxury apartment building, we'd found a charming hotel a bit further down the same coast.

Crystal Waters had been amazing in handling our rebooking after our original plans had been ruined, and when we arrived, they'd kindly upgraded us to a beachfront room. It wasn't exactly waking to the sound of waves crashing on the shore, more of a gentle lapping with a background of the more dramatic waves breaking on the main beach two hundred metres away. It was just what Stuart and I needed after a year we're both keen to forget.

We're still talking about the highlights of our holiday as I turn off the main road onto our lane.

'My favourite has to be The Five O'Clock Club,' Stuart says.

He's referring to the cocktail and nibbles hour that he attended on the hotel terrace every afternoon while I was getting in some lengths of the swimming pool. At the age of sixty-eight, my husband doesn't have an ounce of fat on him anywhere, despite eating exactly what he wants and indulging in wine with most meals, and of course the holiday cocktails. I, on the other hand, must burn hundreds of calories walking and swimming before I can dare to have an espresso martini or the even more decadent mudslide. He would be chatting away happily to other hotel guests, usually women as he's a bit of a charmer, by the time I made a belated appearance dripping wet and smelling of chlorine. We'd joked most days about him abandoning me for one of his conquests, but we only laughed because we're both confident enough in the strength of our relationship to know it would never happen.

'Are you serious?' I ask, flicking on the indicator and slowing to a halt to wait for a gap in the traffic.

'No.' He laughs. 'I just want to remind you of my popularity with Debbie and Tina. Just keeping you on your toes.'

'Debbie and Tina are welcome to you,' I say as a big enough gap between vehicles opens up, allowing me to swing the car across the opposite carriageway and onto our gravel driveway. I love our house of ten-plus years, but I'd love it more if we could pick it up and move it onto a quiet road with a sea view.

The leylandii hedge we planted all those years ago to help screen us visually from the road and absorb some of the traffic noise is now twenty feet high, so neither of us had spotted our daughter's white BMW in our driveway. I smile at the unexpected sight, and as I park next to her car and turn to Stuart, my eyes mist over.

'Bless her,' I say. 'She didn't want us to get back to an empty house. I'll bet she's got the coffee brewing like your mum used to when she used to house-sit for us. What a thoughtful girl we've raised.'

'I'm proud of both Jemma and Callum and the adults they've become,' Stuart says, squeezing my hand. 'He'll probably pop over later after work.'

I release the boot catch for Stuart to retrieve our suitcases and stride across the drive towards our pale green front door, gravel crunching noisily underfoot. I open the door and call out.

'Jemma! What a lovely surprise!'

There's no reply, and that's when I become aware that there is no aroma of freshly brewed coffee. Call it a mother's instinct, but I instantly sense that something is not right. I move quickly down the tiled hallway and open the door to the kitchen-come-family room where everyone always congregates at our house. I breathe a sigh of relief. My daughter, wearing a pale pink sweatshirt and faded jeans, her dark hair tied up in a ponytail, is sitting with her back to me at the round oak table, her hands wrapped around the mug I always give her when she calls round. Maybe she has her earbuds in, listening to her favourite playlist or audiobook and didn't hear me?

'Jemma darling,' I say in an unnaturally loud voice. 'We're back.'

She turns to face me, and that's when I see that she has tears streaming down her cheeks from red-rimmed eyes. My heart plummets. *Oh God*, I silently pray, *please don't let anything have happened to my mum*. My feet feel like lead weights. I'm rooted to the spot, unable to take the few paces across the kitchen to throw my arms around my girl and pull her into my chest to hug away her troubles as I've done since she was little.

'What's wrong?' is all I can manage to ask in a choked voice.

'Will,' she replies through her tears.

For the briefest moment I experience relief. My mum is not the cause of my daughter's obvious distress. Will is Jemma's boyfriend of three years, but I've never been convinced that they are a perfect couple. Earlier in the year they took the committed step of buying a house together and were seemingly very happy, but for the past couple of months I've been caught between a rock and a hard place.

Callum heard a rumour about Will in the summer which has haunted my thoughts since he told me, whilst swearing me to secrecy. It's been tearing me apart to keep it from Jemma, but Callum made me promise until he could find out if there was any truth in it so as not to cause her unnecessary hurt. Callum's wife, Ellie, doesn't know, and neither does Stuart, which has added to my anxiety as we don't do secrets.

My heart drops, taking in Jemma's tear-streaked face. Either Jemma has found out about it herself or she and Will have had a massive argument about something else. Something has brought her round to our house in floods of tears when she's supposed to be working, but what? If she doesn't already know what Callum and I have been keeping from her, now could be the perfect moment to enlighten her. At least she could then decide what to do next in possession of all the facts.

'Oh Jemma,' I say, starting to move in her direction.

'Don't,' she says, holding up her hand with the flat of her palm facing me. 'I don't know if I'll ever be able to forgive you.'

PART ONE

ONE

TUESDAY 26 SEPTEMBER – SIX WEEKS EARLIER

I'm reminded that late September is not the best time to visit Barbados as I watch the rain sheet down and bounce up off the smooth tarmac of the airport runway. They are in the tail end of hurricane season and the weather can be unpredictable, to put it mildly. We probably wouldn't have chosen this time of the year if we weren't celebrating our pearl wedding anniversary.

Stuart and I were married on 1 October 1993 which even to my ears sounds a lifetime ago! We'd flown out to the Caribbean two days after our wedding in Skye, dropping off the suitcase of warm clothes we'd taken to Scotland in exchange for the already packed suitcase of tropical gear. After the wedding and the road journey, followed by a long flight, we were both shattered when we arrived in Barbados, but it certainly didn't dampen our excitement. Neither of us had strayed beyond Europe previously, so even the temperature and the humidity were new experiences. I don't remember it raining on our honeymoon, but that could be my memory playing tricks on me. It probably won't last long, and hopefully it's not a bad omen for our much-needed holiday.

Today, as our plane touches down, I can already see that

there have been some changes since our last visit thirty years ago. The airport is much bigger and less rustic, but no more efficient. We've had an inordinately long wait for our suitcases, so long in fact that we overheard some people whose patience had run out arranging with their travel reps for their luggage to be sent on to their holiday accommodation. Although keen for our holiday to begin, we're not in any great rush, with two weeks of total relaxation stretching ahead of us. We meander around for an hour or so, accepting the free bottles of water offered by the airport staff along with their apologies for the delay, until the conveyor belt finally splutters into life and starts spilling bags of all shapes and sizes from the top of a chute.

For our special occasion, we've stretched the tight budget and upgraded to a private transfer to our hotel in a luxury car rather than trekking around on a bus making lots of drop-offs at other hotels. It's a pleasant relief to sink into the plush upholstered seats of the air-conditioned interior after the long wait in the arrivals hall. I take a swig of water from the bottle handed to me by our tour operator, savouring the cool liquid before swallowing.

'Well, we made it,' I say, reaching for my husband's hand. 'And it's stopped raining. You know, there were times in the past couple of months when I really thought we might have to cancel.'

'Tell me about it,' Stuart says. 'Mum looked so frail when I arrived in Skye, but the further south we headed, the more she seemed to perk up. I think maybe we're going to need another conversation about her coming to live with us. I don't like her being in that big old house on her own, even with Shona calling in for a couple of hours each morning.'

Shona MacLeod has been a godsend. She's worked for the Drummonds for years, but only helped with the cleaning and gardening twice a week before Stuart's dad, Donald, died. Over the past few years, with his mum's health deteriorating, we'd suggested to Eva that maybe Shona could call in every day apart from Sundays and holidays. We'd expected an argument, but Eva had surprised us, and Shona had readily agreed as employment on Skye can be difficult to come by out of the tourist season; she was thankful for the extra money.

'You know what she'll say,' I respond. 'It's her home. She loves it there looking out on the green fields and the sparkling sea.'

'The sea only sparkles when the sun is out,' Stuart says, shaking his head slightly. 'Which on the Isle of Skye, in fact anywhere down the west coast of Scotland, is not that regular an occurrence. Not like here,' he adds, glancing out of the window of the car at the unbroken blue sky. It's only just visible above the height of the sugar cane fields which we are currently traversing, on a road with more craters than the surface of the moon.

'If you're that worried about her, we can have another conversation about it when we get back, but I wouldn't hold your breath.'

Much as I like Eva, she's a very independent woman and stubborn as a mule. Although age is a privilege denied to so many, I haven't enjoyed watching either of our mums steadily decline over the past decade.

Neither Stuart's mum nor mine are in the best of health, but I guess that's to be expected as they are both in their late eighties. It's nothing major for either of them, just the niggles of old age.

My mum was struck down with a bacterial stomach bug earlier in the year, the sort of thing she normally shrugs off easily as she has the constitution of an ox, but it has taken her months to fully recover this time. She only lives a fifteen-minute drive from both my sister, Juliet, and me, but as usual most of her care has fallen to me. Juliet struggles with the concept of shift work. Because I don't work a regular nine-to-five in my role as an editor on a television news channel, she is of the opinion that it's not a proper job and that I therefore have much more free time. To say I was completely exhausted after four months of cooking, shopping and cleaning for Mum, either before work if I was on a late shift or calling in after work if I'd been on earlies, would be an understatement. I still haven't properly recovered from it all. I don't expect to be particularly bright company for the first part of our holiday, so I'm glad our actual anniversary will fall a few days into our stay.

Stuart's mum's health is more concerning. Having spent most of her life enjoying lengthy walks in the area around Staffin, on the north-east coast of Skye, she had to stop a couple of years ago because she started experiencing frequent headaches and dizzy spells. Numerous tests at her doctor's surgery followed by more in-depth investigations at the hospital haven't really given us any conclusive answers.

We were both nervous about her travelling alone on the train to house-sit for us and feed Wilfie, the cat, something she has done over the past twenty-plus years for our various animals. In the end, Stuart drove up to fetch her, and they broke the journey back with an overnight stop in the Lake District, her second favourite location after the place of her birth.

Eva looked happy and relaxed when she arrived two days ago, and Wilfie gave her a warm welcome, brushing back and forth across her legs, purring loudly, his tail all fluffed up like one of those brushes for dusting behind radiators or Venetian blinds. He's not the friendliest cat in the world, having a particular aversion to our daughter and merely tolerating Stuart, but he loves my mother-in-law, and she loves him back.

Both Jemma and Callum have promised to take it in turns to drop in on Eva daily to make sure she doesn't need anything, so we've come away feeling reassured.

The car has now reached the highest point of our journey from the airport and memories of our honeymoon visit come flooding back to me as I drink in the view down to the ocean on the west coast of the island. I sigh. We need to make the most of this holiday as it's unlikely that we'll be able to afford anything so lavish in the future.

'I know,' Stuart says, clearly misinterpreting my sigh as one of satisfaction. 'It's just as beautiful as I remember it.'

I'm not going to spoil the moment by correcting him over the reason for my sigh. Since Stuart accepted early retirement, I've often found myself wishing that we hadn't burdened ourselves with the financial commitment of a hefty mortgage after Stuart came across his dream home while idly scrolling through Rightmove. We weren't actually looking to move and should probably have considered downsizing if anything as our two children would be university bound soon, but I foolishly agreed to a viewing, and the rest is history. The problem is that I'm now solely responsible for making the monthly instalments so money is always a little tight.

'I'm really looking forward to seeing the hotel,' he continues. 'It looked amazing in the photographs.'

'Yes, it did,' I say attempting to mirror his excitement.

My biggest fear is that the photographs might have been Photoshopped and my hard-earned cash, accepting every overtime shift going at the television news channel I work for, has been spent on accommodation in need of a face-lift. Stop it, Lexi, I tell myself sternly. Everything is going to be amazing.

TWO

Fifteen minutes later, the car draws up to a barrier and a woman in a smart uniform, complete with a peaked cap that perches precariously atop her somewhat unruly hair, approaches the driver's window. Our driver gives her our names, and after checking her list, the security guard smiles broadly.

'Welcome to Crystal Waters,' she says, reaching through the window of her small booth to press a button to raise the barrier. 'I hope you enjoy your stay.'

'I'm sure we will,' Stuart replies enthusiastically, as the car proceeds through the barrier and pulls up under the covered entrance to the hotel, a few metres down the driveway.

Within seconds, the rear doors of the car are opened by more uniformed staff, and we are ushered into a small foyer area with a reception desk running down one side of it. They retrieve our bags from the boot of the car, but not before Stuart has slipped a ten-dollar note into the driver's hand. I'm never sure of the tipping etiquette, but tourism was badly hit during the pandemic, and I wouldn't imagine wages are particularly high, so we always tip if we can.

There are two women sitting at the desk behind computer

terminals, both dressed in peacock-coloured shirts in a fabric with a silky sheen to it. The younger of them gets to her feet, her smile lighting up her face and exposing perfectly even white teeth. She comes from behind the desk to greet us.

'Welcome to Crystal Waters,' she says, nodding her head slightly rather than extending her hand. 'Please follow me and we'll get you checked in.'

I'm not going to lie, I was a little underwhelmed by the hotel entrance, which had obviously been photographed from a very good angle – smoke and mirrors as we call it in television – but as we follow her down three wide stairs into an area with low, comfy seating, my breath is properly taken away. From our vantage point we have a view of the resort against a backdrop of an impossibly blue ocean blending seamlessly into a cloudless blue sky. It's the closest thing to paradise that I've experienced in a very long time. I take a moment to fill my lungs with the warm, slightly moist air, and as I do, I feel the worries of the past few months positively lift from my shoulders. We deserve this. We've been putting money aside for almost two years since Stuart suggested a return trip to Barbados. We've cut back on non-essentials, and I've accepted every additional shift at work to cover sickness and people on annual leave.

'Take a seat,' the receptionist says, indicating the rattan sofas. 'My name is Daphne and I'll be checking you in today. I just need your passports and a credit card to get us started.'

I reach into the interior pocket of my handbag for my purse and our passports, which I hand over.

'Thank you,' Daphne says. 'I've made your dinner reservation for seven thirty in the main restaurant as popular times get booked up early. Is that alright or do you want me to see if there is anything earlier or later?'

'That's fine,' we say in unison.

'Would you like a rum punch or a non-alcoholic fruit punch while you're waiting?' Daphne asks.

'Rum punch for me, please,' Stuart says.

The memory of visiting the Mount Gay Rum Distillery flashes into my mind. My new husband had sampled rather too many of the different types of rum on offer and had spent most of the following day in bed, vowing never to drink the stuff again. He'd been true to his word for a couple of days, sticking to the safer territory of beer and wine, but the plethora of rum-based cocktails on offer soon dimmed the memory of the whirling pits he'd experienced. I raise my eyebrows at him now, a smile playing on my lips.

'Same for me, please,' I say.

'What?' Stuart says as soon as Daphne is out of earshot.

'I was just remembering the distillery tour and the aftermath,' I say.

'I'm surprised you didn't ask for an immediate divorce.' Stuart laughs. 'What an idiot I made of myself. You must have been so embarrassed with me staggering around like an old-time sailor on shore leave.' The laughter catches in his throat, and I watch his expression change as he realises what he has just said. 'Oh God, I'm sorry. That was completely thoughtless of me.'

Stuart knows that my maternal grandfather was a merchant seaman who drank away most of his pay packet and wasn't averse to slapping his wife around if she complained about it. There are some things that are not acceptable in a marriage, and it makes me even more grateful for my kind and caring husband.

'I suppose it's not surprising that Joan isn't much of a drinker having witnessed first-hand how it can cause some people to behave,' he adds, lacing his fingers through mine.

'I don't think the alcohol actually causes the behaviour, it just brings out the behaviour that bullies suppress when they are sober,' I say.

'You're probably right,' Stuart says. He adds, 'Let's face it, you are about most things.'

I give an exaggerated shrug, happy to bring the mood up

again. 'I can't help being a genius. Anyway, I don't want to talk about my mum's attitude towards drinking, especially when I'm about to indulge,' I say, gesturing towards the waiter who is heading towards us with two colourful cocktails on a tray.

'Welcome to Crystal Waters,' the waiter says, placing the drinks on the table in front of us. 'My name is Raheem, and I hope to see you most days for the Five O'Clock Cocktail Club as well as pre- and post-dinner drinks.'

'It's a date,' Stuart says, raising his glass and taking a sip. 'Especially if all your cocktails are as good as this.'

Raheem bows his head and says, 'I will do my best, sir.'

'Is it just me,' I say as we watch him disappear back into the small air-conditioned bar from where he'd emerged moments before, 'but does all this "Welcome to Crystal Waters" spiel make you think of *The Stepford Wives*?'

'Do you think the whole place is staffed by robots?' Stuart suggests.

We're both still laughing at the premise when Daphne approaches with a clipboard and pen in hand.

'It's good to see you are already unwinding and getting into the Caribbean spirit, in more ways than one,' she adds, handing me the clipboard and pen. 'I just need you both to sign where marked, and I'll have Hercules show you to your room.'

Stuart can barely control his laughter, and I think I know why. We have some suitcase weighing scales so that I can pack to our full weight allowance. If I know my husband as well as I think I do, he's thinking what an apt name for a porter who must lug around heavy bags. I clear my throat and fix him with a stare that I hope conveys: *pull yourself together*. Not that I mind really; it's good to see him so relaxed. I just hope that I will be able to unwind too, even if it does take me a few days.

. . .

By the time Hercules – who turned out to be much wirier although equally as strong as his namesake – has shown us to our room and we've each taken a shower to freshen up, it's almost time for dinner.

There are two restaurants at Crystal Waters: the main restaurant, where we'll be having breakfast each morning and dinner tonight, and Driftwood, the beach restaurant open from 11 a.m. for drinks, lunch and reserved tables for dinner.

'We've got a few minutes before we need to be at the restaurant,' I say, glancing at my watch. 'Shall we have a wander to get our bearings?'

Stuart smiles. He knows I'm desperate to walk on the beach and feel the sand between my toes while filling my lungs with ozone-infused air. I've always wanted to live by the sea, but it's not been possible with our career choices, unless we factor a two-hour commute in each direction into our working days. Life's too short for that in my opinion, although it would enable me to indulge my latest passion of listening to audiobooks.

'Okay,' Stuart agrees cautiously. 'But not onto the beach because I've just showered, and I can't stand sand on my feet when I'm wearing shoes,' he says, indicating his olive-green deck shoes.

'I said you should have worn sandals,' I tease. 'Then it wouldn't have been an issue.'

'You always have an answer for everything,' he says, shaking his head. 'And of course I won't try to stop you. But I'm going to save the experience for tomorrow morning before breakfast. We'll undoubtedly be up before dawn if I remember rightly from last time we were here.'

I could be mistaken, but I think I detect a risqué hint in his comment. On our honeymoon, we'd ripped the clothes off each other the moment the door to our room had been closed behind the porter. The lovemaking had been urgent and passionate, and we'd had a repeat performance before breakfast the following morning. I love my husband and still fancy him, but menopause has caused havoc with my libido. I hope he isn't expecting too much too soon. I hope I won't disappoint him.

'Alright,' I concede somewhat reluctantly, ignoring what I've perceived as being suggestive in case I'm being oversensitive. I don't want to spoil the evening. 'We've only got about fifteen minutes before our reservation in any case, so let's just have a mooch around to get our bearings.'

We walk hand in hand through the beautifully tended tropical gardens, the soft scent of night-blooming jasmine hanging in the air, towards the sound of waves breaking on the shore. We can see the waiting staff in Driftwood preparing for evening service, covering the tables in pristine white tablecloths, placing silver cutlery and glasses in situ and lighting candles protected by small hurricane lampshades.

'We should book here for our actual anniversary,' I say.

'Absolutely,' Stuart agrees.

We continue our stroll along the path next to the beach, ocean-front rooms to our right and sun loungers, now free of occupants, neatly arranged in pairs either side of small wooden tables beneath straw parasols.

'Maybe we should bring our towels with us on our pre-breakfast walk to reserve our sunbeds?' I laugh.

'I don't think it's that kind of resort,' he replies, a hint of amusement in his voice.

I think maybe he's remembering the package holiday we'd endured, rather than enjoyed, in Sardinia when our children were small. Our hotel was okay despite the lack of air conditioning in the bedrooms, which was far from ideal in the sweltering mid-August heat, but the space around the pool was extremely limited. This resulted in an undignified scramble to reserve sunbeds each morning at 7 a.m. when the pool area opened. It had been worth it though, to have a front-line view of Callum and Jemma, then only seven and six, having the time of their lives. Although younger, Jemma has always been the more spontaneous and confident of our two. She was in the pool before her brother had got his shorts and T-shirt off, insisting that it wasn't cold despite her teeth chattering. Callum has always been more measured which explains why it took him so long to confide in me. We will have to tell Jemma, and I'll have to tell Stuart, but not until after our holiday. As a parent, I've always put our children's needs before my own, but this is mine and Stuart's time, and I don't want anything to ruin it.

'Alghero?' I ask, raising my eyebrows in question.

He nods. 'We certainly learned the hard way that holidaying in Italy in August is not the best idea. No air conditioning and hardly any room to swing a cat, even outside.' He laughs. 'Not that I would, of course,' he adds, responding to my expression of mock horror.

'I'm sure Wilfie will be relieved to hear that. Happy?' I ask.

'I've been happy for the past thirty-seven years,' he says, stopping mid-stride and pulling me into an embrace. 'Ever since I first laid eyes on you in that pokey little wine bar on Frith Street, I knew you were the one for me.'

Then he kisses me. It's soft and gentle and familiar, nothing like the urgent, passionate kisses of our youth, but twice as meaningful. How lucky we were that our paths crossed in the vast metropolis that is London all those years ago. Two souls destined to find each other.

THREE
WEDNESDAY 27 SEPTEMBER

Stuart had been right about the jet lag. I felt him stir and reached my hand out to tap my watch which was charging on the bedside table. The bright green display informed me that it was 4.45 a.m. Despite my best efforts to close my eyes and clear all thoughts from my mind in an attempt to doze off, further sleep eluded me. I had thought about retrieving my iPad from the top of the chest of drawers to check my work emails. Two things stopped me. Firstly, the possibility of waking Stuart and, secondly, his subsequent annoyance at my inability to switch off from work. We'd eventually reached an agreement over dinner last night that I would only check work emails twice a day. If truth be told, that was twice too often for Stuart, but I feel the need to keep my finger on the pulse of my demanding job, especially with all the current restructuring.

An hour has passed, and I've been lying as still as I can because, judging by the gentle, rhythmic snores coming from the other side of the bed, it appears that my husband is not struggling in the same way. The trouble is, I now need the loo. I wriggle towards the edge of the bed and try to roll out without disturbing him.

'You're awake then,' he says.

'Sorry. I didn't mean to disturb you,' I respond.

'You didn't. I've been awake for ages.'

I could dispute this, citing his snoring as my evidence, but there's no point. He'll just deny it exactly as he does at home when he falls asleep on the sofa while I'm trying to listen to a television drama. Instead, I say, 'Well, we might as well get up and go for that pre-breakfast beach walk then if we're both awake.'

'Or we could stay in bed a bit longer,' he says, his hand reaching out towards me and lazily grazing my thigh with his fingertips.

I love my husband as much as I ever have, but intimacy with him is something that has become less and less frequent over the past couple of years. Apparently, if all the television programmes and magazine articles that bombard us with information about the menopause are to be believed, loss of libido is one of the most common problems faced by women at this stage of their lives. Being commonplace doesn't make it any easier to deal with, and I've found myself making all sorts of excuses to try and avoid having sex with a man I still love so deeply. I must admit, I was relieved last night to discover that Stuart had fallen asleep while I was in the bathroom taking my make-up off and cleaning my teeth. He'd been very tactile while we'd sat on the sofas under an inky blue sky speckled with stars, sipping our cocktails so expertly prepared by Raheem. I hadn't needed to find an excuse then, but I'm glad to have one now.

'I'm desperate for a wee,' I say, getting up out of the bed and groping my way towards the bathroom in the darkness. I flick the switch to turn on the light, my eyes blinking against the unfamiliar brightness. As I close the door behind me, I'm sure I hear Stuart say, 'Of course you are.'

Whilst I'm certain that Stuart still loves me as much as I love him, I do sometimes worry that our lack of intimacy might eventually drive a wedge between us. Maybe being away from the relentless pressure of work and the day-to-day family dramas will give me space to relax and enjoy lovemaking again.

Even if I was going to change my mind, it's too late by the time I emerge from the bathroom a couple of minutes later. Stuart is out of bed and dressed in T-shirt and cargo shorts and is slipping his feet into his Birkenstock sandals. He's opened the curtains to reveal semi-darkness, but a hint of pale orangey pink is creeping into the sky as the dawn threatens to break. I reach for a bright yellow cotton sundress from my side of the wardrobe and a bikini from the top drawer of the dresser.

Two minutes later we're on the path that takes us down to Driftwood. Unsurprisingly, no one is around, but the tables are now stripped of their linen and all signs of the finery from the previous evening, leaving a much more rustic appearance. We cross the restaurant then kick our sandals off before dropping down onto the soft sand which feels cool underfoot at this early hour. At this part of the beach, it's only a few steps to reach the water gently lapping at the shore, although further along the beach is much broader and the waves more powerful, as we'd observed from the terrace yesterday evening. There's something about a newly washed beach that I've always loved. With each tide comes the chance to start afresh. If only life itself was like that without the baggage of what has gone before.

'Watch out for the coral,' Stuart says over his shoulder.

He's walking ahead of me, and I just heard him curse, so presumably the warning comes from a place of experience.

'Thanks for the heads up,' I say, trying to extend my stride to walk in his footsteps and minimise the risk. After a few steps I give up. Stuart is six foot two and long-limbed while I'm five foot three at a pinch.

Thankfully, both our children are more like their dad in their physical stature, but neither has his colouring. Stuart's strawberry blond hair and fair skin tone are an indication of his

Scottish heritage, which is why my husband will be plastering on factor 50 sunscreen when we get back from our walk and reapplying at intervals throughout the day. An application of once-a-day factor 30 will be fine for me, especially as I'll be under the shade of a parasol reading one of my books throughout the hottest part of the day. I'm so looking forward to completely relaxing. It's been a tough few months worrying about our mums, and work hasn't exactly been a barrel of laughs either.

Most of my emails lately have been about the 'restructuring' of our department. I hate the term restructuring which almost inevitably means redundancies. Editors are essential to keep the news we are broadcasting current, along with any developing stories. I'm in the gallery for the live shows, and I also need to be keeping an eye on social media and other news outlets for breaking stories, as well as checking in with reporters out in the field. It's very full on, and I sometimes wonder if I'm getting a bit too old for the intensity of the job, particularly the social media angle where I'm making crucial decisions on what is real and what is fake news. It's unlikely that I'll be made redundant, but nobody's completely safe with the new American owners on a cost-cutting drive. To be honest, if they offered me a decent redundancy package, one that would cover paying off my mortgage, I'd bite their hand off.

We've now reached the end of the wide powdery stretch of sand. If we want to go any further, we're going to have to time a quick dash into the next small bay in between the waves crashing onto the shore.

'How daring do you feel?' Stuart asks, the challenge clear to see in his eyes.

'I'm game if you are. What's the worst that can happen?' I say, giving a slight shrug of my shoulders, acting braver than I feel.

. . .

It was worth getting drenched, I think, as I watch my husband making his way back across the restaurant with a glass of orange juice in each hand. He doesn't look anywhere near to his sixty-eight years, either in his clothes or out of them. I feel the heat of a flush creep up my neck.

We'd successfully navigated between the waves on our way past the rocky outcrop to get to the next stretch of beach on our early morning walk. We'd continued along to the next barrier of rocks where we'd sat in the comfortable silence of two people who've known each other a long time and watched the sun make its dazzling appearance on the horizon, beginning its ascent into a cloudless sky with the promise of a beautiful day ahead. What neither of us had realised was that the tide was on its way in. When we got back to the divide between the two beaches, there was less time to make our dash between the waves, and we got caught with the full force of one, soaking us both to the skin.

We got back to our room, laughing at our stupidity in getting caught by the wave and looking like a pair of drowned rats. We'd both gone straight into the bathroom to strip off our wet clothes rather than dripping all over the bedroom floor, and in that confined space, feeling relaxed at the comedy of our situation, I hadn't had the time or the desire to think of excuses not to make love with my husband. It was urgent and passionate from both sides, almost as though we needed the intimacy to rediscover each other. Lying next to Stuart in the afterglow, with only the sheet covering our nakedness, I realised how much I'd missed that part of our relationship. I'm hopeful that getting over this psychological hurdle will allow us, in time, to fully rediscover each other physically.

'Your orange juice, madam,' Stuart says, placing the glass in front of me and bowing slightly from the waist.

'You idiot,' I mutter, taking a long swig of the freshly squeezed juice.

'Thank you for this morning,' he says, his eyes connecting with mine. 'More of the same tomorrow?' he asks, raising his eyebrows.

For some reason, I find his words irritating. Thanking me for having sex with him and then either expecting or hoping for more of the same has spoiled the whole episode for me. Why can't he just enjoy the moment? It now feels like he's pressuring me to have sex with him again. I shift uncomfortably in my seat, acutely aware that the issue surrounding the physical side of our relationship is not yet fully resolved.

Is it all down to me? Probably. I'm always so damn busy sorting everyone else's problems I have a tendency to put mine on the back burner rather than facing up to them. I'm wondering how to respond without sounding arsy when my phone vibrates in my crossbody bag. I've got it on silent because I have an aversion to people who have telephone conversations in restaurants. To buy myself some time before replying to Stuart, and possibly bursting his happiness bubble, I unzip my bag and steal a quick glance at my phone screen.

A message from Jemma lights up my screen, starting with the words, *Hi, Mum, call me when you get this. I called round to see Nana this morning, but...*

I feel the hairs on the back of my neck stand up. I'm pretty sure Jemma would not be messaging me on holiday about something trivial. She prides herself on her ability to deal with most situations, often only revealing there was a problem once she's found a solution. I suspect there are some things I will never know about my daughter's private life, and that's probably how it should be. My mum certainly doesn't know everything about me.

'Is everything okay?' Stuart asks, eyes down as he butters a slice of toast.

'I'm not sure. It's from Jemma. She wants me to call,' I say, pushing my chair back from the table.

I don't tell him that she mentioned his mum. It could be nothing, and if so, it's pointless worrying my husband.

'I'll just pop up to the reception area and give her a quick call,' I add, trying to keep the concern from my voice. 'I noticed yesterday that I have more bars of signal up there.'

'Do you want me to come?' he asks, lowering the piece of toast he was about to take a bite out of back onto his side plate.

'No, I'm sure everything's fine,' I lie, already experiencing the churn of anxiety in my stomach. I notice Devonia, the waitress allocated to us at dinner last night, approaching. 'Can you order for me?' I ask. 'I'll have the eggs Florentine. I won't be long.'

I smile at Devonia as I hurry past her on my way out of the restaurant and make my way up the stairs, phone in hand. I open the whole message as soon as I'm on level ground and my heart misses a beat.

Hi Mum, call me when you get this. I called round to see Nana this morning, but she didn't answer the door when I knocked, so I let myself in. Try not to worry, but she'd had a fall and was sitting propped up against a kitchen cupboard and was clearly in a bit of pain. I called 111 and they said to call 999 for an ambulance because of her age. We're just waiting for it now. Nana didn't want to bother you on your holiday, but I said I thought you should know. Love you xx

FOUR

Jemma picks up on the third ring, sounding very far away. Well, I suppose she is.

'Mum?' she says.

I can hear the relief in her voice across the four thousand miles that separate us.

'Hi love. Of course you did the right thing in contacting me,' I say, wanting to immediately reassure Jemma. 'Has the ambulance arrived yet? What did they say? Are they taking Nana to the hospital?' I realise I'm firing questions at my daughter like bullets from an automatic weapon, so I add, 'Sorry, take your time, it was just a bit of a shock to get your message.'

'You took ages to ring,' Jemma says, sounding a little odd. Do I hear a hint of reproach in her voice? 'I sent it two hours ago.'

'Oh? It only just pinged through. The signal is a bit hit and miss, but it's okay here in reception. So, where are you now?'

'I'm at the hospital. The paramedics were a bit concerned with how pale Nana looked so put an oxygen mask on her and they've brought her in for some tests,' Jemma says. I can detect a wobble in her voice. Maybe it was worry rather than reproach I heard previously.

'What sort of tests?' I gently probe, my fingers tightening around my phone.

'They don't know if she might have banged her head when she fell. She seemed a bit confused when I asked her and was equally non-committal with the paramedics. They did a bit of feeling around, asking her what was hurting, and they suspect she might have fractured her wrist attempting to break her fall. I'd been holding that hand, Mum, squeezing it to reassure her that help was on its way, and she never said a word about it hurting. What if I've made it worse?'

I'm aware that Jemma is becoming emotional. I need to calm her down as I haven't got all the facts yet.

'Of course you haven't, Jem. Nana would have said if it was hurting her.' We both know this is a lie as Eva would never want to upset either of her precious grandchildren. 'So,' I say, quickly moving the focus away from Jemma, 'are they doing X-rays just now?'

'Yes. They wheeled her straight off to the X-ray department after checking her in.'

'At least it sounds as though they're looking after her well,' I say before taking a breath and adding, 'And how are you holding up, Jem? Is anyone there with you?'

'If by anyone you mean Will, then no, I haven't been able to reach him. But I messaged Callum and he's on his way.'

'Good,' I reply, feeling relief that it is Jemma's brother who is on his way to be with her at the hospital rather than her boyfriend. The situation I find myself in, knowing what I think I do about Will, but having been sworn to secrecy by Callum, is becoming untenable. I hate keeping this a secret from both Jemma and her dad. 'You shouldn't have to deal with this on your own. I need to go and let Dad know what's happened, but we'll come up to reception straight after our breakfast and call you back for any updates.'

'Okay,' my daughter replies before ending the call.

I take a deep breath, trying to process the information Jemma has just shared. I need to decide how serious the situation is. Should we attempt to get on the next flight home in case Eva takes a turn for the worse, or do we wait for the result of the X-rays and any further tests the hospital deems necessary? We've saved so hard for this special holiday, but if there's even the remotest possibility that Eva won't pull through, we'll have to return home. I'd never forgive myself if anything happened to her while we're lounging on some faraway beach.

I make my way back down the stairs to the restaurant much more slowly than the speed I'd ascended them ten minutes ago. A queue of guests waiting to be shown to their tables has formed at the desk, and there are a few disgruntled mutterings as I ease my way past. Devonia is standing by our table with a plate in her hand. I'm guessing it's probably my eggs Florentine, and she and Stuart are deliberating whether it should go back to the kitchen to be kept warm. I raise my hand to catch my husband's attention, plastering a smile on my face. Our waitress turns her head in my direction and then lays the plate down just as I arrive back at the table.

'Perfect timing,' I say.

'I can take it back to the kitchen to be warmed up if you like,' Devonia says.

'It'll be fine, thank you,' I reply, slipping into my chair, picking up my napkin from where I'd abandoned it and laying it across my lap.

She smiles and heads off in the direction of the queue I've just bypassed, collecting some guests and showing them to their table in the increasingly busy restaurant.

'You were a long time,' Stuart says. 'Is everything okay?'

'Let's eat our breakfast before it does actually get cold, and then I'll tell you about it.'

My husband doesn't need to be told twice. He loves his food and has demolished his full English with fried plantain as the Caribbean twist within a few minutes. I've barely touched my eggs Florentine despite it looking and tasting delicious from the small amount I've managed to swallow because of the tightness in my throat.

Stuart sits back in his seat and pats his non-existent stomach.

'I was ready for that after our energetic morning,' he says.

The only thing missing from his remark is a knowing wink, which might have been coming until he clearly notices my barely touched food. The concern in his eyes is evident as he raises them to meet mine.

'Something's wrong. What was Jemma messaging about?'

I lay my knife and fork side by side on my plate and take a sip of black coffee to wet my mouth. It feels as dry as a desert.

'Well, it seems Eva had a fall this morning.'

The panic is instant in my husband's eyes.

'Is she alright?' he asks.

'Jemma went round to ours when Eva didn't answer her mobile and found her sitting on the kitchen floor propped up against the cabinets. She called 111 who in turn advised 999 because of your mum's age. They've taken her to the hospital with a suspected broken wrist.'

'Jesus! I knew we shouldn't have left her on her own in the house,' Stuart says, a pink flush of anger colouring his cheeks.

His remark is directed at me. I'd backed Eva when she said she didn't need to be babysat. 'I live on my own for eleven months of the year, Stuart,' she'd said when he'd suggested that maybe our kids could take it in turns to stay with her at our house while we were away. 'What would be the point of me travelling all the way down from Skye to look after the house and Wilfie if Jemma and/or Callum need to be here too?' she'd demanded. 'I want to still feel useful in my old age. Surely you wouldn't want to deny me that?'

Once Eva had gone to bed, tired after her journey but otherwise well, Stuart and I had discussed it. He admitted that he'd been shocked by his mum's frail appearance when he'd arrived to drive her down to ours. 'I wish now I'd just said no to her coming. She's deteriorated quite rapidly since we went up in July,' he'd said. I'd talked him round, sticking up for Eva needing to still have a purpose in life, and he'd reluctantly agreed. I'm now on the receiving end of an accusatory glare.

'Let's not overreact. This could have happened anywhere and with more serious consequences,' I say gently while reaching across the table to take his hand in mine. 'She could have had a fall outside in her own garden shortly after Shona had left for the day and been lying there undiscovered for hours. At least Jemma was on hand to call the emergency services.'

I'm saying this to comfort my husband, but also to appease my guilty conscience. I'd come up with the idea of Jemma and Callum popping in from time to time during our fortnight away, and despite his reservations, Stuart had eventually agreed to it. Eva had been more difficult to persuade, but I'd pleaded with her, telling her how much Stuart and I had been looking forward to the return trip to Barbados and how he was digging his heels in about leaving her alone in our home. 'Just for you, then,' she'd whispered conspiratorially when I'd taken her early morning cup of tea up to her room. 'He's always been a worrier, that boy,' she'd added.

I'm not sure I'd describe my husband as a worrier, but he has a kind and considerate nature that has certainly softened some of my forceful edges over the years.

'I suppose,' Stuart concedes. 'But what do we do now?'

'Let's head up to reception. I told Jemma we'd give her a call back once I'd filled you in on everything and there would be more likelihood of some test results.'

'Why not call from our room?' he asks. 'I'm not sure it's a conversation I want to have in a public place.'

'The signal is stronger there,' I remind him.

He nods as though he's just remembered how hit and miss it was when we'd rung Jemma and Callum last night to let them know we'd arrived safely. It had been too late to call Eva because of the delay in getting our luggage and the time difference, but I wish now we'd spoken to her from the airport. I don't allow my thoughts to spiral into 'what if' territory as I follow my husband across the restaurant and back up the stairs I descended only ten minutes previously. Halfway up the stairs he stops abruptly.

'Do you think we should call Mari?' he asks.

To be honest I have no idea if we should worry his sister over in Canada at this stage. True, her mum has been admitted to hospital, but it seems a little premature until we've got the results of the X-rays and any other tests they perform. Eva's had medical issues for over a year now, and Mari hasn't shown much inclination to come and visit.

'Let's talk to Jemma first and see how the land lies,' I say. 'There doesn't seem to be much point in worrying her unnecessarily. After all, there's not a lot she can do from the wilds of Canada.'

'About the same as we can from the Caribbean, I'd say,' Stuart mutters.

His remark is unkind and out of character, but I don't respond, putting it down to fear of the unknown. He turns away from me and continues up the stairs to reception. I follow, silently sending up a prayer. *Please let her be okay*.

FIVE

Stuart hasn't spoken much all day, but not at all since we arrived in the departure lounge of Grantley Adams Airport for our flight home after being fast-tracked through check-in and security. His leg is vibrating involuntarily, and he's alternating between staring off into the middle distance and dropping his face into his hands in a gesture of despair.

I've tried to keep the mood positive since our phone call with Jemma, but without much success. We hastily packed the suitcases that we'd unpacked less than twenty-four hours previously, accompanied by the squeals of happy holidaymakers enjoying the glorious sunshine. It doesn't feel fair.

Jemma had tried to dissuade us from flying straight back to the UK to be with Eva, saying that she and Callum were both now at the hospital with their nana.

'Honestly, Mum,' she'd said, 'there's nothing you and Dad can do for Nana that me and Callum can't. It was a clean break to the bones in her wrist, so they haven't got to reset it or anything. She hasn't even got to have a cast on it, just an elastic support with metal in to keep the bones aligned so that they can mend. Nothing else is broken, and she's in good spirits. They've told me and Callum that they're only going to keep her in overnight for observation because of her age.'

I knew what Jemma was saying made perfect sense and that it probably wasn't necessary for us to fly back, but neither Stuart nor I would have been able to relax and enjoy ourselves, which was the whole point of the holiday. There would always be that little voice in my head asking *What if*. I think Stuart had reached his decision while we were still on the phone to Jemma that we would get the earliest possible flight back, and I wasn't going to try and change his mind.

Jemma had one more attempt at preventing us from cutting our holiday short. 'Nana will be furious with you both, you know that for a fact,' she'd said.

Of course, we knew she was right, but sometimes you must put your own feelings ahead of others.

The hotel staff have been brilliant. They contacted our Virgin Atlantic rep, who in turn managed to get us on the evening flight and arranged our pick-up for mid-afternoon. The hotel even offered to pack for us, but we declined, believing that keeping busy would take our minds off worrying.

I'd forced myself to eat some lunch as I was starting to feel a little light-headed having skipped breakfast, but Stuart just toyed with his food.

My phone vibrates in my pocket, Jemma's picture appearing, and I quickly answer.

'Hi Jem, we're all checked in and just waiting for boarding to start.'

'It's not too late to change your minds,' Jemma says. 'It seems crazy to come all the way home when Nana is fine. They gave her a mild sedative so that she'll get a decent night's sleep, and she was barely able to keep her eyes open to eat her dinner, even though dessert was her favourite.'

Despite the seriousness of the situation, I allow myself a smile. I can't think of much worse than rice pudding with a dollop of jam on the top, but maybe that's because it brings back memories of disgusting overcooked school dinners. My pet hate was Tuesday's offering of steak and kidney pudding with suet pastry the colour and weight of a wet dishcloth.

'I'm glad she managed to eat something. It's surprising how quickly older people get weak if they haven't been able to eat for a while,' I say, thinking of my own mum earlier in the year when everything she was eating went straight through her.

She'd been convinced that her 'time was up' and it was awful watching her waiting to die. Funnily enough, it had been Callum's news that he and Ellie were expecting their first baby, Mum's first great-grandchild, which had caused her to rally, although she did experience a setback when Ellie miscarried at fourteen weeks.

Eva had been over the moon with the news too. She already had two great-grandsons, but she'd yet to meet them. She's only met her granddaughter, Fleur, twice as she'd been born after Mari had moved to Canada. The move had devastated Eva, and I don't think she has ever truly forgiven Mari for denying her the pleasure of being around her granddaughter. It had, though, worked in my favour. When Stuart's dad, Donald, had died, Eva turned to me for support, having held me at a distance for most of the fifteen years that Stuart and I had been together. We grew closer and closer, with her often confiding in me before her own flesh and blood. Without realising it, I'm sending up another little prayer that Eva will be okay and will be around to meet any future children Callum and Ellie may have.

'Are you still there, Mum?' Jemma says.

'Oh yes, sorry. I just allowed my mind to wander off for a moment with you mentioning rice pudding. Don't ask,' I say before she has the chance to. 'And it's too late to change our minds about coming home. I don't think the other passengers would be best pleased at having the flight delayed because two old fogies want their bags taken off. We must have been last to check in so our luggage would have been chucked in the hold first.'

There is silence from Jemma's end of the call.

'Besides, Dad and I both agree that it's the right thing to do.'

'Okay,' Jemma says eventually. 'It's your call.'

I smile. I can hear the tight acceptance in our daughter's voice. She doesn't agree with what we're doing but knows she won't change our minds.

'Are you and Callum still at the hospital?' I ask.

'No. Cal left while Nana was eating, and the nurse didn't seem too keen for me to stay beyond visiting hours. I've given her my number, and I've got the number for the nurses' station which she said I can call at any time for updates as it's manned or should that be "peopled" all night.'

It's a relief to hear that my daughter's sense of humour hasn't deserted her after such a traumatic day. Apart from their colouring, our children resemble their father in appearance, but I'm pleased to say they have both inherited my sharp wit.

'I hate to have to ask, but would you mind popping in on your way home to feed Wilfie? Poor thing. He's so sensitive, he'll know something's not right.'

'Are we talking about the same cat?' Jemma asks. 'The one that bites my hand when I go to stroke him. Fortunately for you and him, Cal offered to feed him on his way home. I can call in in the morning if you like?'

I can hear the reluctance in her voice.

'No need. Our house is between the airport and the hospital. We'll drop our bags and feed Wilfie on the way to see Nana.'

'Well, if I can't persuade you to change your minds, have a safe flight and let me know the moment you land.'

'Will do. And Jemma...'

'Yeah?'

'Thanks for today,' I say, a slight tremble in my voice.

I'm proud of the way our daughter has handled the emergency, particularly as she's seemingly had little or no support from her useless boyfriend. Not for the first time, I wonder what our beautiful, clever, hardworking girl ever saw in Will apart from his looks.

It makes my stomach churn to think about how Jemma will react when she finds out that her boyfriend might not be so 'perfect' after all.

'Nana will be fine, Mum,' Jemma says, dismissing the thanks. 'She's as tough as old boots. You and Dad need to stop worrying. See you tomorrow.'

The line goes quiet, and I breathe a small sigh.

'Was that Jemma?' Stuart asks. His voice sounds muffled which is hardly surprising as he's sitting forward in his seat with his face resting in his hands, his fingers gently massaging the area just above his eyebrows as though he has a headache. He's not the only one, but I'm hoping to sleep a bit on the plane, particularly as the airline has very kindly upgraded us to business class. 'Any change?' he adds.

'They gave her a mild sedative and she's sleeping,' I reply. 'Jemma's given the nurses' station her number if they need to call during the night.'

Stuart grunts, and silence falls between us again.

SIX

My hope of falling asleep on the plane as soon as we were in the air didn't materialise. Despite the extra wide seats and footrests, I couldn't seem to get comfortable. I gazed out of the window for the first hour or so watching the sky turn from blue to shades of orange, the sun glinting off the silver wings of the aircraft, but once night-time engulfed us, I pulled the window blind down to shut it out. There was something almost suffocating about the endless velvety black sky, with no little pinpricks of light from houses far below, as we flew over the Atlantic Ocean.

Dinner was served with wine in real glasses rather than plastic ones and proper metal cutlery which would normally have impressed me, but I couldn't get remotely excited by it. Nor could I focus on the movie I selected after scrolling through the choices twice. Stuart eventually emailed his sister to tell her their mum was in hospital despite us initially agreeing that there wasn't much she could do from Canada. He hadn't heard anything back from her before we boarded the flight, but at least she was aware of the issue. If something were to happen to Eva, Mari had as much right to be with her mum as Stuart did. Whether or not she travels to the UK will be her decision.

In terms of distance, Mari lives much further away from the Isle of Skye than we do, but when it comes to travel time there's not much in it. If we drive from Berkshire it takes us a good twelve hours with no stops and light traffic. Mari can be back on Scottish soil in around seven hours. It's then a short flight from Glasgow to Skye, followed by a taxi ride, but Mari has rarely chosen to return since her departure forty-two years ago. Although my mum and I don't always see eye to eye, I can't imagine not being in her physical presence for more than a week, unless we're away on holiday, so I find the idea of years without personal contact somewhat baffling and, to be honest, a little sad.

I finally doze off at around 4 a.m. UK time, so just about midnight in Barbados, and am woken a couple of hours later when the cabin lights go on for the crew to start serving breakfast. I take the offered croissant but pass on the scrambled eggs, as does Stuart. We both accept the black coffee though.

'Did you manage to sleep?' I ask.

'On and off,' he replies. 'Probably about the same as you. An eight-and-a-half-hour journey has never felt so long, and we're not done yet.'

I place my hand over his on the armrest separating our seats.

'Not long now,' I say, keeping my voice calm, which belies my true feelings. What if Eva has taken a turn for the worse in the long hours we've been in the air? Would Stuart ever be able to forgive me for taking Eva's side and persuading him to come away on holiday?

'I'm sorry,' he says, turning his hand over to squeeze mine and angling his head so that our eyes meet.

'You're feeling anxious,' I say, not admitting that I am too. 'It's only to be expected.'

'No, I mean for blaming you for us coming away and leaving Mum on her own. She's a stubborn old bird, and you're right that she could have had a fall at home. It's these damn dizzy spells she's been having. I just don't get why they haven't found out what's been causing them,' he says, irritation creeping into his voice. 'Thank goodness Shona persuaded her that driving on the island roads isn't a good idea any more. She could have blacked out and ended up in a peat bog or off a cliff.'

My husband is being somewhat melodramatic, but I don't care. It's much better for him to let his emotions out rather than bottling them up.

'I feel really bad for the kids as well,' he adds. 'It doesn't feel right that they're having to deal with this.'

'They're fully grown adults, Stuart, not teenagers. Jemma seemed completely in control of things and made all the right decisions. And Cal must have left work early, which, as we both know, goes against the grain, to support his sister. I'm bloody proud of the pair of them.'

Stuart nods in agreement.

'They're good kids. We've done a decent job in raising them.'

I wouldn't normally turn on my mobile phone until we've cleared passport control, but circumstances today demand otherwise. Moments after the wheels of our Boeing 737 make contact with the tarmac and the applied brakes reduce our rapid speed, I reach into my handbag for my phone as one of the flight crew makes the usual announcement, welcoming us to London and requesting that we all remain seated until the captain has turned off the seatbelt sign.

I press the top button on the side of my mobile and a white apple with a bite out of it appears in the middle of the black screen. When it requests my passcode, I hold the device up, hoping for facial recognition, but nothing happens. I tap in the four digits of my code wondering if I really am that unrecognisable after the stress of the preceding hours and an almost sleepless night. A visual message alert from Jemma pops up almost immediately, and I'm relieved that I have it set to silent when I see the first few words: *Don't stop by the house, Mum...* There's no point alarming Stuart unnecessarily, but I feel a dreadful sense of foreboding as I open the message with shaking hands. There's no *Hi, Mum* or *Hope you had a good flight*.

> *Don't stop by the house, Mum. You and Dad need to get to the hospital ASAP. They called around five thirty and said Nana had buzzed for the nurse during the night complaining of a sharp pain in her head. They gave her some painkillers, but when the nurse went to check on her an hour later, she was still in a lot of pain. That's when they called me. Cal and I have just arrived at the hospital. I'll message again when I've seen Nana, but I think you should come straight here from the airport xx*

I check to see what time the message was sent. 6.19 a.m. That's over an hour ago. My heart is pounding. The plane is still taxiing towards its allocated stand and is moving at what feels like a snail's pace. Because we're in the front section of the plane, we should be able to disembark quite quickly, but there's bound to be a queue at passport control despite Stuart and I both having newish passports which means we can use the electronic gates.

I cast a sideways glance at my husband. He's busy gathering his belongings from under the seat in front of him and placing his used headset in the seatback pocket, so doesn't appear to have noticed me checking my phone. I decide not to mention anything to him until we're through passport control. We'll probably have to leave our bags if our last experience of Heathrow is anything to go by. We landed after a trip to New York, and it took more than an hour for our cases to make an appearance on the baggage carousel. Judging by the urgency in the tone of Jemma's message, we don't have the luxury of time.

We'll have to let someone in authority know about the bags though or they will be seen as unattended and could be deemed a security threat, maybe even destroyed in a controlled explosion. All these thoughts are running through my mind when I feel my phone vibrate in my hand. It's another message from Jemma.

Are you down yet?

I type out a one-word response – *Just* – as the plane jolts to a halt and the sound of people releasing their seatbelts fills the air. Stuart is on his feet, reaching our hand luggage bags down from the overheard lockers like a whippet out of the traps on race day. I get to my feet too, glad to stretch out after hours of sitting as another message flashes up on my phone screen. This time Stuart does notice.

'Is that the kids?' he asks nodding his head towards the phone.

The cabin doors are not open yet, and there's a crush of people blocking the aisles. We're not going anywhere for a while.

'Just O2 welcoming me to the UK,' I say after glancing down at the screen. It's a lie. The message is Jemma again and simply says: *Call me when you can.*

SEVEN

THURSDAY 28 SEPTEMBER

There was no queue at passport control after all, but in fairness Stuart and I were among the first from our flight to arrive after striding along the walkways at a very brisk pace. There was no one in front of us placing their passport down on the glass the wrong way round or not looking up into the camera, and no technical hitch with the gate itself. As soon as we've cleared the arrivals hall where the signs stipulate you are not permitted to stand, I pull Stuart to one side.

'It wasn't O2,' I say in response to the question in his eyes. 'Jemma wants us to call.'

The flash of panic in his eyes is unmistakable.

'Has something happened to Mum?' he asks.

While I'm waiting for Jemma to answer my call, I quickly explain to Stuart about Eva having a disturbed night with a bad headache and how the hospital rang Jemma to let her know. After six rings it goes to voicemail.

'Hi Jem, it's Mum,' I say. 'We're just through passport control and we're going to head for the long-stay car park once we've let an official know that we've got an emergency and haven't got time to wait for our bags. We should be with you in forty-five minutes or so. Can you WhatsApp me the name of the ward Nana is on, please?'

Less than fifteen minutes later we are at the exit of the car park waiting for the barrier to lift, and Stuart is moaning that we'll need to stop for petrol because he didn't fill up before we parked due to the heavy traffic making us late. My phone rings. It's Jemma. I decide not to put her on speakerphone and instead press the handset close to my ear.

'Hi Jem, we're just coming out of the car park,' I say. 'How is she?'

There is a pause and then a sniff before my daughter speaks in a shaky voice. 'She's gone, Mum,' she manages, before sniffing again and adding, 'Nana has died.'

Somehow, I suppress a gasp. Stuart is driving, and we're on a dual carriageway with no immediate place to stop. There's an expression about blood turning to ice when you suffer extreme shock, but in all my fifty-six years, I've never experienced it... until now. An icy paralysis grips my heart, spreading rapidly through my body. I swallow. Our daughter is clearly distressed, but I must be careful what I say.

'Okay darling,' I say. 'We'll be with you as soon as we can.'

'Is Dad driving?' Jemma asks, seeming to understand my lack of a more comforting response.

'Yes, that's right. We just need to make a quick stop for petrol then we'll head straight there.'

'What on earth are you going to say, Mum? I just can't believe this has happened. Poor Dad.'

All I want is to hold my darling girl in my arms and let her give way to the emotion she is undoubtedly feeling. Jemma displays to the world a persona of strength and always being in control, something else she has inherited from me. I suspect she developed this hard outer coating around the time that she had a falling out with Nicola, her best friend at junior school. All the other children in their class took Nicola's side in the disagreement, and for a while, none of them spoke to Jemma. My daughter pretended she didn't care, but as her mum, I knew she was terribly upset by the whole experience. Like most arguments at that age, it was soon forgotten by Nicola, and they were best pals again within a couple of weeks, but it had a profound and lasting effect on Jemma. It was as though she'd made a promise to herself that no one would ever see weakness in her again. But deep beneath Jemma's outer shell there lies a softness and vulnerability that even I only rarely see. I can hear it in her voice now.

Up ahead is an illuminated sign for a petrol station. I know Stuart has been casting me sideways glances wanting to know what Jemma has been saying, so I gesture towards the garage and say, 'We might as well fill up here.'

He pulls off the road onto the brightly lit forecourt, and I end my call with Jemma by reiterating, 'We'll be there as soon as we can.'

'So, what's happening then?' Stuart asks, stopping next to the pump for unleaded fuel and turning the engine off. 'I couldn't really tell from your end of the conversation.'

I need a few moments to plan how I'm going to impart this devastating news to my husband.

'I'll get us both a coffee while you fill her up.' I'm already halfway out of the car to avoid discussion. 'Pull into one of the parking spaces in front of the shop when you've finished,' I say, indicating them vaguely with my left hand while striding purposefully towards the shop. 'That way you won't be blocking the pump while I'm waiting to pay,' I add, noticing the queue at the cashier's till.

I'm not certain that Stuart heard the last part of my sentence delivered over my shoulder. It might have been lost in the swoosh of the automatic doors as I approached them, but hopefully he got the gist of what I was saying. He won't be in a fit state to drive once I've delivered the bombshell about Eva. It will be easier to swap places if we're in a proper parking space, although I'm not sure I'll be much more capable of tackling the M25 than him, I think, noticing the shake in my hand as I reach out to select a flat white on the coffee machine.

'You need to put the cup under first,' a friendly male voice from behind me says. 'You'll be wearing it otherwise.'

'Oh, yes, of course,' I say, quickly sliding the paper cup onto the metal grid just as the machine begins depositing steaming liquid. 'Thank you,' I add, turning to see a man who looks to be around Callum's age. 'I was miles away.'

'Are you okay?' he asks, genuine concern evident in his voice. 'You look as though you've seen a ghost.'

Without warning, a tear starts to trickle from the corner of my eye which I brush away briskly.

'Not really,' I reply, shaking my head slightly as I try to regain control. 'I've just had some awful news, and I've no idea how I'm going to tell my husband.'

The man follows my gaze out to where Stuart is just returning the fuel nozzle into its holder.

'Is that your husband?' he asks.

'Yes,' I reply.

'What's his name?'

'Stuart,' I say.

'I'm Andy,' he says, reaching for the coffee which has now finished dispensing. 'Is this for Stuart?' he asks.

'I'm supposed to be getting us both one, but I was just trying to buy myself some time while I worked out how I'm going to tell him.'

Andy hands me the paper coffee cup having first slipped a corrugated sleeve over it so that it won't be too hot to hold.

'Same again?' he asks, placing another paper cup onto the metal grid, his finger poised over *flat white*.

'Yes. Thank you for being so kind.'

'Kindness doesn't cost anything,' he says, pressing the

button to set the machine in action again. 'Is there anyone else with you?'

I shake my head.

'So, can whatever it is wait until you get to where you're going, because you don't look in any fit state to drive, and if this awful news has a similar effect on your husband, he probably shouldn't be behind the wheel of a car either once you've told him.'

'But he's going to ask me how his mum is because our daughter rang just now from the hospital. What can I say to him? I can't lie,' I say, the words spilling out of me.

'How bad is she?' Andy asks. 'I'm a detective, but I'm currently off duty. If it would help though, I can blue light you to the hospital.'

'It's too late. We're too late,' I manage, suppressing a sob. 'Eva had come down from Skye to house-sit and look after our cat, but she had a fall yesterday and ended up in hospital. We flew back early from our holiday, but we're too late. She's died.'

It's as though the pressure that has been building and building inside me from the moment of Jemma's first call, while I tried to stay strong for Stuart, has been released. The kindness of this total stranger has twisted the valve, allowing my emotions to pour out of me like a gush of steam. Stuart is now getting back into our Ford Kuga. In a couple of minutes, I'm going to have to reach some kind of decision.

'So,' Andy says gently. 'If Eva has already passed, what benefit would there be in telling your husband now? Wouldn't it be better to get to the hospital to be with your daughter and tell him when you're all together?'

What Andy has just said makes perfect sense. I can't help wondering if part of his role in the police either now or in the past has been as a family liaison officer.

'But what will I tell Stuart about the phone call? It doesn't feel fair to keep this from him.'

'Life isn't always fair,' Andy says.

Something approaching sadness flickers in his eyes momentarily. Perhaps I was wrong about his empathy and understanding coming from his training in the police. That pained expression suggests he has personal experience of life not always being fair.

He picks up the second cup of coffee, and instead of getting one for himself as had clearly been his original intention, he ushers me towards the cashier's queue which is now a good deal shorter than it was.

'It's sometimes about taking the course of action which will lead to the least amount of hurt,' he says. 'Message your daughter and tell her that you've decided to hold off telling her dad the terrible news until you're all together. She'll understand, and I'm sure your husband will too.'

'But what do I say to Stuart?'

'Be vague. Maybe something along the lines of: your daughter was letting you know that the hospital will need to speak to you when you get there. It's true, they will, so you're not lying to your husband.'

I'm still not sure, and he can obviously sense my hesitation.

'Or my original offer to drive you both to the hospital stands if you'd rather tell him straight away. Which hospital is Eva in?' he asks.

'St Peter's,' I reply.

'I'm heading in that direction, so it's not a problem for me to take you if you'd prefer.'

I take a moment to consider. It won't benefit Stuart to find out about losing his mum here at an airport service station. It would be much better to be with Callum and Jemma so that we can all try to come to terms with what has happened together.

'No, you're right,' I say. 'Telling Stuart now won't bring Eva back. I'm sure St Peter's will have a relatives' room.'

Andy gives me a reassuring smile.

'Are you okay to take it from here then?' he asks.

'Yes. Thank you for your advice and for being so kind.'

'No worries. I'll get back in the coffee queue. I've been on nights, so I need a black coffee before I go and pick my little girl up from my ex. It's my weekend to have her,' he says, his eyes lighting up.

I watch him walk back up the aisle between the crisps and confectionery and wonder how someone as seemingly thoughtful and caring could be split from the mother of his child, a child he clearly adores. I'm glad he felt able to share a small part of his personal story with me after I'd unloaded on him.

'Next please,' the cashier says in a voice that manages to convey boredom and irritation in just two words.

I step forward and set one of the coffees on the counter before tapping my card against the machine to pay. Having my drink to sip on will reduce the need for conversation, at least for the first part of what is going to feel like an endless journey.

EIGHT

We eventually find a parking space in the hospital car park, get a ticket from the machine to display in the windscreen and head towards the main entrance. I'd sent Jemma the message suggested by Andy, and she'd texted back a few minutes later to say that there was a relatives' room on the second floor near the ward where she and Callum had sat with their nana as she took her final breath.

It had been difficult on the journey to steer the conversation away from talking about Eva, but I'd somehow managed it. I'd kept my voice light, chatting about Callum and his job as a recruiter and the long hours he put in. It earned him great money but meant he was tired and stressed most of the time, and that worried me as his mum.

I'd then moved the topic of conversation to Jemma and how, despite being so savvy in her job in marketing, she had a questionable choice in boyfriends. Ever since she started dating at sixteen years old and went out with Ryan, who we later found out used to help himself to his dad's whisky and his mum's antidepressants, I can't think of one that Stuart and I met that was good enough for our daughter. I suppose all parents feel the same way, but you can't say anything for fear of being accused of interfering, or worse, losing them from your life altogether. It's been particularly tricky with Will. They've been in a relationship for three years, and I must admit he exudes charm and is very good-looking, but after Callum's revelation I have difficulty trusting him.

Jemma has invested a lot of time and energy into the relationship, which doesn't appear to be reciprocated, but maybe that's because he is borderline lazy, the total opposite of our daughter who has a wonderful work ethic. It hasn't been helped by the current 'working from home' trend. The operative word is working, but according to Jemma he doesn't do too much of that when he's not in the office. He's been known to spend the morning playing golf or going to the gym for a couple of hours on company time. I can't quite get my head around why he thinks it's okay, but maybe that's because I have no opportunity to do my job from home.

The mini-rant about Will has passed the time, although Stuart, who normally chimes in with his own thoughts, has been predominantly silent. I was starting to run out of things to say that would avoid any mention of Eva as we turned into the entrance to the hospital. Stuart's knee had begun its customary nervous jiggle as we began our second circuit of the car park looking for likely signs of people who were about to leave. I'd just started talking about our cat, Wilfie, saying that I hoped he would have enough hard food to keep him going until we got home, when I spotted a Prius edging out of a space a few yards in front of us. Stuart exhaled heavily, clearly relieved to have found a parking space, but also, I suspect, pleased to not have to listen to any more of my inane chat.

As we wait for the lift to take us to the second floor, a sense of overwhelming dread settles like a lead weight on my shoulders, and I'm more aware than usual of the rhythmic beat of my heart, underlying the fact that Eva's heart is now still. I honestly have no idea how Stuart will react to the news that his mum has died. She's been frail and we've been concerned about the fainting episodes, but neither of us could have foreseen that she would have been taken from us so soon.

I messaged the word *here* as I'd agreed with Jemma as Stuart was concentrating on parking our car in the ridiculously small space, so I knew that she and Callum would be there to meet us, but as the doors open and I see the undisguised pain on their faces, the enormity of what they've had to deal with hits me.

'Hey, Dad,' Callum says, reaching his arms around Stuart in an awkward man hug. 'I'm sorry you've had to cut your holiday short. I know how much you and Mum have been looking forward to it,' he adds, giving me a much more comfortable embrace.

Of the two of us, I've always been the more tactile parent, but I notice over Callum's shoulder as he stoops to hug me that Stuart is clinging on to Jemma. In that instant, I know he's realised that something monumental has happened. He might be thinking a stroke or a heart attack, but I'm not sure whether he'll have considered that Eva might have actually passed away.

'Come on,' I say, urging our children to lead the way to the relatives' room. 'Let's get ourselves some privacy.'

The room is only a few yards down the corridor. Jemma and Stuart are walking ahead of Callum and me, and she is holding his hand. For a moment I'm transported back to a time when our children were very young and were not permitted to walk along the road without holding our hands. It feels like something of a role reversal, with Jemma anxious to absorb some of the shock that is hurtling inexorably towards her dad like an out-of-control juggernaut. I grip Callum's arm tighter, and he smiles down at me, his face unable to hide the apprehension he is feeling.

'I'm glad I waited to tell him until we could all be together,' I whisper.

'So am I,' he replies in an equally hushed tone.

The room we follow the others into is lit unusually softly for a hospital and is furnished with upholstered chairs in a pale sage-green colour. It's like walking into someone's living room, which is probably the desired effect.

We're all standing in the middle of the room, when a woman appears in the doorway.

'You must be Stuart,' she says, walking towards my husband and extending her hand. Stuart takes it briefly, shooting me a mildly panicky sideways glance. 'And Alexis?' she says, a slight question in her voice as she repeats the gesture. 'I'm Dr Constantine, and I was the doctor on call last night. Can I offer any of you a tea or coffee?' she asks, indicating the vending machine in one corner of the room.

I shake my head and mutter, 'No thanks.'

'Nor for me, thanks,' Stuart says. 'Could you please just give us the update on Mum? It's been a long journey, and I just want to see her.'

I don't think Stuart notices Dr Constantine glancing over to Jemma who gives a slight shake of her head. The doctor is clearly trying to ascertain if Stuart is already aware of his mum's passing.

'Shall we sit down?' she says, sitting herself to encourage us to do the same. I take her lead, and the rest of my family follow suit.

'I got a call from the nurses' station at six thirty this morning saying that Eva had been kept awake most of the night with a headache which wasn't responding to painkillers.'

I like that Dr Constantine has referred to Stuart's mum as Eva rather than Mrs Drummond. It feels much more personal.

'Your son and daughter were with their grandma when I got to her room about fifteen minutes later and although she was clearly in pain, she was asking them what they had ordered for her breakfast. She said she hoped it was porridge rather than toast as she thought the crunching would be worse for her headache.'

Despite everything, I allow myself a smile. Eva would have hated hospital porridge. Nobody makes porridge like my mother-in-law. The smile freezes on my lips. *Made* porridge, I correct myself. She won't ever make porridge again.

'I checked the blood pressure readings on the machine at her bedside and asked her if she could remember when she'd last had painkillers. When she said she couldn't remember, I popped out of the room to go to the nurses' station to check as I didn't want to overmedicate.'

I notice both Jemma and Callum flinch. It must be awful for them to sit here and listen to the doctor recounting the last moments of their nana's life, but nowhere near as bad as actually experiencing it. It's going to be a tricky time helping my children navigate their way through their grief.

Dr Constantine had paused briefly, but now continues.

'While I was at the nurses' station, one of your children pressed the emergency buzzer, and by the time I got back to Eva's room with the nurse, she was lying back on her pillows and had lost consciousness.'

The room is silent. Only the distant clatter of breakfast trolleys as the catering staff collect patients' trays invades the hush that has fallen.

'How long was she out for?' Stuart says, his tone anxious.

All four pairs of eyes are trained on him. My husband still hasn't grasped the situation.

'I'm so sorry, Stuart,' Dr Constantine says. 'There was nothing we could do.'

'I don't understand,' he says, the volume of his voice increasing. 'She's in a bloody hospital surrounded by nurses and doctors and medical equipment. What do you mean there was nothing you could do?' he demands.

'Dad,' Callum says, trying to calm his father. 'It wasn't the doctor's fault. One minute Nana was talking quite normally and the next she...' his voice falters.

'Callum's right, Dad,' Jemma agrees. 'The doctor buzzed for help immediately, but I think Nana had already gone. It was just so quick.'

Stuart is looking from one to the other of his children, clearly struggling to comprehend what they are telling him. I'm looking at them feeling enormous guilt that they've had to deal with this.

'No,' Stuart says. 'I can't accept that. There must have been something you could have done. Is it because she was an old lady? Did you all just make the decision that it wasn't worth trying to save her?' He's shouting now, in a most un-Stuart-like way.

I reach for his hand, but he shakes my hand away.

'Believe me, Mr Drummond, we always do everything we can to save our patients no matter what their age,' the doctor says. The shift from Stuart to Mr Drummond illustrates how upset she must feel because of his accusations. 'Although we don't know for sure, and won't know until we've done a post-mortem examination, we think your mother may have had an aneurysm that had gone undetected for years. It might have leaked a small amount of blood, which could have been the cause of the dizziness and headaches she'd been experiencing, but the fall could have weakened it to the point of rupture, which is what we believe happened this morning.'

Stuart has closed his eyes while listening to the doctor's explanation and is taking deep breaths, presumably to calm himself after his angry outburst.

'And if it was a ruptured aneurysm as you suspect, there is absolutely nothing that could have been done to save my mother?' Stuart asks in a more controlled tone.

'If it had been detected earlier, there might have been a slim chance of operating, but once ruptured there is very little that can be done. I'm so sorry,' she adds. 'If it's any consolation to you, after a sharp burst of pain which Callum and Jemma told me that your mother experienced, she would have been unconscious and wouldn't have felt any further discomfort.'

I reach for Stuart's hand again, and this time he doesn't pull away from me. His anger is spent it would seem. Now he must accept his new reality. Those of us who are lucky enough to live a good number of years are all orphans in the end.

'There's nothing more I can tell you for the moment,' Dr Constantine says gently. 'Would you like to see your mum now?'

Stuart raises his eyes to mine. It's such a difficult decision for him to make knowing that the life has gone from his mum's body.

'What do you think, Lexi?' he asks. He sounds so sad and lost, it's heartbreaking.

'I think you'll always regret it if you don't,' I say after a moment's hesitation, during which I try to imagine Eva's face without her twinkling cornflower-blue eyes meeting mine.

'Will you come with me?' he asks.

'Of course,' I say. 'I loved Eva too.'

Stuart gets slowly to his feet with the reluctance of a five-year-old on his first day at school.

'I'm sorry I got angry,' he says to Dr Constantine. 'It's not your fault.'

I get up to follow Stuart and the doctor out of the relatives' room, then turn back to look at my children sitting side by side holding each other's hands. It's their first experience of being present as someone took their last breath, and it fills me with dread that it could one day be repeated. The thought of our children bearing witness to mine or Stuart's passing is almost inconceivable.

'Are you okay?' I mouth silently to them.

Jemma nods while Callum gives a slight shake of his head.

We will all process Eva's death differently, and it will be my job to try and steer everyone through this dreadful time. It's going to be a challenge.

I raise my fingertips to my lips and blow them a kiss before catching up with Stuart in the corridor.

'Are they alright?' he asks, reaching for my hand and gripping it tightly.

'They will be,' I say, trying to reassure myself as much as my husband. What they've had to deal with is huge for anyone of any age and I don't really know how either of them will process it. I guess only time will tell.

NINE

Callum drives us home from the hospital in our car with Jemma following behind in hers. I shake my head slightly as I get out of the back seat wondering how we were in a plane only a few short hours ago.

Seeing Eva lying still and lifeless in the hospital bed had been every bit as awful as I'd feared. People often say that the person 'looked at peace' or 'looked as though they were sleeping', but I didn't get that feeling at all. I'd tried not to cry as I wanted to be strong for Stuart, but I couldn't stop the steady trickle of tears from rolling down my cheeks. I had to run the back of my hand across my chin periodically to prevent them from dropping onto my bright yellow linen blouse, which seemed loud and inappropriate given the situation. But we hadn't called in at home as originally planned, so I hadn't had the opportunity to change.

Callum releases the boot catch, probably assuming that our luggage is in there.

'We didn't wait for our cases,' I say. 'I explained the situation and they're hoping to send them over this afternoon. Not that there is any real rush,' I add, as Jemma's BMW pulls onto the drive next to us.

'Oh right,' Callum replies, going round to the back of the car to close the boot.

'I'll get the kettle on,' I say, retrieving my front door keys from my crossbody bag and linking my arm through Stuart's to guide him towards our front door. He looks totally lost, which must reflect how he is feeling. Stuart had a great relationship with both of his parents, but although he loved his dad dearly, he was undoubtedly closer to his mum. Maybe it's because they had similar personality traits, although my husband has always refuted any suggestion that he's stubborn.

'Not for me, Mum,' Callum says, following us across the gravel. 'Let's get you both inside, and then I'll need to show my face at work.'

'Are you sure you feel up to it?' I ask, as Stuart moves past me into the hallway and bends to stroke Wilfie.

Wilfie is my cat, and while he's always very affectionate with me, he's normally not so with other people, Stuart included, so I'm surprised to see him brushing himself against my husband's legs as he crosses backwards and forwards, preventing Stuart from advancing towards the kitchen. He must have heard the tyres on the gravel and come to investigate, but it's a little odd that he hasn't come straight over to me as he normally would. It's as though Wilfie knows he needs to comfort Stuart.

I pull my keys out of the lock and lean back against the door, holding it open for Jemma and Callum to pass while keeping an eye on Wilfie. He's a house cat so not allowed outside because we live on such a busy road, and I can't bear the thought of anything happening to him. A couple of weeks after we moved in, our neighbour's cat was knocked down and killed. I'd been wavering about whether to let Wilfie roam free or not, but that decided me against it.

'Are you sure you feel up to what?' Jemma asks, clearly only having heard the tail end of our exchange.

'Cal is going to have to go in to work,' I say.

'What?' Jemma exclaims. 'Are you joking? Surely they'll understand if you call them and explain what's happened.'

'Recruiting doesn't work like that, Jem,' Callum is saying as I close the front door and usher Stuart and Wilfie towards the kitchen.

If I know our daughter, she isn't going to let this drop, and I don't want Stuart to hear her raised voice.

'Why can't you just put your family first for once?' Jemma demands. 'Mum and Dad need us.'

I don't hear our son's response as I hastily close the kitchen door to block out the sound of a potential argument. I fill the kettle from the tap, hoping the noise of the running water will drown out their voices, then sit it back on its base and flick the switch, illuminating the red light.

'We need to ring Mari before she leaves for work,' I say, glancing up at the kitchen clock whose hands are both standing to attention, pointing at the twelve on the oversized face. 'It'll be about 7 a.m. in Canada now, won't it?' I add, turning to face Stuart who is sitting on one of the chairs at the kitchen table, but still bending forward to fuss the cat.

He raises his eyes to mine.

'That's not a call I'm looking forward to,' he admits. 'What on earth am I going to say?'

I go over to where he's sitting, pull out the chair next to his from its neatly tucked in position and sit down, reaching for his free hand.

'We'll have it on speakerphone,' I say. 'If I feel like you're floundering, I'll take over.'

'You're my rock, Lexi. I don't know what I'd do without you,' he says, a distinct wobble in his voice.

'For better or worse,' I say, gently reminding him of our

wedding vows. 'We're here to support each other. We always have been.'

The kitchen door is flung open and Jemma is standing there, her eyes glinting dark. I shake my head slightly, trying to defuse her obvious anger, but she either doesn't notice or decides to ignore me.

'Sorry, you two. I'm going to have to drop Cal back to his house to collect his car so that he can go into work!' She almost shouts the final word. '*I'll* come straight back once I've dropped *him*.'

Our children get along better than most siblings. There's only eighteen months between them and Cal has always looked out for his younger sister. It doesn't mean they have similar personalities and always agree about everything though. They are both quite stubborn, like their dad and Eva, but of the two, Callum is usually the first to capitulate, preferring a quiet life unless he feels strongly about something. This is clearly one of those occasions where neither is going to compromise on their opinion.

Cal appears behind his sister in the doorway.

'I'll come straight from work tonight,' he says, before turning on his heel and heading for the front door.

'I'm furious with him,' Jemma hisses. 'But he's adamant that no one at work can pick up on the discussions he's been having. I'll be back as soon as I can,' she adds, flouncing across the hallway and out of the front door, slamming it hard behind her.

'She'll calm down,' I say to Stuart, who is looking upset and a little bemused by our daughter's outburst. 'They've both had a terrible shock.'

Stuart nods. 'Do you think we should wait for Jemma to get back before we ring Mari?' he asks.

'I think we should do it sooner rather than later,' I say gently. 'Mari has a right to know.'

Stuart lets out a sigh and picks up his mobile phone.

TEN

As promised, Jemma came back to our house after dropping her brother at his home and stayed with us for most of the afternoon. She helped me unpack the suitcases when they were delivered and put the dirty clothes through a wash cycle, not that there were many. We'd been away for less than forty-eight hours and had spent most of that time in the outfits we'd travelled to and from Barbados in, apart from the orange flowery dress I'd worn to dinner on the first night and the yellow sundress I had on at breakfast yesterday morning when I'd received Jemma's first worrying message. *How could that only have been yesterday?* I find myself wondering as I put away my newly bought straw sunhat without having had the chance to wear it. It doesn't seem possible.

Stuart went for a lie down shortly after Jemma and I finished unpacking the cases. He was physically exhausted from all the travelling and emotionally drained after what had happened to his mum. The call to his sister was the final straw. He'd hauled himself up from the kitchen chair while I was loading the washing machine, smiled apologetically at Jemma and excused himself.

In a way, I'm glad. I want to spend some time alone with Jemma after the traumatic experience she went through this morning. It was bad enough that she'd found her nana collapsed on the kitchen floor and had to call an ambulance, but to be with her as she took her final breath is something I've never had to deal with. I thought she might want to talk about it, but although I tried to broach the subject several times while we were upstairs unpacking, Jemma was uncharacteristically guarded. She clearly isn't ready to have the conversation, and I don't want to force things. If I know one thing about my daughter, it's that the more you push, the more she clams up. I decide it's better to let her open up to me in her own time and instead tell her about the earlier phone call with her Auntie Mari in Canada.

I don't think I'll ever get over Mari's reaction to Stuart after he'd gathered all his courage to make the call and gently explain what happened.

'Well, there's no point in me coming over now if she's already dead,' Mari had said when he'd finished.

Stuart had visibly flinched. There had been no emotion in her voice and no attempt to consider her brother's feelings.

'I'll see if I can get time off from work to come over for the funeral, but we're moving into the busy pre-Christmas period so they may not be agreeable,' she'd added.

I could hardly believe my ears. Mari works in a gift shop. It's not as though other members of staff wouldn't be able to cover her absence for a few days so that she could be there when her mother is laid to rest.

'Obviously, we'll have to communicate about selling the house and dividing up her possessions,' she'd then continued. 'I'm assuming Mum left a will, and everything is split fifty-fifty, so it should all be pretty straightforward.'

I was aghast at the callousness of her behaviour. The image of Eva's lifeless body swam before my eyes and threatened to overwhelm me again. Mari's main reaction to her mother passing was how her worldly goods should be disposed of. I'd wanted to say something, but I was pretty sure it wouldn't have made much difference to Mari's attitude, and it might have upset Stuart further, so I stayed quiet.

The call had lasted five minutes, if that. It was as though Mari couldn't wait to get off the phone. I've only met Stuart's sister on two previous occasions, the most recent being their father's funeral fifteen years ago. It had been a fleeting visit, and obviously emotions were running high, so my opinion of her has always been predominantly formed by things that Eva and Stuart have told me over the years. Both had focussed on happy family memories of growing up in their close-knit community on the Isle of Skye while we'd been going through photographs for Donald's memorial service. So many pictures of happy red-cheeked faces, walking on the windswept, pristine beaches, or dancing at a Ceilidh. On these occasions, Donald's ruddiness would more likely have been caused by an overindulgence in his favourite tipple, Scotch whisky.

There were very few photographs of Mari in the family albums, especially since her move to Canada. Maybe she hadn't sent many, or perhaps her parents had chosen not to display them. Whatever the reason, it was apparent that distance had not made their hearts grow fonder.

There were a couple of Mari holding Eva and Donald's first grandchild, my niece, Fleur, and a few snowy exterior group shots of them gathered in front of the log cabin where Christmas was always celebrated with Mari's in-laws rather than her ever making the trip to spend it with her side of the family.

Before we had the children, Stuart and I always made the lengthy trip to Skye, usually in pretty dire weather conditions, to spend Christmas and New Year with his mum and dad. The

November Callum was born, we all agreed that it was much too long a journey for a five-week-old baby to undertake, so Donald and Eva travelled south to spend Christmas with us, although they left on 29 December to be back in time for the *first footing* on Hogmanay.

That set the pattern for the next few years, a pattern that continued after Donald died. Initially, Eva had been reluctant to come to ours, but I was determined that she shouldn't be on her own, and I wasn't taking no for an answer. Stuart went to fetch her as I was working up to the 23 December. We'd all done everything in our power to make Eva's first Christmas without her husband as good as it could be in the circumstances. She'd sat with our children, then aged twelve and fourteen, watching films or reality television, not that she was a particular fan of the latter, but she did find it fascinating.

'They should do a reality show with the contestants abandoned on an island in the Hebrides in winter. That would be a true test of reality,' she'd said to me while we were decorating the Christmas cake together after the children had gone up to bed on Christmas Eve. I couldn't help but agree with her, remarking as I often did about the 'snowflake' generation I worked alongside at News 24/7.

'They want everything, and they want it now,' I'd replied. 'None of the younger ones seem to appreciate the years of hard work my generation has put in for News 24/7 to get the ratings it does. Those of us who've been there from the start have worked our way up the ladder to our current positions, but if they don't get a pay rise or a promotion in a year or so, they move on.'

'It's that whole "the grass is always greener on the other side" mindset,' Eva had responded. 'A bit like Mari moving to Canada.' She'd shrugged her shoulders and added, 'Oh well, her choice,' before changing the subject.

No one has ever elaborated on Mari's reason for emigrating. All I knew for sure was that it had fallen to Stuart and me to care for his parents as they'd grown older, and subsequently support his mum emotionally after Donald's accident. Whatever the reason, I would have expected the person on the receiving end of such sad news about her mother to show more compassion.

If I'm honest, I don't have the warmest of relationships with my own sister, Juliet, but I'm pretty sure she would have reacted very differently from Mari if I'd been the one making this devastating call about our mother.

Stuart looked utterly bereft after Mari terminated the call.

I tried to soften the blow, saying, 'She's probably in a state of shock. The full impact of losing her mum hasn't hit her yet.'

Stuart took a few moments before he responded.

'No, I don't think that's the case at all,' he said sadly. 'She knows Mum never truly forgave her for moving to Canada and preventing her from having a proper relationship with her granddaughter and great-grandsons. Although they did try to patch things up when she came over for Dad's funeral, I think the sad truth is that she's been waiting for Mum to die so that she could sever her last connection with the Isle of Skye.'

I watch Jemma's face, searching for a reaction as I fill her in on the details of her dad's call with Mari. When she eventually comments, I find what she says surprising.

'I thought something else must have happened,' she says. 'When he excused himself to go for a lie down, he suddenly looked all of his sixty-eight years.'

I know what she means. Stuart left the room with his shoulders slumped forward, his feet almost shuffling across the pine floorboards. But he's her dad, and my husband, and I feel the need to jump to his defence.

'I think Mari should shoulder the blame for that,' I say. 'I'm appalled by her lack of feeling on hearing that your nana has passed away. Even if she doesn't care she should at least have shown some consideration towards your dad. She wasn't the one juggling work and long trips to Skye on a regular basis before he retired. It's part of the reason we needed the trip to Barbados so desperately. We're both exhausted.'

'Maybe Nana, and Grandad too when he was alive, are partly responsible for her reaction,' Jemma says.

'What's that supposed to mean?' I ask. My daughter has a habit of playing devil's advocate. Usually I support her, because it makes you consider other points of view that may differ from your own. But this is not the time or the place to debate Mari's motivation for her reaction.

'I just mean, they might not have shown her how much they loved her after she left for Canada. Maybe she felt like the second child, not just in age but in their affections.'

And there it is. Jemma hides it well most of the time, but she does have a ridiculous belief that I favour Callum over her. I don't. I love both my children equally.

'Well, perhaps if Mari had come back for a visit a little more often, they would have been able to show her how much they cared about her,' I say, determined not to get into a discussion about Jemma and her brother.

'Did they ever go to Canada?' Jemma counters. 'It's not exactly the other side of the world. It wouldn't have taken much longer than the road trip down here, but I don't remember them going.'

Jemma has a point, which brings me back to wondering what the circumstances of Mari emigrating were in the first place. But point or no point, I'm uncomfortable apportioning blame for Mari's lack of compassion at Eva's door only hours after her death. I'm about to react to Jemma's comment when it dawns on me why she's behaving like this. It's her way of coping with what has happened, protecting herself by going on the attack. I need to diffuse the situation as quickly as possible because I don't want us to be arguing if Stuart should suddenly reappear.

'No, they didn't go,' I say. 'I think it was something to do with your grandad having an inner ear condition which made it painful for him to fly.'

I'm not lying. Donald did have a problem with his ears, something to do with an explosion at very close proximity when he was in the army. It was one of the reasons he was invalided out in his early thirties. But whether that was why they didn't visit Mari in Canada I'll never know for sure.

'Oh,' Jemma says, looking slightly embarrassed. 'I never knew that.'

'It wasn't something your grandad talked about really. He was old school. His generation were very private about disability and just got on with things the best they could. I suppose your nana could have gone on her own, but perhaps she was a nervous flyer.'

I feel as though I'm babbling, and Jemma goes quiet, staring down at her hands resting in her lap. Judging by her lack of response, I think I've successfully calmed the situation, and we go on to talk in general terms about the funeral. Obviously, it will be held on Skye, and Eva will be laid to rest with Donald, but we also touch on what music she might like and whether or not she would have wanted flowers. I think yes, because she loved her garden and Jemma thinks no, for the same reason.

'Nana always preferred leaving them in the garden rather than cutting them and bringing them into the house,' she is saying when Stuart pushes the kitchen door open.

'Yes, to flowers,' he says. 'She deserves a beautiful send-off, but just from close friends and family.'

At the mention of family, I realise that I've yet to impart the awful news to my mum. It will have to wait. Today I need to concentrate on my close family unit and their feelings.

'Flowers it is then,' I say, casting a hopeful glance in Jemma's direction.

'Agreed,' she responds, clearly wanting to agree with her dad's wishes.

ELEVEN

Before she left, Jemma insisted that Stuart and I should try and eat something. Despite neither of us being in the least bit hungry, I open a tin of soup and get some bread out of the freezer to make toast while she's still there, which seems to satisfy her.

Twenty minutes later I'm clearing the barely touched bowls of tomato soup off the table when the doorbell rings, and we hear someone letting themself in. Both our children have keys to our home, but neither enter unannounced if they know we're home.

'How's it going?' Callum asks, walking into the kitchen. He clearly notices me pouring the soup down the sink because he adds, 'You need to eat something. It wouldn't do for you two to get ill.'

I can't help wondering if he's arrived at this conclusion on his own or if he's been talking to his sister on the phone on his drive to ours.

'I know,' I reply, rinsing the residual orangey-coloured liquid from the bowls before stacking them in the dishwasher.

'I'll do us a milky coffee or hot chocolate later, I promise. Can I get you anything?'

'I can't stop long. Ellie's making dinner.'

'A cup of tea, or a beer if you prefer?' I offer.

Callum raises his eyebrows. We've never encouraged our children to drink and drive.

'Just the one,' I clarify.

'Tea'll be fine, thanks, Mum. How are you holding up, Dad?' Callum asks, squeezing Stuart's shoulder before sitting down next to him.

'I still can't quite believe it, Cal,' Stuart replies. 'She's not been that great health-wise for a while, but she was on such good form on the journey down from Skye, apart from feeling tired when she got here. I hope that's not why she had the fall. You know, because she was overtired.'

'You can't think like that. She's been unsteady on her feet for ages. She could have had a fall at home and died alone. At least she had me and Jemma with her, holding her hands when...'

I had my back to Callum and Stuart, busying myself with a mug and a teabag, but when he stops talking, I turn. The sight that greets me is heartbreaking. Callum is holding his head in his hands, his shoulders heaving up and down, and Stuart has his arms around his boy. I give them a moment before crossing over to them and enveloping them both in my arms.

'Hey,' I say. 'That's good. Let it all out, darling.'

He's properly sobbing now, something I've never seen my son do, even when he got home to discover that Max, our twelve-year-old labrador, had crossed the rainbow bridge while he'd been at school.

'God, Mum,' he says, struggling to regain control, 'I never in my worst nightmare imagined what it would be like to be holding someone's hand when they died. One minute she was talking to us, albeit a little bit groggy from all the painkillers, and then she kind of went a bit rigid before collapsing back on her pillows.'

I shoot a quick glance at Stuart. His eyes are closed, and I'm unsure whether he's ready to hear about his mum's final few minutes.

'Then what happened?' he asks, his voice gruff with emotion.

'She... Nana,' Cal corrects himself, 'said, "Oh, that hurts... that really hurts," and Jemma pressed the buzzer for the nurse and we both held her hands tightly. She was gripping back hard and then her grip relaxed. I – I think she might have died before Dr Constantine and the nurse came rushing in, and it was only a couple of minutes,' he finishes, exhaling as though exhausted from reliving it.

Stuart nods his head gently.

'I'm glad she didn't suffer for long,' he says. 'When it's my time, that's how I want to go.'

'Don't say that,' Callum and I say in unison.

'We all have to go in the end,' Stuart says. 'I'm just glad it was quick for Mum and that she had you and Jemma with her as she passed,' he adds, squeezing Callum's forearm. 'I wouldn't be able to forgive myself if she'd been alone. She was so often alone after Dad died. She missed him terribly.'

I can't speak. Eva and I had become so much closer after Donald's death, but it hadn't happened immediately. She'd bottled her feelings up for months, almost as though she still expected him to walk back through the front door asking what was for supper. Then one night, six months to the day since he passed, she'd rung up in floods of tears saying that she'd given all his clothes to charity because he wouldn't be needing them any more. Stuart was in the middle of a project at work which he couldn't get out of. I rang in sick, took the next flight to Glasgow, hired a car and drove for hours. I stayed with Eva on Skye for two weeks, at the end of which I persuaded her to come back to Berkshire with me, where she stayed for a month. As she was leaving to go back to Skye, she'd leaned in for a hug and whispered, 'I'll never get over losing Donald, but I'll never forget your kindness in helping me try to. You're like a daughter to me.'

'Yes, she did,' I agree. 'I hope they are reunited now.'

'Do you think there is life after death, Mum?' Cal asks with a touch of hope in his voice.

'None of us knows the answer to that for sure, but I like to think so,' I reply.

'Me too,' he says. 'You didn't think badly of me for going in to work today, did you?' he asks. 'Keeping busy was my way of dealing with things, although to be honest I wasn't really on it. Maybe Jemma was right, and I should have stayed here with you guys.'

'You're here now,' I say. 'That's the main thing.'

Callum's face contorts.

'I just wish Nana could have lived a bit longer,' he says. He looks on the edge of tears again.

'She had a good life,' Stuart says, trying to reassure his son. 'And a long life too. Imagine all the things she's seen and experienced in eighty-eight years.'

'I know. But she never got to hold a great-grandchild.'

It takes a moment before I realise what Callum is saying.

'Is Ellie pregnant again?' I gasp.

'Yes,' Callum says, his voice sounding shaky. 'We wanted to wait until she was further along before telling anyone, after last time, but I wish now that we'd told Nana when we popped round on Wednesday. I wanted to, but Ellie said she looked tired after her journey, so we were going to do it when you got back off holiday. And now it's too late.'

'Oh, Cal,' I say, flinging my arms around him. 'I know the timing seems off, but this is just the best news. It feels like the whole circle of life thing. Does Jemma know?'

'No. Nobody else knows, not even Ellie's mum. I'll be in trouble for telling you without Ellie here. It isn't how I would have wanted you to find out.'

'Well, I'm glad you've told us. It will help us have a happier memory of 28 September,' I say. 'And don't be too sure your nana didn't know about it.'

Callum looks puzzled.

'What do you mean?' he asks.

'Just that she knew I was pregnant with you before I did. She had a bit of a sixth sense for that sort of thing.'

'If it's a girl, we're going to call her Eva,' Callum says.

I raise my eyebrows, wondering if he's consulted Ellie about this.

'It's okay, Mum,' he says, clearly reading my expression. 'Ellie and I agreed on it when I rang her from the hospital earlier. In fact, she suggested it. She knows how close we all are as a family and what a huge part of that both our nanas are.'

I'm not looking forward to breaking the news to my mum. The two nanas weren't super close, but they got on well despite being quite different personalities. On Monday lunchtimes they loved to have catch-up conversations about the latest celebrity to be voted off *Strictly Come Dancing*, and sometimes compared notes on the *Sunday Times* crossword if either was stuck on a clue.

Come to think of it, I realise with a twist in my stomach, she doesn't even know we're back in the country, but I can't face calling her today. Maybe I'll pop over tomorrow. It will be easier to tell her in person, although I'll have to be careful not to reveal Callum's news.

Mum will be so pleased about the baby, not least because she really likes Ellie and was devastated when she miscarried earlier in the year. Not for the first time, I think how lucky our son is to have found his wife among all the undesirables. Most of my friends with adult children have told me horror stories about partners their offspring have been involved with and how difficult it is to watch a child you've nurtured from birth be the victim of physical or mental abuse. I'm grateful that I haven't had to support either of our children in recovering from a messy break-up, although in Jemma's case it could just be a matter of time.

I've no idea how she will react when Callum and I eventually tell her how Will landed his brilliant new job. We were all so proud of him. It's every recruiters' dream, my son included, to put themselves forward if a role comes up that they would be perfect for. There is so much competition though, particularly if a company is looking to fill the post through a recruitment agency. Will obviously wanted the job badly enough to go to any lengths to secure it, probably mainly because of the huge increase in salary, according to Jemma. Callum was appalled when he heard the rumour in August and was all for confronting Will until I made him realise that it could destroy his and Jemma's sibling bond if the rumour proved to be untrue. My suggestion for me to mention it to Jemma so that she could ask Will directly was rejected by Callum for the same reason.

Instead, we agreed to hold back on saying anything at all to Jemma until Callum had done a bit of digging. It's been a couple of months now and as much as I want to know whether anything damning has been flagged up, now is not the time to ask. There is also the slight problem that Stuart knows nothing about it. He's not a violent man, but I think Will would be on the end of a punch on the nose if it turns out to be true.

Will is thirty-six years old, a full ten years older than Jemma, which is a similar age difference to me and Stuart. Until this business, I'd occasionally found myself wondering why he hadn't been snapped up before. Maybe now I have the answer.

Ellie and Callum are the same age. They were married three years ago, only a year after they met, but it was like they had been looking for each other and didn't want to waste any more time. When I'd expressed surprise, after Callum had told me they were moving in together only a few months after their first date, he'd simply said, 'When you know, you know.'

I'm certain Ellie will make a great mother, and Callum is desperate to be a dad. Despite my suggestion that Eva might already have guessed about the pregnancy, it feels cruel that the two of them were denied the pleasure of being able to tell her and watch the delight in her cornflower-blue eyes. At least they will have the joy of telling Mum, for whom their new arrival will be a first great-grandchild. My sister, Juliet, and her partner, Heather, decided not to have children so there won't be any familial grandchildren or great-grandchildren on her side of our family.

Stuart is sitting quietly, listening to the exchange between Callum and me, but when he speaks his voice is loaded with emotion.

'That is truly great news, son. Your mum's right. It will give this date a much happier significance rather than it being the day we lost Nana.'

Callum hugs his dad again and downs the rest of his cup of tea.

'I'm sorry, I'm going to have to go, but call if you need to talk, okay?'

I follow Callum out into the hallway and wait for him to put his coat on before reaching my arms around him and resting my head on his chest.

'Look after him,' he says. 'Dad isn't usually one for getting emotional, but he seems very fragile.'

'I will,' I assure him, mumbling the words into his wool coat and holding onto him tightly.

'And Mum. This whole business has put everything into perspective for me. As soon as the funeral is over, I think we should tell Jemma regardless of whether I've been able to find out anything else or not.'

TWELVE
FRIDAY 29 SEPTEMBER

It takes me a few minutes to remember where I am and why I'm here when I first wake up. The reality soon hits and with it a heavy weight descends. I feel as though I'm pinned to the bed under a duvet of lead rather than down and feathers. Stuart is still sleeping soundly at my side, inhaling through his nose and making a kind of spluttering sound with his mouth as he breathes out. He always does this when he's sleeping on his back. I usually give him a sharp dig in the ribs accompanied by instructions to turn onto his side, but I haven't the heart this morning. The longer he stays asleep, the longer he'll be protected from his new normal.

I lie in bed for a while trying to decide on the best way to tell my mum about Eva. I'm torn between ringing her to tell her that we've had to come back from holiday because Eva has had a fall, as preparation for delivering the news about her death in person, or simply turning up on her doorstep. Neither is ideal. If I call Mum first, she'll most likely get herself into a state worrying about Eva's condition, which is pointless in the circumstances. But if I just turn up on the doorstep, will the shock of seeing me and Stuart when we're supposed to be four thousand miles away be too much for her?

Then with a flash, I realise there is a third option. I could call my sister, Juliet, explain that I've had to come back from holiday because of an emergency and ask her to head to Mum's as a kind of early warning system and then meet me there. We don't always see eye to eye, but I have a feeling she'll come through for me even if I don't reveal the full extent of the circumstances which have forced our early return.

Normally I would ask Stuart's opinion, but he's probably not in the right frame of mind to decide. In the end, I think that option three will probably cause Mum the least amount of anxiety. Decision made, I'm trying to slip out from under the covers to go and call my sister without disturbing my husband. My feet contact the plush carpet, and I'm manoeuvring myself upright to reach for my dressing gown when Stuart speaks.

'I'm not asleep, you know,' he says.

I turn to look at him. His eyes are still closed, but he is no longer making the spluttering noise.

'I'm sorry,' I say. 'Did I wake you?'

'Not really. I've been awake off and on all night.'

'Do you want me to bring you up a cup of tea?' I ask.

'Thanks for the offer, but I'll get up,' he replies. 'I think part of the reason I didn't sleep well is because my stomach has been rumbling. My mind is finding it hard to face the thought of food, but my body has other ideas.'

'I'll make some toast and coffee,' I say, slipping my arms into my silky robe. 'And I'll turn the heating up,' I add. 'It's freezing.'

'I'll be down in five minutes,' Stuart says. 'I need a shower. I just couldn't face it last night.'

Callum had left at around seven the previous evening, and I made Stuart and myself a hot chocolate drink using the long-life almond milk my sister has when she visits, as we hadn't got any fresh milk in. Juliet is lactose intolerant, so I never risk giving her cow's milk in case she has a reaction. It's a good job the cartons have a very long shelf life, although I hate to think what they contain to keep them fresh enough to consume. I think we've had this carton since Easter, which is the last time Juliet was in our house. I do see her at Mum's sometimes, but most of our interactions are on WhatsApp with an occasional phone or Facetime call. The thought of speaking to her this morning is already filling me with dread.

Stuart and I had carried our mugs of hot chocolate through to the lounge last night and were sat cuddled up together on the sofa, under a throw, when Wilfie decided to join us, kneading his paws into the soft fleece and purring. I don't know who derived the most comfort from the action: me, Stuart, or the cat. Once Wilfie had settled, no longer needing one or other of us to stroke his sleek black fur, Stuart and I sat staring at the television, which was broadcasting a repeat of *Who Wants to Be a Millionaire*. I wasn't paying attention to it, and I don't think Stuart was either as he normally shouts out the answers before the options have appeared on screen, much to my annoyance. It wasn't even 9 p.m. when we decided to call it a day, me via a bath in which I fell asleep only to be woken about an hour later by the tepid water devoid of bubbles. Stuart was out for the count when I climbed into bed.

The frozen slices of bread are poised in the toaster, the filter coffee machine has finished its noisy preparation of our morning drink, and Wilfie is tucking into his chicken and green beans breakfast when Stuart appears in the kitchen doorway wearing grey jogging bottoms and a black T-shirt, his silver-streaked hair wet from the shower. I find it quite amusing that my husband dresses in a sporty manner because he is the most unsporty person I know. He doesn't mind watching it, particularly Formula 1 and rugby, but taking part is altogether different. He does however love walking and will happily disappear for an hour or two to 'blow the cobwebs away' as he describes it.

Maybe it stems from his childhood on Skye. His parents' house is quite remote, and most organised clubs and activities centre on Portree, which is almost an hour away and a drive involving a lot of narrow and winding roads. Walking was what they did as a family and Stuart still enjoys it, as do I when I'm not too busy. I always made time for walks when we had Max, but I've become a little lazier without an excuse to get out in the fresh air.

'Better?' I ask, depressing the lever on the toaster.

'Much,' he replies, walking over to the coffee machine and filling the two mugs I've already got out ready on the work surface. 'I think I'll have mine black,' he says. 'I'm not fond of that nutty milk you buy for your sister.'

I allow myself a smile. He has been known to use that adjective about my sister herself rather than the milk she drinks.

'Speaking of who,' I say. 'I thought it might be better to ring Juliet, tell her we've had to come back early from holiday and organise to meet her at Mum's. That way she can tell Mum we're home rather than us just turning up unannounced, so it will be less of a shock for her.'

'Good idea,' Stuart says, carrying the mugs over to the table. 'I suppose you'll have to let work know what's happened too.'

For once in my life, I haven't given work any thought. I'm not expected back on shift for just over two weeks because I've taken an extra few days to get over the jet lag. Maybe I should try and get myself back on the roster, because we're going to need a couple of trips up to Skye to sort out Eva's house, but the thought of going into work at the moment is beyond me.

'Let's get today out of the way first,' I say, retrieving the golden slices from the toaster and spreading them thickly with golden butter. 'We can't really start to plan anything until all the official stuff is done with the coroner, so I'm not going to be able to give precise dates when I can and can't work.'

'How much compassionate leave do News 24/7 give?'

Stuart asks, taking the plate I'm handing him and dipping a spoon into the honey jar.

I watch him drizzle the amber-coloured liquid over one slice, working outwards in concentric circles, before dipping the spoon again and repeating the process on the other slice. He offers me the spoon, but I decline, at which point he pops it in his mouth to get the remaining honey rather than wasting it. Then he lifts a piece of the toast to his mouth and takes a bite. I'm relieved to see Stuart eating after he couldn't even finish the chocolate drink last night.

'I'm not sure. I think most companies give four or five days, but I'll have to ask Jenny when I speak to her,' I say, sinking my teeth into the unadulterated toast and butter. I like honey and jam and marmalade and even Marmite on occasion, but nothing beats a thick slice of farmhouse bread toasted to golden brown perfection and spread with French butter with salt crystals in my humble opinion.

Breakfast continues in silence, apart from the munching sounds. I get the distinct feeling that Stuart is reliving moments from his past and wouldn't appreciate the intrusion of me talking.

My silence is not only in preparation for the call I'm going to have to make to Juliet once the dishwasher is loaded but also the thought of how we go about telling Jemma about Will once the funeral is over. Not for the first time, I wonder if she will try and forgive him. She seems totally committed to their relationship and has sometimes expressed to me her fear of being single in her thirties. But is that any reason to accept what he's allegedly done? My head is spinning at the thought of what the next few weeks hold.

THIRTEEN

It's almost 10.30 a.m. by the time we're turning into the end of my mum's road. There had been a call from the hospital to deal with, confirming that they would be performing an autopsy on Eva to determine the cause of death.

On both sides of my mum's street there are bungalows as far as the eye can see. She and my dad moved here when he retired, thinking that it would be a nice community to grow old in together – a lot of the other residents at that time were retirees too. Within two years my lovely dad had suffered a stroke and died, and gradually the street started to fill up with families with young children as bungalows tend to have bigger gardens. If Mum doesn't like it, she doesn't complain, but it is my idea of a living hell.

As I hoped, Juliet's car is already in the driveway of number seventeen where Mum's Honda Jazz used to stand. We'd been on at her to sell it for the past few years as none of us were very comfortable with the thought of her driving with the lack of tolerance in today's fast-moving world. It would have been awful for her to be on the end of abusive road rage, but even worse was the thought that her reactions might not be as quick as they used to be. Her excuse not to sell has always been that she would lose her independence without the car, but she knew it wasn't true really. There is a bus which stops right outside her neighbour's bungalow and goes into the local town. She's made very good use of it since her car was sold to the daughter of the woman who does her garden, and she's enjoyed having some extra cash to spend.

There is just enough room to squeeze onto the drive behind Juliet's Honda Juke, although Stuart does mutter something about, 'She could have pulled further forward,' as he edges closer to her bumper.

I have a front door key, but as with our kids, I never just let myself in when I know there is someone home. I press the bell to announce our arrival and am about to put the key in the lock when the door opens.

'Oh, hi Heather,' I say, trying to regain my composure. 'I didn't realise you'd be here too. I thought you'd be at work.'

Heather is my sister's significant other and has recently been made a partner in the law firm where she's worked since graduating. The two of them have been together for over twenty years and did consider getting married when the law changed, but they haven't got around to it yet.

'Jules asked me to come. It's not a problem, is it?' Heather asks.

'Not at all,' I say brightly. I'm never quite sure how to greet Heather. I have occasionally given her a hug when she arrives at our house with Juliet, but it always feels a bit awkward. Mum's hallway is not very big, and she is pressed as far back against the wall as it is possible to be for me to pass without touching her, so she obviously feels the same way.

'In here, love,' Mum's voice calls out, and I take the cue to edge past Heather into her front room with Stuart closely following me.

Mum is sitting in her favourite chair next to the gas fire

which is on and has made the room uncomfortably warm and stuffy. I have an overwhelming desire to fling the windows open to let some fresh air in, but it's not my place to do that so I slip out of my coat and drape it over the back of the sofa before bending down to embrace Mum. She accepts the hug without really reciprocating. Her attention is already on my husband.

'Come here, you gorgeous man,' she says, arms outstretched towards Stuart. 'Give your mother-in-law a cuddle.'

This treatment isn't exclusively reserved for Stuart. Mum is like it with Callum too and was like it with Juliet's husband, Nigel, before they were divorced.

To his credit, Stuart obliges as he always does.

'You're looking well, Joan,' he says when he's finally extricated himself from her bear hug.

'Oh, not too bad for an old lady,' she twinkles.

My mum was faithfully married to my dad for almost fifty years as far as I know, but she's always had a flirtatious edge with men she encounters, including, much to mine and Juliet's embarrassment, our senior school headmaster. It makes me blush to think about it. I wonder what she would do if any of them responded in a similar manner. Run a mile is my best guess.

'How is Eva?' she continues. 'I tried to call her on Monday after that dreadful pop singer won the dance-off, but there was no reply. Then I remembered she was on her way down to yours to look after Wilfred while you were away. I wasn't expecting you back so soon,' she adds, confusion wrinkling her brow.

She must notice the look that passes between me and Stuart.

'What is it?' she asks. 'There's something wrong, isn't there?'

I notice that her pale, blue-veined hands are gripping the arms of the multi-coloured velvet chair that she bought on a whim from a shop on the high street a couple of years ago. She likes sitting in it because it gives her more support than the chairs in her three-piece suite. She has a point. Even with Juliet's light frame, the chair pulled up next to Mum is positively sagging. Mum's chair doesn't match the other furniture in her lounge, which is upholstered in a tasteful shade of grey, but at least it doesn't clash. I can feel my heart thumping in my chest. The whole reason for coming round to Mum's to tell her about Eva face to face was to do it as gently as possible to cause her the least amount of distress, but we can't lie.

'Stuart?' she persists.

'The thing is, Joan,' he says, dropping to his haunches in front of Mum and releasing her hold on the chair to take her hands into his, 'Eva had a fall in our kitchen.'

Mum inhales sharply, as does Juliet.

'So that's why you've come home,' Heather says. 'Eva can't look after the house and the cat. Couldn't the kids have rallied round?'

Her add-on about Jemma and Callum is infuriating, especially after what they've endured.

'They did rally round, as you put it,' I reply through gritted teeth, working hard to control my anger which is fuelled by my emotional state. 'Jemma called an ambulance, and Cal joined them both at the hospital.'

'Oh, I'm so sorry to hear she had to go to the hospital, Stuart,' Mum says. 'Is that why you're here? Are we going to visit? You'll have to give me a moment to change into something more suitable,' she adds, releasing her hands from Stuart's to press them down on the arms of her chair and aid her into a standing position.

While Mum was talking, I'd caught Juliet's eye, my flash of anger gone, and given a slight shake of my head. Her eyes had widened as she'd realised the gravity of the situation.

'That's not going to be possible, Joan,' Stuart says.

'Oh, well maybe later on then,' Mum says, sinking back down onto her chair with something approaching relief on her face. 'They're sticklers for visiting times, aren't they? Poor Eva stuck there alone. I hope she's got her knitting or the crossword with her. It's my biggest fear, you know. You're admitted with some minor complaint, then you catch that bug thing and come out in a coffin.'

The silence following Mum's words is deafening, and as it stretches into several seconds, I can almost see the penny drop. Her eyes flick from Stuart, who is still crouched at her feet, to me.

'Alexis,' she says, panic mounting in her voice. 'Tell me it's not true.'

'I'm sorry, Mum. We wanted to tell you in person because we knew it would be a shock for you. Eva passed away early yesterday morning. Callum and Jemma were with her,' I add, shooting a meaningful look at Heather.

To her credit, she looks suitably remorseful.

'I'll go and make us all some tea,' she offers.

'I'll come and help,' Juliet says, almost jumping out of her seat as though it is suddenly scalding hot.

I move into the vacated chair and reach for one of Mum's hands. I'm expecting her to ask what happened, whether they had established the cause of death, and I'm preparing myself to explain it to her as gently as I can. She doesn't say either of these things though.

'I'm going to miss our chats,' she says. 'Who am I going to chat with now?'

I've always hoped that my mum would become less self-centred with her advancing years, but it seems that's a forlorn hope.

Belatedly seeming to realise what's expected of her, she

says, 'This is just awful for you, Stuart, but looking on the bright side, at least she won't have to keep going for tests to find out what was wrong with her. Perhaps she didn't mention it to you because she didn't want to upset you, but they were really getting her down.' She turns to look at me. 'Maybe you should have put the cat in a cattery rather than expecting an elderly lady to make such a long journey. Animals are such a tie. You shouldn't have them if you can't commit to looking after them.'

'Mum! That's not a very nice thing to say,' Juliet exclaims from the doorway through to the kitchen. 'Stuart has just lost his mum, and you're pointing the finger of blame at him and Lexi. I do wish you'd think before you speak.'

For a moment, Mum is as taken aback as I am. I've never heard my sister criticise our mother in this way or be so supportive of my feelings, for that matter.

'Don't you dare speak to me like that!' she shouts at Juliet, fixing her with an angry glare. 'This is my house, and I'll say whatever the hell I like to whoever the hell I like. Do I make myself clear?'

The shocked silence that follows my mum's angry outburst seems much longer than the few seconds it undoubtedly was and is broken by Stuart.

'Try to calm down, Joan,' he says in a soothing tone of voice that I would have been unable to muster. 'We're all shocked and emotional. I'm sure Juliet didn't mean to upset you.'

Juliet presses her lips together. Like me, she clearly doesn't trust herself to speak. I'm appalled by my mum's behaviour.

'Sometimes it hurts to hear the truth,' Mum says, her voice calmer but her jaw set firmly. 'It doesn't mean it shouldn't be spoken.'

I'm not surprised that Mum won't accept that she's out of order. I'm fuming that she is criticising me, which is not unusual, but to also lay blame for Eva's death at Stuart's door at a time like this is unforgivable. What I really want to do is get out of this stuffy space, away from Mum with her self-centred view of the world, and breathe in deep lungfuls of air to calm myself down. But if we leave now, who knows what future impact it might have on our relationship with her? I tell myself she's old and in shock, but deep down I know it's simply who she is. The world according to Joan.

'I'll come and help you with the tea,' I say to Juliet. To be honest, it feels a bit cowardly leaving my grieving husband to deal with my mother, but he has a much better chance of smoothing things over than me. I can't speak right now, or I might come out with a few home truths of my own that will drive a proper wedge between us.

'I only came through to ask if you've got any alternative milk,' my sister says as I push past her on my way to the kitchen. 'I can't see any in the cupboard where you usually keep it.'

'No, I haven't. I wasn't expecting you all to just drop in on me unannounced,' I hear Mum say belligerently before the rumble of the kettle boiling and the door closing behind me obscure her words.

Heather has her back to me getting the mugs down from the cupboard. I'm pretty sure she will have heard much of the exchange, but my sister's partner has always tended to stay out of family disputes. Maybe it's her legal training that makes her cautious and unwilling to get involved in things that don't directly concern her.

Mum's kitchen is compact, to use estate agent's terminology, so there isn't really room for three of us to be preparing hot drinks, but I had to get away from Mum. I sit down on one of the chairs at the two-seater table underneath the window with a view out over the back garden. It's as neat and tidy as it was when my dad was alive, but no credit can be attributed to my mother, who has no interest in it other than to sit outside with her morning coffee on sunny days.

I hear the kitchen door open and am aware of Juliet behind me before she places her hand on my shoulder.

'That was completely out of order,' she says, giving my shoulder a gentle squeeze. 'Are you okay?'

'Thanks for sticking up for me, sis,' I say without turning to face her but reaching my hand up to place it over hers. I don't want her to see the tears in my eyes. We don't always see eye to eye when it comes to Mum, each of us thinking that she favours the other. I sometimes wonder if she does it deliberately to play us off against each other. She's like a puppeteer pulling the strings. 'The only reason I didn't shout back at her is because I think she will miss Eva terribly,' I continue. 'They only saw each other occasionally, but they both enjoyed their telephone conversations even though they didn't always agree. It will make her feel more isolated, especially in the winter months when she can't get out as much.'

'It's not just that,' Heather says.

I turn my head in her direction, surprised by her interjection.

'What do you mean?' Juliet asks, her tone suggesting that she's as surprised by Heather's comment as I am.

'They're a similar age. Eva dying is a graphic reminder of Joan's own mortality. Maybe she should be more mindful about the impact her words have on others, but I think in this case she's just scared of what the end of her life might be like,' Heather concludes before turning back to deal with the hot drinks. 'Still milk and one sugar for you and Stuart?' she asks, a teaspoon poised above the white ceramic container with the word *sugar* embossed on it.

'Yes, thanks,' I reply as she plunges the spoon into the golden granules once for each of us before stirring each mug. Mum would approve. She doesn't like the spoon to go back into the sugar wet.

If either of us had said what Heather just said to the other, it wouldn't have sounded so reasonable, but coming from her it makes perfect sense. My heart unexpectedly twists thinking of my mum being lonely, and anxious about her own death.

'Come on,' Juliet says, picking up two of the hot drinks that Heather has finished preparing and encouraging me to do the same. 'Let's go and make our peace.'

FOURTEEN
FRIDAY 29 SEPTEMBER

Stuart and I had delayed making the call to Shona the previous evening as neither of us had felt up to it emotionally. We suspected she would be very upset by the news of Eva's death, but neither of us realised how utterly devastated she would be, in stark contrast to the way Mari had reacted to her mother's passing.

Between us, we'd managed to smooth things over with Mum before we'd left her house around lunchtime. Heather's words about Mum being afraid of her own mortality had a ring of truth about them and had certainly helped calm my anger at what I'd perceived to be another example of Mum's self-centred attitude. She's not selfish, far from it. She loves treating us all to surprises just to see the joy on our faces, but she can be very tunnel-visioned. I've warmed to Heather after her insightful input into Mum's reaction to Eva's death. I don't dislike Heather; it's just we don't really have much in common, apart from Juliet of course.

I'd rung Jenny, my boss at News 24/7, on her personal number to tell her about Eva while we were on the drive home from Mum's. She was very sympathetic and is going to see if and where I can be put back on the roster before I would have been back from holiday. I explained we'd like to be able to rebook our holiday for a later date; I didn't have much annual leave left to use before the end of the year. She's also promised to check the compassionate leave allowance for me. I'll probably have to top that up with annual leave as I'm guessing we'll need to be in Skye for a week or so around the time of the funeral.

Neither of us wanted to make the call to Shona from the car. She was so much more to my mother-in-law than a carer and an extra pair of hands. Although I'd become much closer to Eva after her husband died, I wasn't always on hand for a good old gossip about the latest overheard conversation in the supermarket in Portree. Shona had become Eva's friend and confidante as well as being her employee.

Shona answers on the third ring, an element of surprise in her voice suggesting to me that Eva must have given her my mobile number along with Stuart's to dial in case there was an emergency. She must have it stored on her phone.

'Hello,' she says tentatively in her soft Scottish accent. She's probably wondering why on earth I would be ringing her from Barbados.

'Hello, Shona. It's Lexi, Stuart's wife,' I say.

My phone is lying on the kitchen table between me and Stuart and is on speaker.

'Yes,' she says followed by silence on the other end of the call. I'm pretty sure she's guessed that something is wrong; otherwise, why would we be phoning from our holiday? I thought I could do this, but I'm struggling to find the words. I shake my head at Stuart.

'Shona, it's Stuart,' my husband says.

I can't be certain, but I think I hear an exhalation of breath. Maybe she thought I was ringing to tell her that something had happened to Stuart and that I was phoning to enlist her help in breaking the news to Eva of an accident while jet-skiing or some such thing. This is agonisingly painful. It's so much more difficult than either of us had envisaged.

'Erm, I'm afraid we have some sad news,' he continues. We lock eyes, and I urge him to continue speaking, but he's faltering just as I'd thought he might.

'The thing is, Shona,' I say, swallowing back the tears that are threatening to prevent me from speaking. 'The thing is, and I'm so sorry to have to tell you this over the phone, but I'm afraid Eva has passed away.'

A terrible wailing sound comes from the phone. The only discernible word is, 'no', followed by more wailing. In the background I can hear a man's voice, although I can't hear what he is saying. I wish now we'd thought to ask Shona if she had anyone with her. This is awful news to hear alone, especially as it's so unexpected.

'Who is this?' a man's voice demands, sounding agitated. 'What's going on?'

Stuart picks up the reins.

'Is that Rory?' he asks.

'Aye.'

Shona's husband is one of less than half the older male population of Skye to have a name other than Donald.

'It's Stuart Drummond. Eva's son. I'm so sorry we had to be the bearers of such awful news to your wife, but we'd rather she heard it from us than anyone else,' Stuart says.

The sound of sobbing is almost drowning out Rory's voice.

'What news?' he demands, although I suspect he might already have guessed judging by his wife's reaction.

'I'm afraid my mum passed away suddenly yesterday morning.'

'Well, you have my condolences, lad. Eva was a fine woman. If it's all the same to you though, I'm going to end the call to look after my wife. She'll probably want to call you back to find out what happened when she's over the shock, if that's alright?'

'Of course,' Stuart says before the call is terminated.

'Oh my God, that poor woman,' I say. 'She's been a constant companion to Eva since your dad died. I hope she'll be okay.'

'She's in shock, which is completely understandable. It's going to be a massive change for her not going up to Mum's every day. It's going to take a bit of getting used to,' he says.

What he doesn't add, and doesn't need to, is what we discussed before making the call. There isn't a huge amount of work for the local residents on Skye outside of the tourist season. Not only will Shona miss Eva's physical presence, but she will also miss her wages. Stuart and I have agreed we will keep her on for the moment, if she can bear being in the house without Eva there. It's a big old house and will need to be kept clean and tidy for when we put it on the market. That will probably take several months, but once it's sold, I'm not sure what she will do for work. Poor Shona, her friendship and her livelihood ended in the space of a few minutes.

Stuart and I have just finished beans on toast for our lunch when my phone rings. I snatch it up expecting it to be Shona, but it's Jenny from work.

'You're in luck, Alexis. Amanda has called in sick. Apparently, she has Covid... again!' she says with more than a hint of scepticism in her voice. 'She's supposed to be in from tomorrow for the next four days on the late shift. I thought I'd offer it to you first if you feel up to it?'

'Can you give me ten minutes, Jenny? I'll just run it past Stuart, but put me down as a heavy pencil.'

'Sure,' she says, ending the call.

Stuart's eyebrows are raised.

'A heavy pencil for what, Lexi?' he asks.

I explain about the potential shifts.

'Are you sure you're ready to go into work?' he asks. 'You've had a hell of a shock yourself, plus the upset of breaking the news to other people.'

'There's nothing much we can do for now though, until we can start planning the funeral,' I say carefully, making no mention of autopsies and coroners' reports. 'I think I'd rather keep busy at work. But I won't go in if you'd rather me be here with you.'

Stuart takes a moment, clearly weighing things up.

'I'll be fine,' he says. 'But I agree with you about keeping busy. I might go up to Mum's to make a start on sorting things out. You know what a terrible hoarder she is...' he pauses before correcting himself. 'I need to start getting used to thinking of Mum in the past tense. I guess it hasn't fully sunk in yet.'

'Oh Stuart,' I say, reaching across the table for his hand. 'You can't go to Eva's on your own. I'll ring Jenny back and tell her it's a no, and we'll both go.'

He smiles and squeezes my hand.

'Thank you for saying that, but from a practical point of view it makes no sense. The burden of the mortgage payments has fallen on your shoulders since I accepted early retirement. I had hoped the lump sum that Pixton's gave me would last a little longer, but it's surprising how quickly you go through it when there isn't a regular pay cheque coming in.'

Stuart's right. What had seemed like a lot of money was quickly consumed by having to replace the fencing all down one side of our property, not to mention some of the roof tiles which were dislodged during the same storm. I love our house, but it positively eats money.

'To be fair, they didn't give you much of a choice. Just like News 24/7. Restructuring almost always means getting rid of older members of staff,' I say.

'Well, it's history now, but if you need to take unpaid leave at any point to top up your compassionate leave, you'll be worrying about affording the next instalment, and that's not fair. I'll be fine going up on my own, and I'm sure Shona will help me while I'm there.'

I know he's right. The amount of money I have left out of my pay cheque each month once the mortgage has been paid is frighteningly low. I'd love to be able to take early retirement so that Stuart and I can enjoy our lives together, especially considering that both our dads died in their early seventies, but we're committed to three more years on our current fixed rate if we don't want to pay the early repayment charge.

Alongside saving for our Barbados trip, we've been squirrelling away two hundred pounds a month into an ISA. Those savings, combined with taking a tax-free 25% lump sum out of my company pension, should just about give us enough to pay off the mortgage completely at the end of the fixed term, but that seems such a long way off.

'Ring Jenny back and tell her you'll do it,' Stuart is saying. 'You won't be able to stay off work until after the funeral anyway, and as you say, being busy will keep your mind off things.'

'Are you sure?' I ask. 'The holiday has left us scrabbling around for cash a bit, even though I'll probably be able to get some overtime shifts in the run-up to Christmas. The younger members of staff that I work with call in sick for the slightest thing. There's no dedication to the job any more.'

'I agree,' Stuart says. 'But just be careful who you share that opinion with.'

'I always watch my back,' I say. 'So, are you okay for me to call Jenny and tell her I'll do it before she books someone else?'

'Yes, but only if you're sure you're up to it,' he says.

I nod and smile reassuringly before picking up my phone to call Jenny back.

'And Lexi,' he adds. 'Try not to worry too much about money. There'll be some from Mum's estate when we're eventually allowed to sell the house.'

I wonder if the thought of selling his family home fills Stuart with as much sadness as it does me.

Later, snuggled up on the sofa watching Friday night television, we open the half bottle of champagne that I'd bought at the supermarket earlier. We won't be celebrating our pearl wedding anniversary on Sunday, as I'm now working and Stuart will be on Skye, but neither did we want it to slip by completely unacknowledged.

'Cheers to us,' I say, chinking my lead crystal champagne flute against his.

'To us,' he responds.

It couldn't be further from the celebration we had planned, but somehow it doesn't really matter. We have each other and that's all that really counts.

FIFTEEN
SUNDAY 22 OCTOBER

I glance up at the corner of the screen on the top left of the bank of monitors in front of me. There's only another fifteen minutes to go before I'm done for the night, and it can't come soon enough. The thought of climbing into my comfortable king-sized bed warmed by the fluffy hot water bottle that Stuart will have placed on my side is incredibly appealing.

I hated finishing my night shift at News 24/7 and going home to an empty house while Stuart was away in Skye. Empty apart from Wilfie who, I must confess, I allowed to sleep on the bed next to me rather than in his cosy cat basket in the utility room. He's been a bit miffed that he's once again been relegated to the utility room since Stuart has been home.

I finish at midnight tonight, but my head still won't hit my pillow much before 2 a.m. after a quick debrief, writing a shift report and the drive home. I could have done with a few extra hours in bed as we have to be up at 7 a.m., but it was another extra shift that I didn't feel as though I could turn down. Everything is already packed for the week away from home, and we are flying from Heathrow to Glasgow on this trip to accompany Eva's coffin. We've arranged to hire a car from Glasgow and

Stuart will do most of the driving, so I'll be able to grab forty winks on the way. To be honest, I think I could sleep almost anywhere at the moment after the three weeks I've just endured.

It's been tough both physically and emotionally since we arrived back from Barbados. Although Amanda is now back at work after her latest bout of Covid, she'd apparently managed to infect two of the other editors, Carlotta and Tarkin, both of whose shifts I was able to pick up. I worked seven days straight, which is the maximum we're allowed to do at News 24/7, then had two days off before going back in for four days. I also managed a couple of swapped shifts with my bestie, Lucy, so that I can take a week off for the funeral. Two days off, then the four days, or rather nights, I've just completed, which I was down to do anyway after my original holiday dates. At least it was all late shifts, so my body clock wasn't flipping from earlies to lates, but it's little wonder that I'm feeling exhausted.

Lucy was as appalled as I was when I received the email from Jenny on the final day of my run of seven days straight regarding compassionate leave.

Hi Alexis,

I'm sorry to have to tell you that it is not News 24/7's policy to grant compassionate leave on the death of a non-relative. I did go back to HR and ask them to reconsider in light of your twenty years of service with the company and how close you were to your mother-in-law, but it was a flat no, I'm afraid.

Obviously, I'll approve any unpaid leave you need to take around the funeral dates, and I'm fine for you to swap shifts if others are willing so that you don't eat too much into your remaining paid holiday, but apart from that, I'm afraid my hands are tied.

Jenny

I'd sat staring at the screen for several minutes, unable to comprehend what I was reading, before forwarding the email to Lucy with a message.

> Callous bastards! When I think of all the times I've come into work feeling less than a hundred per cent, rather than taking a sickie like some do, mentioning no names… (Snowflake Personified), it makes me wonder why I've bothered. Seriously! How valued do I now feel?!?!?

Lucy doesn't respond to my email but instead appears at my desk a few moments later.

'Can you believe it?' I start to say in a raised voice.

'Not here,' she says, glancing around the production office. There are only a handful of people in here, but Lucy is clearly bothered about the volume of my voice. 'Let's get a coffee,' she adds, taking hold of my elbow and steering me towards the double doors that lead to the stairwell and lifts up to the cafeteria on the top floor.

'Go and grab us a table in one of the booths, and I'll get the cappuccinos in,' Lucy says, gesturing to the far corner near the window.

If she's hoping I will have calmed down a bit by the time she places the frothy coffee on our table, she's sadly mistaken. If anything, I'm even more agitated sitting there thinking about all the occasions I've worked overtime to help News 24/7 out in a crisis, missing some special moments with my kids, like sports days and Christmas carol concerts, all because of my misplaced sense of duty.

'Can you actually believe they're refusing to give me a few days of compassionate leave after all I've done for them over the past twenty-odd years?' I say, launching straight into a rant before Lucy has had the chance to sit down. 'Twenty bloody years of my life, and this is how they repay me. You couldn't make it up,' I say, taking a gulp of my drink and instantly regretting it. It's still far too hot and scalds my tongue, not to mention the roof of my mouth, where I'll probably develop a blister.

'I know,' Lucy says, sensibly blowing on her drink before taking a small sip. 'It doesn't seem fair. You'd think they might make an exception in certain circumstances rather than sticking to the rule book. But don't do anything stupid. You're emotionally wrought and physically tired after seven days straight on shift. Take a minute to consider your options.'

'You know what's really infuriating?' I say, ignoring Lucy's attempt to calm me down. 'If I'd known they wouldn't grant compassionate leave, I could have called in sick like all the snowflake generation do. *Sorry*,' I say in a simpering tone, '*I can't come into work today because I've got a cold.* Boohoo! Take a bloody Day Nurse like the rest of us do and get on with your job! Do you know how many days of sick leave I've taken since I started at this company?' I demand.

Lucy shrugs and shakes her head.

'Eight!' I almost shout. 'Eight days off sick in over twenty years.'

'Impressive,' Lucy says, taking another sip of her coffee. 'I think I've had more than that,' she admits.

'But I'll bet not as many as Snowflake Personified. She's been here less than two years, and I know for a fact that she's been off at least a quarter of that time because she's on the same shift pattern as me. It's a joke! Honestly, Lucy, if I could afford to resign, I would. I'm sick to death of the place and the internal politics. It's pathetic.' I take another huge gulp of my coffee, which has thankfully cooled down to a more manageable temperature while I've been raving.

'If you can't beat them, join them,' Lucy says, her voice so quiet that I almost miss what she says.

'What do you mean?'

'They owe you those days off for the funeral, which you are going to have to take as holiday. Agreed?'

'Well, not officially, but morally, I guess,' I reply becoming slightly calmer.

'So, next time you want a few days paid leave, catch a cold or flu,' she says, winking. 'Or have a raging migraine. You can self-certify for up to seven days, so you don't even need to see the doctor who signs you off.'

'You're joking?'

'Nope. Stop being so fiercely loyal to a company that doesn't value the sentiment. Do what everyone else does; only in your case, you've earned it.'

'No wonder companies have to restructure and let people go,' I say, using my fingers as speech marks. 'The work ethic of the twenty-something brigade is virtually non-existent. What a sad state of affairs.'

'The point is, Lexi, if everyone does it, why should you be the exception? Don't let the bastards win,' she adds, downing the rest of her drink.

I spoon the last of the froth into my mouth. It's the bit with the chocolate shavings on it, which is the only reason I ever order a cappuccino, if I'm honest. Lucy has talked me down off my high horse and has offered to swap any of her shifts with mine if it will help.

'Thanks, Lucy,' I say. 'I don't know what I would do without you.'

'That's what friends are for,' she says as we place the tray with our two empty mugs onto the rack to be cleaned. At least News 24/7 have got something right and are no longer using disposable plastic cups.

I'm still seething at the injustice as we make our way back downstairs, but no one will ever realise it from the response I'm planning to send to Jenny.

> Thank you for trying, Jenny.
>
> Lucy has offered to swap some shifts with me. I'll let you know the dates in question when the funeral arrangements have been finalised.
>
> Alexis

I hit the send button so hard that I'm surprised I don't break the computer.

The previous day, not long after Stuart had surfaced from his long drive back from Scotland, we'd heard from the coroner's office stating that the autopsy had confirmed Eva's cause of death was a bleed in the brain caused by a ruptured aneurism, exactly as Dr Constantine had suspected. They were happy to release Eva's body to the undertaker who was to prepare her for the journey to Skye in readiness for her funeral.

It gave us some closure, knowing that once the aneurism had burst, there was very little that could be done medically to try and save her, and even if they had been able to, the chances were very high that there would have been some brain damage. Both Stuart and I knew that Eva would not have wanted to continue living a shadow of her former life. Devastating as it was for us that we were unable to say our goodbyes, it was undoubtedly the best thing for Eva.

At around the same time as I was contemplating marching into Jenny's office and handing in my resignation, Stuart was confirming the date of Eva's funeral, which had been reserved with Donald Campbell and Co. in Portree. But that was not all he was organising. He'd gone behind my back to secretly rebook our holiday in Barbados because he thought I looked completely exhausted when he got back from Skye. He told me all about it over breakfast the next morning and looked so pleased with himself. Eva's funeral was on a Friday, we would stay on Skye for the scattering of her ashes on the following Monday and then head back to Berkshire to prepare for our second attempt at the Barbados trip. It wasn't going to cost us anything, thanks to the compassion of the hotel and the airline, something not mirrored by my employers.

I hadn't wanted to burst Stuart's bubble, so I decided not to tell him about News 24/7 refusing me compassionate leave. With the swaps Lucy had offered me and a couple of extra shifts, I would be able to cover the time away on Skye for the funeral, but I wouldn't have enough paid holiday left for the whole Barbados trip, so I would have to take a couple of unpaid days leave if I couldn't get any overtime shifts.

'Am I running the VT?' I hear my director, Frankie, ask.

'Yes, sorry, I was just checking on a breaking news story on social media,' I lie.

Frankie doesn't comment but plays in the pre-recorded piece from the previous hour about a suspected sighting of a black panther on the loose in the Surrey Hills. The footage is grainy, and I strongly suspect it's a domestic cat not dissimilar to Wilfie that someone has manipulated for their five minutes of fame, but it's a slow news night, and it will fill the final few minutes of the show.

As the footage comes to an end, the newsreader, Janine Frost, says, 'If you see the creature, do not approach it as it could be dangerous.'

Tired as I am, an image of Wilfie bearing his fangs and hissing at Jemma fills my mind, making me smile.

SIXTEEN
WEDNESDAY 25 OCTOBER

The sunlight glittering on the expanse of ocean and the cloudless cerulean sky are deceptive. I'm just back from a walk along the deserted beach and can confirm to anyone who might be interested that the day hasn't climbed into double digits and is unlikely to now as it's the middle of the afternoon. I remove my knitted bobble hat, unravel the colourful scarf from around my neck, both hand-knitted by Eva, and deposit them on the white ceramic hook in the hallway where I've just hung my quilted coat. The whole house is struggling to warm up despite Stuart and I arriving a couple of days ago, and a shiver runs through me as I head to the warmest room, the kitchen.

I've never craved a Rayburn or Aga as so many people do. I've always thought it was a yuppy-led trend that was a lot more bother than it was worth. I'm an okay cook, but I don't do a lot because of my shift work at the television channel, so for us it would mostly be used for heating and hot water. I open the door to the kitchen and the warmth envelopes me as I cross the flagstone floor to the Belfast sink, collecting the kettle on the way. The water trickles rather than gushes from the old-fashioned tap, but I'm in no rush. Once full, I cross back to the Rayburn and use an oven glove to lift the lid that covers one of the rings. I'm grateful that Shona had lit it in advance of our arrival. We had hot water for a bath after our long journey and something to cook on, not to mention one room in which we weren't compelled to wear several layers of winter woollies.

Eva's kitchen is huge and is so much more than merely a place to prepare food. It is, and always has been, the absolute heart of her home, large enough to accommodate a generous rectangular wooden table in the centre of the room that permanently has eight chairs positioned around it and has, on special occasions, seated twelve people. The Rayburn is in the centre of one wall with plentiful work surface space on either side, above which are tall cupboards that Eva had painted a delicate shade of primrose a few years ago. Before then, they had been a dark oak shade that allowed for the appreciation of the natural grain of the wood but felt a little oppressive. The yellow brightens the space immensely and Eva also had the three-seater sofa, which stretches along one of the other walls, reupholstered to match. The addition of cushions decorated with flowers and bees adds to the warm, homely feel.

On the wall opposite to the Rayburn is the door from the hallway and the door to the scullery-cum-boot room, separated by more cupboards above the work surface and a big American-style fridge freezer. Stuart had initially questioned his mum's £2000 investment in something that he wasn't sure she would get full use of, but she'd said she was finding it difficult to reach down into the old chest freezer in the scullery. Similarly, reaching into her under-worktop fridge was awkward for her, and she added that it was never big enough when people were staying.

By people, Eva meant us. As far as I know, no one else stayed with Eva, and we didn't visit that often. A pang of guilt clutches my heart as I place the kettle on the Rayburn. There were times when Stuart and I took a holiday from work when we could easily have come to stay, but we didn't. It seems selfish to me now, but at the time, I'd wanted to lie on a beach and read a story in a book rather than listen to someone relating real-life stories.

I cross back to the sink, resting my hands on the curved enamel edge and gaze out on a sight that Eva would have enjoyed almost daily since she and Donald had inherited the house from his grandparents five months before Stuart was born. I've heard so many tales about the near-seventy years she had lived in this house, but I can't help wondering how many more stories she shared with Shona, and yet more that will go with her to her grave. I've been tearful on and off since Eva's passing, shocked at times by how emotional I feel, but now, feasting my eyes on the green fields spread out before me, leading to the ocean with its white-capped waves and the mainland in the distance, the tears start to flow in earnest.

The whistle of the kettle several minutes later has me reaching for the linen tea towel both to mop my eyes and also to wrap around the handle of the kettle, which inexplicably is made of metal rather than something heat-resistant. That's when I become aware of my husband standing in the kitchen doorway.

'You were a long time,' Stuart says, no hint of reproach in his voice.

'I lost track of time,' I reply. 'I didn't realise how far I'd walked until I turned around to come back. It was cathartic being alone with my thoughts on a deserted beach with only the seagulls for company.'

'A penny for them,' he says, pulling out one of the kitchen chairs with its faded floral seat cushion and sinking down onto it.

'What, the seagulls?' I tease.

'I wouldn't give you a penny for them,' he replies. 'Nasty,

vicious creatures. I'll have a brew if you're making one. It's still a bit nippy in the rest of the house.'

Not usually one to bear a grudge, Stuart still hasn't forgiven the seagull who assaulted him when we were on a day out in Brighton when the children were young. It was an accident, of course. The bird caught the back of Stuart's hand with the point of its sharp beak while in the process of nicking a chip from the polystyrene tray he was carrying. He dropped the rest of his chips, such was his shock, and he's borne a grudge against seagulls ever since.

'You seem to have got the hang of that thing again,' he adds, indicating the Rayburn, where I'm closing the ring cover to keep the heat in with the oven glove, having first removed the kettle.

'To me, this thing is as vicious as the seagulls,' I reply. I don't know how many times I've burnt myself on it over the years because I forgot the handles get scalding hot, and it isn't a good idea to touch them with your bare hand. 'I will concede though, that it's very efficient at heating the room. It's flipping freezing out there.'

Stuart grins. 'Once a southern softie, always a southern softie. We're not quite into November yet. This is positively mild.'

'Says the man who was just complaining about it being nippy in the rest of the house,' I reply, chucking the tea towel at him.

It feels good to be having a bit of harmless banter after everything we've been through since Eva's death. I'd hated seeing her lifeless body lying in the hospital bed. But even worse for me was the thought that they weren't going to leave her in peace.

The doctor had requested the autopsy be performed to absolutely establish the cause of death. As suspected, it was a ruptured aneurism, but what the report couldn't establish with any degree of certainty was how long Eva had had a ticking time bomb in her head. The pathologist's report suggested it could have been there for as long as twenty or thirty years. The thought that it might have burst while she was driving along the treacherous roads on Skye while she had the precious cargo of my two children in the car when they used to stay with Stuart's parents each year during the summer holidays had brought me out in a cold sweat. Losing Eva at the age of eighty-eight is of course a tragedy, but does anyone ever really get over the death of a young child? I'm pretty sure I wouldn't have been able to.

After ducking to avoid the inexpertly aimed tea towel, Stuart stoops to pick it up from the floor then comes round to my side of the table and pulls me into a hug. We've been doing a lot of hugging since Eva died, each gaining strength from the other when we're at a low ebb.

'You look like you've been crying,' he says, gently brushing his fingers across the top of my cheek.

'Guilty as charged,' I say. 'I guess it's being here knowing that your mum isn't and thinking of all the times she looked out of that window at that beautiful view,' I add, biting down on my lip to prevent myself from blubbing again.

If I'm feeling this way, goodness knows how Stuart must be feeling. He obviously knows what's going through my mind, which isn't surprising considering how long we have been together, as he answers my unspoken question.

'It feels strange being in my childhood home without either of my parents here,' Stuart says, resting his chin on the top of my head. 'I keep expecting to see Mum sitting on the sofa knitting every time I open the door to the lounge or calling up from the foot of the stairs that breakfast is ready. I've got this weird feeling that her spirit hasn't left yet.' He pauses briefly. 'It's almost as though she wasn't ready to go.'

I pull away from my husband and look into his eyes questioningly.

'No,' he says, shaking his head. 'I don't mean like a ghost

haunting a building. It's more as though she's waiting for something.'

I agree with everything that Stuart has just said. I can feel her presence in every inch of this wonderful old house. It's little wonder she didn't want to move into a care home nearer to us so that we could keep an eye on her. Why would anyone choose to leave this splendid solitude to be surrounded by the sound of shuffling feet and moans about the aches and pains of old age, not to mention the smell of boiled cabbage or, worse still, urine. I've had plenty of time for contemplation over the past four weeks while we waited for the coroner's report so that we could then go ahead and organise Eva's funeral. I've concluded that the way she died, although more prematurely than we would have hoped, is what she herself would have wanted.

Eva wasn't one to complain, but over the past year she'd said to me on more than one occasion, 'Growing old is for the healthy. I don't want to be hanging on to life either physically or mentally incapacitated. I'd rather die a quick death than a lingering one.' Recalling those conversations has helped me accept what happened, but I'm still filled with guilt and regret that Stuart and I weren't with her to say our goodbyes.

'It's this whole limbo period we've been in,' I say. 'Maybe once the funeral is over, we'll be better able to remember the happy times rather than the tragic circumstances of her death, and that in turn will allow us to let her go.'

'I hope the weather stays like this on Friday,' Stuart says. 'It would be good to give her the send-off she would have wanted.'

Between us, Stuart and I have done our best to carry out Eva's wishes. Perhaps she had an inkling that she didn't have much time left because she'd written a very comprehensive list of who she wanted to attend the service and what music she wanted playing, complete with the reasons why, which had made writing the eulogy so much easier. She also left strict instructions about what was to happen to her ashes. She wanted half to be buried in the roots of a new rowan tree to be planted in her garden and the rest to be scattered along the shoreline.

I think Eva presumed she would die in this house, so the starting point of her final journey will be from here. She is currently resting at Campbells, the funeral directors in Portree, having travelled up from Berkshire with us on Monday. It had been sobering watching her coffin being loaded into the hold for the flight up to Glasgow, where we were met by Donald Campbell himself for the coffin to be transferred into a hearse for the onward journey.

'I checked the forecast,' I say. 'This current high pressure is set to last for a week, so Friday should be perfect for the service, and hopefully Monday will still be good for planting the tree and scattering the ashes.'

'It seems so final,' Stuart sighs. 'It was bad enough when Dad died, but this is the end of their era. It just leaves me questioning, what was the point of it all?'

'The journey,' I say. 'That's why we need to make the most of every moment because our time is running out too.'

'Is it selfish to say that I hope I go before you?' Stuart says, bringing my hands up to his lips and imparting a kiss on them. 'I can't imagine my life without you in it. It would have no meaningful purpose.'

'Don't let Jemma and Callum hear you say that,' I say, a smile playing at the corners of my mouth. 'They already think I'm more important in your life than they are. Don't give them actual ammunition.'

'You are,' he says. 'I love my kids, but I didn't choose them, they're blood relatives. Same as I didn't choose my sister,' he adds, a shadow passing across his face.

'What time do you think Mari will get here tomorrow?' I ask.

'Early afternoon, I'd say. Probably about the same time as the kids.'

Jemma, Will, Callum and Ellie are all driving up together so that they can take turns with the driving and share the cost of the fuel. They're planning on leaving very early, 5 a.m. was the last I heard, so as not to get caught in the morning rush hour. Ellie's in her second trimester now so I'm hoping her morning sickness has eased off. I did tell Callum that we'd all understand if she didn't feel she could face the long journey, but she wouldn't hear of it. Will has volunteered his Audi A7 for the trip as the largest and most luxurious vehicle, which should make it a more comfortable journey.

'Then we'd better make the most of tonight,' I say.

A hopeful look appears on Stuart's face, and I immediately regret my choice of words, although weirdly, the physical side of our relationship has dramatically improved since our pre-breakfast lovemaking in Barbados. That all seems such a long time ago now. Both the hotel and the airline offered us a choice of a refund or a credit note for the cost of our aborted holiday. I'm glad we decided on the latter, and now I've accepted that Stuart made quite a big decision without checking with me, I'm happy that we'll be flying back to the Caribbean next week.

'I meant continuing to sort through all your mum's paperwork,' I say.

His face falls.

'But if we plough on, I might be up for an early night,' I add, a hint of suggestion in my voice.

SEVENTEEN
THURSDAY 26 OCTOBER

The whole house is feeling much warmer this morning thanks to the Rayburn finally warming up the dozen or so radiators. It's just as well as we have six people arriving today.

Stuart and I made up beds in four of the bedrooms yesterday evening before we sat down to our dinner of cauliflower and broccoli cheesy bake. It was always one of Eva's favourites when she stayed at our house, so I wanted to make it in her honour. I would have done it for everyone tonight, but Ellie is not keen on cauliflower, and Will rarely eats cheese. He's not lactose intolerant like Juliet, but he is into his fitness and describes cheese as the enemy. I'm quite happy to go to war with a slice of cheddar on a hot buttered crumpet or slivers of Comté or Manchego on my favourite crackers. To be honest, I'm not sure whether it would have been to Mari and her daughter Fleur's taste either so it made sense to cook it last night for the two of us.

We've given Mari and Fleur a room each. I'm fairly sure that Mari would be happy to share a bedroom with her daughter, but not so sure about them sharing a bed. All seven of the bedrooms in Eva's sprawling house have double beds which in fairness have seen better days. It's one thing for a couple to be on a slightly sagging mattress, resulting in a roll together, but something else entirely for a mother and daughter.

Mari's husband, Todd, had been unable to make the trip to Scotland, saying he had no one to look after the animals on his smallholding, and Fleur's husband, Brett, was staying home to look after their two boys. Todd has a point about getting someone you trust to look after your animals. It's bad enough getting someone to feed Wilfie. Despite my mum's suggestion, I can't bear the thought of him going into a cattery, and I wouldn't trust her to have him at her house as she would forget he's a house cat and leave her windows or back door open. Not that she's ever offered to have him, so it's irrelevant. Callum and Jemma have taken it in turns since we left home on Monday and have promised to do the same while we're away in Barbados, even though it adds a thirty-minute round trip to each end of their working day. But while we're all away, I've had to beg a favour from our next-door neighbour which no doubt we'll have to repay at some point.

Annette has six cats, none of whom go out after what happened to their first cat soon after we moved into our house, so litter tray duty will be a bit of a mission. At least she's used to being around cats though, and Wilfie seemed to give her a sniff of approval when she popped round for me to show her where everything was.

After dinner and the washing up, we'd made a start on going through more of Eva's paperwork. Stuart had brought our shredder up with him on his first visit, and it's just as well that he did. Eva had kept utility bills from the 1950s when they'd first moved into Rowan House, not to mention all the accounts from Donald's motor repair business. I hate to think how many trees were chopped down to produce all that paper, but at least it could all go into the recycling after shredding.

We did get an early night but fell asleep cuddling in the dip of the mattress rather than anything more romantic.

Shona is coming up to the house after breakfast to make sure that the dining room is spotlessly clean for Eva's arrival around lunchtime. We opted for a sealed coffin. My family have all seen Eva since her passing, and neither Shona nor Mari and Fleur expressed the desire to see her. I'm sure funeral parlours know how to make the deceased look as though they are just sleeping, but I'd rather remember her as she was.

I'm just washing up at the kitchen sink when I notice a car which looks as though it is driving across a field. It isn't. The road is not visible from the vantage point of the kitchen window, giving the impression that the Drummonds' land stretches down to the beach and the sea beyond. If it is Shona, she will be here in a few minutes, taking a left turn off the coast road and driving up the single-track lane with its passing places before turning onto Eva's driveway.

She did ring us back on the day we had broken the tragic news of Eva's death to her, apologising for overreacting, which of course we dismissed, saying it was good to know how much Eva had been loved. She was also at the house a couple of times when Stuart was here three weeks ago, and again on Monday morning to light the Rayburn for us. There is quite a large woodstore at the side of the house, which is well-stocked at the moment, but we'll have to check with Shona about replenishing it. The last thing we want is for the house to get damp with no one living in it.

Shona only stays for an hour, saying she doesn't want to be here when the hearse carrying Eva's slight body arrives. Donald Campbell has brought his son, and between the four of us, we carry the coffin through to the dining table, which Shona has covered with a white jacquard tablecloth. The official flowers will be brought up by Donald tomorrow to adorn Eva's coffin for her final journey, but I've picked some greenery and some dahlias from the garden and put them in a vase on the centre of the casket. I've also lit some lavender candles. I started buying them for her every Mother's Day after Stuart's dad died, and she claimed it was her favourite scent. I'll leave them burning in the fireplace, protected by the ornate fire guard until they are burned through.

Stuart and I decide to go out for a walk before everyone arrives. It might sound strange, but Eva lived in this house on her own for many years after her husband died. It feels right that she should spend a little bit of time here without us.

We've only been back long enough to have a bowl of soup accompanied by the crusty bread that Shona had brought up with her from the village when we hear the squeak of the metal gate rolling along its runner. It's only just after 3 p.m. so it can't be Jemma and Callum with their respective partners unless they left in the middle of the night.

'Do you want me to make myself scarce?' I ask.

'Why would I want you to do that?' Stuart says, replying to my question with one of his own.

'I just thought you and Mari might need a bit of space,' I say, giving a light shrug of my shoulders.

'I don't think so,' he says, opening the kitchen door and beckoning for me to follow him out into the hallway where I can already see the shadowy outlines of two people through the glass panels of the inner door. The outer door is solid wood and encloses the porch when winter properly sets in.

'Mari and I are siblings, but we barely know each other, and we certainly have nothing to say that I wouldn't want you to hear,' he adds.

With that, he opens the door, and I'm not sure if he is being ironic when he says, 'Welcome home, Mari.'

'You always did have a sharp sense of humour,' Mari says, allowing Stuart to embrace her briefly. 'This is Fleur,' she continues, indicating a tall, slim woman with long copper-coloured hair standing at her side. 'Meet your Uncle Stuart and Aunt Alexis.'

'Lexi, please,' I say. 'I'm only ever called Alexis by my boss at work and my mum when I've done something she disapproves of.'

'Really?' Mari says. 'That's odd, because Mum always referred to you as Alexis.' There's an edge to her voice, but I'm not sure of the point she is trying to make. 'Is she here?' Mari continues, returning her attention to Stuart. 'Mum,' she clarifies, responding to Stuart's confused expression.

'Oh, yes. She's in the dining room. The coffin's sealed, but go in.'

Mari gives her brother a withering look which seems to convey that she doesn't require his permission to see their mother.

'Or I can show you up to your rooms if you'd prefer to freshen up first,' I offer, anxious for there not to be an unpleasant atmosphere.

'Rooms?' Fleur says. 'Aren't we in together? I'm not sure I want to be in a room on my own. This house is a bit spooky.'

She has a shrill voice that sounds a bit whiny, and I can't help wondering if Mari's daughter is going to be as uncomfortable to be around as her mother is.

'It does have a feel of the Addams Family about it,' Mari says, stepping into the hallway, dropping her holdall-type bag on the tiled floor and hanging her coat on a free peg. 'I'm sure someone will love it though.'

I can sense Stuart's irritation rising. His sister is barely through the door and she's already dropping hints about the inevitable sale of their family home.

'The kitchen is quite welcoming though, if I remember rightly,' Mari continues. 'Any chance of a coffee?'

'Of course. Come on through and I'll put the kettle on,' I say leading the way through the hallway. 'And you're welcome to share a room if you want, Fleur, but it's all double beds so I thought you might be more comfortable in a room on your own. There's no need to decide just yet,' I add, noticing her uncertain expression.

I don't remember the tension between Stuart and his sister being this obvious when she was here for their dad's funeral, but maybe that's because Eva was there. I'm secretly hoping that our kids did manage to get away from Berkshire early and will arrive soon. As uncharitable as it sounds, I'm relieved that Mari and Fleur will only be staying for two nights. When I'd asked via email if they wanted to stay for the scattering of the ashes on Monday, it had been a resounding no. I'm now starting to wish that Mari hadn't been able to get time off work to make the trip at all. But she's here, and I'm going to make it my job for things to run as smoothly as possible.

Once we've finished our coffee, during which Fleur has reached the decision that she would prefer a room on her own, I head upstairs with them to where Stuart has deposited their bags on the landing while he goes out to fetch in more wood for the Rayburn. I'd originally thought about putting Mari in the better of the two rooms with the view down to the sea, but she's been borderline unpleasant to me, so I've changed my mind.

'This is seriously cool,' Fleur says when I open the door to the room that I've now allocated to her. 'What's the coastline I can see? Ireland?' she asks.

Mari makes a tutting sound and shakes her head. As I correct Fleur, I wonder if maybe her mother is unpleasant to everyone.

'No. That's the Scottish mainland,' I say. 'We're on the east coast of Skye here.'

There are already a few lights illuminated over the water as the evening is starting to descend. I glance at my watch. It's after five now. I hope Jemma and Callum won't be too much longer as they are unfamiliar with the roads. Even as I'm thinking it, I hear the metal gate rolling back.

'I've put you in Stuart's old room,' I say to Mari over my shoulder as I head for the stairs. 'I'm sure you remember where that is.'

Greeting my children and their partners after their long drive is far more important to me than making small talk with Stuart's sister, I think, rushing down the stairs just as Stuart opens the kitchen door.

'They're here,' he says.

'Yes, I heard the gate,' I reply, reaching the front door before him and flinging it wide just as Will's car pulls to a halt.

'I told Cal to park at the front so we can get their bags in. We can move it in the morning before Donald Campbell turns up,' Stuart says.

All four doors of the Audi open simultaneously, as does the boot hatch.

'I'd forgotten how long the drive is,' Callum says, unfolding himself from the driver's seat and stretching his arms above his head to illustrate his point.

'Made a little longer by me needing the loo so frequently,' Ellie says apologetically, climbing out of the rear passenger seat behind the driver.

Jemma is getting out of the other rear seat and shoots me an accusatory look.

'Yeh, Mum. You could have told me that Cal and Ellie were pregnant. I thought maybe she'd had a dodgy curry last night and that's why we needed to keep stopping.'

'It wasn't your mum's news to tell,' Stuart says, immediately jumping to my defence.

'Standard,' Jemma and Callum chorus in unison.

'What is?' Ellie asks, looking from one to the other.

'Dad always takes Mum's side on everything,' Jemma says, but there is humour in her voice now.

'Guilty as charged,' Stuart says, holding his hands up as if in surrender. 'Hi Will, welcome to Rowan House,' he adds.

Jemma's boyfriend is gazing up at Eva's home as he closes the passenger door.

'Wow! This place must be worth a fortune,' he says.

Jemma looks mortified, and I feel Stuart bristle at my side.

'Let's get you all inside,' I say. 'Now that the sun is setting, there's a proper chill in the air, but thankfully the Rayburn is behaving itself.'

'What's a Rayburn?' Will asks, seemingly unaware of how inappropriate his previous comment was.

'It's like an Aga on steroids,' Callum says, a hint of humour in his voice as he goes round to the back of the car to unload the selection of bags.

I think maybe my son is poking fun at Will's bodybuilder physique, but if he notices, he doesn't react.

The two of them have known each other since before Will and Jemma were an item when they worked together at Shipton Garnet Recruiting. Will had been invited to Callum and Ellie's wedding and had asked to be introduced to their beautiful bridesmaid, who'd taken his breath away in her gorgeous pale-green silk bridesmaid gown. Callum hadn't revealed at the time that Jemma was his sister. He's told me that it's a decision he regrets since finding out that Will most probably slept his way into his new job.

Jemma was feeling sorry for herself having been dumped by someone she was really keen on after only three dates. She never went into the details of what went wrong between them and I hadn't felt that I could ask without upsetting her further. Jemma has always been more secretive than her brother, preferring to handle things herself rather than asking for my or her dad's help.

She started seeing Will on the rebound, but much to everyone's surprise, the rebound lasted. Although there was no sign yet of making their relationship official, they'd demonstrated their commitment to each other when they'd bought their house. If only Callum had made his discovery about Will before they'd completed on it, I thought, my mouth going dry. It will make things much more complicated if Jemma decides she can't get past what he's done, and the moment to tell her is moving inexorably closer.

'Do you want to give me a hand with these, Will?' Callum continues.

'Sure,' Will replies. 'It's okay, Stuart, we've got these,' he adds as my husband starts to move in their direction.

Stuart and I exchange a glance, both trying to suppress our amusement. Will spends hours in the gym bulking up his biceps, toning his triceps and perfecting his pectorals, so why wouldn't he take every opportunity to show off his strength?

'Thanks,' Stuart says, redirecting his steps towards Jemma and Ellie. He links an arm through each of theirs and goes into the house while I wait for Callum and Will, now laden like two pack mules.

Callum allows Will to go up the front steps ahead of him casting me a sidelong glance as he passes. As his mum, I know how much Will's comment about the value of Rowan House has irritated my son, but now is not the time or the place to lock horns with his sister's boyfriend.

In response to his look, I give a slight shake of my head. I need Callum to hold his feelings in check for a few more days, not only for his dad's sake but also to give Eva the respect she deserves.

EIGHTEEN

We settled on spaghetti bolognese for dinner after checking that everyone was happy with our choice of meal. I made a point of telling Will that the Parmesan cheese would be served in a separate bowl, and he acknowledged with a thumbs-up gesture before disappearing up the stairs to his and Jemma's room.

Stuart and I are preparing the meal together as cooking for eight is no mean feat. We've treated it like a military operation, with all the chopping and dicing done in advance. Everything is in the pan apart from the generous slug of red wine, which I'm wondering if I should omit with Ellie being pregnant.

Right on cue, I hear Callum say, 'Mmm, that smells good.'

I glance over my shoulder briefly to see him standing in the kitchen doorway.

'One of the few dishes in my repertoire,' I say, turning back to the saucepan to give it another stir. I pick up the bottle of red wine and continue, 'Actually, I was just wondering whether to leave the red wine out with Ellie being pregnant?'

'Thanks for thinking of it, Mum, but unless I'm mistaken, the alcohol is burned off during the cooking, so it'll be fine, won't it, Ellie?' my son says.

With my back to the kitchen door, I don't realise that his wife has followed him into the room.

'Yes, absolutely fine,' she confirms. 'I'd hate to spoil the delicious taste unnecessarily, but I'll pass on having a glass of wine with my dinner.'

My daughter-in-law has moved to sit on the sofa, so I can see her out of the corner of my eye. As she speaks, she places her hands protectively on her belly even though there is no sign of a bump yet. It's going to be a nervous few months for the two of them until the baby is viable after what happened earlier in the year.

'What will you have to drink with your dinner, Ellie?' Stuart asks. 'We've got lemonade, coke or sparkling water. Or tap water, of course,' he adds.

Stuart has moved on to laying the table with place mats and cutlery now that the ingredients have all been added to the bolognese sauce, and Callum is reaching glasses down from the cupboard.

'I'll have a sparkling water, please,' Ellie replies, starting to get up off the sofa.

'You stay there, darling,' Callum says. 'I'll get it.'

The love in his voice gives me a warm, fuzzy feeling. They are so right for each other. I've turned my attention to the huge pan of water for the spaghetti now. I take a big handful of dried pasta and carefully coil it into the bubbling water, a process I repeat several times with so many mouths to feed.

'Shall I call everyone down for dinner?' Stuart asks.

My heart lurches. That had always been Eva's role.

'Probably a good idea,' I reply, lifting the lid of the sauce to give it a stir. 'It'll be another ten minutes or so, but it will give people time to get down and settled.'

'Are you having red, Mum?' Callum asks, lifting one of the two bottles that Stuart has uncorked to allow it to breathe.

'Yes, please. And your dad will have red too,' I say as

Stuart's voice calls out from the foot of the stairs, summoning everyone.

'That kind of goes without saying, Mum,' Callum replies catching my eye and giving me a meaningful look. Both he and Jemma have expressed concern about the amount their dad drinks, but to be honest, I think they are overreacting. He's a social drinker and enjoys a few glasses when we're in company, but I haven't seen him drunk since our trip to the Mount Gay Rum Distillery on our honeymoon, so I'm not worried. Callum pours the garnet-red Malbec into three glasses before setting the bottle back down.

'Does it matter where we sit?' he asks, picking up two of the glasses.

'You decide,' I say.

'What's Cal deciding on?' Jemma demands.

I should have known it was her from the heavy footfall on the stairs. For someone of her stature she's always made a heck of a racket thundering up and down. The question is typical of her. She doesn't like Callum to be given the final word on anything. It was the cause of the few arguments they had when they were growing up, especially as teenagers, but Callum has been more amenable since he's been with Ellie and doesn't rise to provocation so easily.

'Just places for dinner, but you choose if you'd rather,' he says with a light shrug of his shoulders.

'I'll let you have that one,' Jemma concedes. 'Where would you like me to sit?' she adds, a trace of sarcasm in her voice.

'I thought couples could sit opposite each other, with Mari and Fleur at either end? What do you think?' Callum says, deliberately seeking his sister's approval.

'Have they always been like this?' Ellie asks, making eye contact with me.

'Yep,' I reply, swishing a fork through the spaghetti to keep the strands separated. 'Where's your dad got to? I'm going to need a hand lifting this pan over to the sink to drain it into the colander.'

'Sounds like my sort of job,' Will says, coming into the kitchen. 'I just passed Stuart on the stairs. I think he's gone to knock on Mari's and Fleur's doors because they didn't respond when he called. Is it ready to be drained?'

I notice the look exchanged between Callum and Ellie. Will really doesn't help other people's perception of him being something of a meathead when he always volunteers for anything that requires a bit of muscle. At least, I'm hoping that was all the look was about. I would hate for Ellie to be burdened with mine and Callum's secret about Will when she must already be feeling emotional about saying our final goodbyes to Eva tomorrow. As though he's reading my mind, Callum catches my eye and shakes his head almost imperceptibly. Considering the enormity of the wrong he believes Will has committed against his younger sister, I think Callum is showing huge restraint.

'Thanks, Will. It just needs another couple of minutes then we'll be good to go,' I say.

'Well, isn't this cosy,' Mari says a few minutes later as I'm ladling out pasta onto the eight plates Stuart has laid out along the work surface. I think I detect a hint of derision in her voice, but at least she is less snippy than earlier. 'Does it matter where I sit?' she asks.

'I've got you and Fleur on the ends if that's okay?' Callum replies.

'Yes, of course it is,' Fleur says before her mother can respond. 'I'll go at the other end, Mum,' she continues. It places her between Callum and Ellie who are already waiting expectantly for their food. She probably thinks they'll have more in common to talk about as they are more her age group, although there is still over a ten-year age difference.

Stuart is sitting between Ellie and Jemma, while I'll have Callum to my right and Will to my left, with Mari between him and Jemma, in what always used to be Donald's place when he was alive.

'I think my first impression was totally off,' my niece says as she pulls out her chair and sits down. 'My room is beautiful. I sat staring out of the window at the twinkling lights across on the mainland for ages. It was so relaxing that I fell asleep in the chair.'

In my eyes, Fleur has totally redeemed herself after the comments she made earlier, but her mother views it differently.

'Probably the jet lag,' Mari says. 'There's nothing relaxing about this place in the depths of winter when the pipes freeze or the Rayburn malfunctions. Hopefully, an incomer with no knowledge of the awful weather will buy it. I'm pretty sure they'll soon realise it needs knocking down and rebuilding to modern standards.'

I feel Stuart stiffen at my side as I'm spooning bolognese sauce onto the mounds of pasta. I place my free hand on his forearm in warning. We'll only be around Mari for two days, and with Eva laying in rest in the next room, I think the least we can do is be civil to one another. If he was about to say something in response, he obviously thinks better of it. He remains silent as he picks up two plates of food and places them in front of Fleur and Ellie.

'This looks delicious,' Ellie says graciously.

'Yes, it does,' agrees Fleur. 'And for what it's worth, Mum, I think it would be a tragedy to knock this place down and lose all its associated history. Sure, it needs a bit of modernising, a few more bathrooms and toilets, but it looks as solid as a rock, and anything more modern would be out of place in the surroundings.'

I see the glare Mari gives her daughter as I deliver the next two plates of food to her and Jemma.

'And you're an expert architect all of a sudden are you, Fleur?' she snipes.

Everyone else at the table is waiting until all the plates are handed out and Stuart and I have sat down to join them, but Will digs straight into his food the moment his plate hits the place mat, much to Jemma's obvious displeasure. It isn't good manners, but at least it breaks the tension when he says, 'Bloody hell! This is the best spag bol I've ever eaten, Lexi. We should go over to your parents' house for dinner more often, Jem.'

His fork plunges back into the tomatoey meat sauce and is halfway back to his mouth before he realises that everyone else is patiently waiting for Stuart and me to sit down before eating.

'Oh, sorry,' he says, lowering his fork back to the plate. 'I should have waited.'

'Don't worry about it, Will,' I say, slipping into my place at his side. 'I'm glad you approve, but I thought maybe we could each say a silent little prayer and raise a glass to Eva before we tuck in.'

Jemma is glaring at her boyfriend, and once again I wonder what kind of spell Will has her under and whether the spell will be permanently broken if our suspicions are proved true or whether she will give him a second chance.

We all raise our glasses and take a moment of silence before Stuart says, 'To a wonderful mother and grandmother.'

We all chink glasses, murmuring, 'To Eva.'

NINETEEN

It was after 10 p.m. by the time all the dishes had been washed, dried and put away. All the guests decided on an early night after a long day of travelling, and Stuart and I are in our room getting ready for bed.

'What do you make of Will?' Stuart asks unexpectedly.

Under most other circumstances, this would be the perfect opportunity to tell Stuart what I think about Will, even if it would mean breaking the promise I made to Callum, but it doesn't feel appropriate the night before we lay his mum to rest. I'd almost confided in Eva when Callum had come to me because I desperately wanted another female opinion, but I'm glad now that I didn't as she would have died without the issue being resolved one way or another.

'Well,' I say, choosing my words carefully so as not to inadvertently arouse my husband's suspicions, 'I think we both agree that Jemma makes odd choices when it comes to boyfriends.'

I wipe my mouth on the plush towel that Shona has allocated for my use in the en suite bathroom, having just cleaned my teeth. Ours is the only bedroom in Rowan House that has full en suite facilities, giving weight to the comment Fleur had made earlier.

En suite makes it sound grander than it is. There is a toilet, a small, enclosed shower cubicle and a single pedestal-style wash basin. All three are in a disgusting shade of green which Stuart tells me is called avocado and was all the rage when his parents had it installed. The mirror above the basin is failing at the corners, and the glass shelf beneath it on which all my toiletries are lined up like soldiers on parade has a small crack emanating from the supporting bracket. It's quite a big space, which could easily accommodate a bath, walk-in shower and large vanity unit with double handbasins, but that wasn't the style apparently when Eva and Donald had this part of their huge master bedroom sectioned off in the 1980s. I'm glad they had the foresight to install a generous heated towel rail powered by the Rayburn. I inwardly admonish myself for not rinsing the toothpaste from around my mouth properly as I notice the white mark it has left on my deep pink towel.

'I didn't mean her choice of boyfriends generally, I meant more specifically the current one,' Stuart says, taking his dressing gown off and hanging it on the back of the bedroom door before padding across the room and getting into bed. He's wearing grey cotton jersey pyjama bottoms and a white T-shirt top. We're both comfortable sleeping in just our skin when we're at home, but we always wear night clothes when we're away anywhere.

'He's nice enough,' I reply noncommittally while pulling the bedcovers back and climbing into bed. 'He could do with filtering his thoughts though before he says them out loud.'

'You're not wrong,' Stuart says, shaking his head. 'Some of the things he came out with over dinner were insensitive to put it mildly. Although I did warm to him with his put-down about Mari's job.'

Will had asked Mari what she did for a living, and she'd

gone into a lengthy explanation about her role as a retail advisor.

'Oh, so a shop assistant then,' he'd said after she'd finished speaking.

Mari had bristled before commenting, 'At least I'm helping to keep the high street alive rather than shopping online.'

'That comment about shopping online was a dig at me, you know,' I say to Stuart. 'I mentioned that I don't have much time to go to actual shops when she was over for your dad's funeral, and she's never let me forget it as though I'm single-handedly destroying the high street. I don't know what her issue with me is.'

'Really?' Stuart says reaching his arms around me and snuggling into my back so that we're lying together like spoons. 'She's jealous of the way you filled the gap when she swanned off to Canada. You became more of a daughter to Mum than she was, especially after Dad died, and she hated it.'

'But that's not true,' I say, wriggling myself free from Stuart's tight embrace so that I can turn to face him. 'I never tried to take Mari's place in her affection. I was in Eva's life because I'm married to her son. I was very fond of her, but I never viewed myself as anything other than her daughter-in-law.'

'I know,' Stuart says, 'but I'm not sure if that's how Mari saw it.'

'Why did Mari go off to Canada to live?' I ask. It's a question I've always wanted to know the answer to but had hoped that Stuart would divulge rather than me having to ask outright. 'She must have known it would cause a rift in her relationship with Eva and Donald.'

Stuart takes a deep breath as though he's debating whether to tell me something.

'Nobody ever spoke about it because my parents were both mortified that she struck up a relationship with a pen pal who the school introduced her to when she was studying for her Highers.'

I'm puzzled as to why that would have been such a deep, dark family secret until Stuart continues.

'He – he was a prisoner serving a ten-year sentence for aggravated burglary and was ten years older than her. Our dad went berserk with the school when he found out, but his objection to her communicating with the guy just made Mari do it behind his back.'

Stuart and I have always been mindful of trying to get the balance right between being too strict with our children and allowing them enough freedom. It's something most parents must deal with at some point in their teenagers' lives.

'The shit really hit the fan when he was about to be released on parole. He invited Mari to join him in Canada to help him start over and build a new life together. She'd turned eighteen two months previously, so my parents couldn't legally do anything to stop her going.'

'So that was it?' I ask. 'She just upped and went to Canada to be with Todd?'

'Not Todd,' Stuart says. 'Mari met him because he was an orderly at the hospital she was rushed into after the guy she'd gone out to Canada to be with had beaten her to within an inch of her life.'

'Oh my God,' I say, horrified that I'm only just discovering this now. 'Poor Mari.'

'I know. I suppose it goes some way to explaining why Mari can seem so heartless and downright rude on occasion. I'm not sure she ever truly forgave Mum and Dad for not going over to Canada to see her while she was in the hospital. Dad's view was that she'd made her bed and so should lie in it,' Stuart says ruefully. 'The sad thing is, if they'd gone to visit her, I think she would have come back home to Skye with them. Dad was too pig-headed to back down and as a result Mum suffered. It put a strain on their marriage for a while. Not only did Mum no longer feel close to her daughter, but when Fleur came along, she missed all the things a grandmother looks forward to.'

I think of Callum and Ellie and the way she had protectively laid her hands on her belly earlier. I'm beyond excited to meet our first grandchild and shower them with love. I can only imagine how awful it must have been for Eva to be denied that closeness.

'It's all so sad, but at least Mari found happiness with Todd, and they had Fleur,' I say.

Stuart is giving me an odd look.

'What?' I ask.

'The thing is, and you mustn't ever tell anyone this, Todd isn't Fleur's dad.'

I'm confused now. Why are there so many secrets surfacing now that Eva has died?

'Go on,' I urge.

'Mari doesn't know that I know, but she told Mum about it when she came over for Dad's funeral. I guess she was feeling emotional and wanted to get it off her chest.' He pauses briefly. 'Mari discovered she was pregnant by the ex-con, and that was why he beat her up.'

The bitter taste of bile fills my mouth, and a shudder runs through me. What a disgusting piece of humanity. How could any man behave so appallingly towards any woman, let alone one who is carrying his child.

'Poor Mari,' I say again, putting aside all the hurtful things she's said to me and about me over the years. 'It must have been difficult telling Fleur that Todd is not her dad. I wonder if she told her anything about him?'

I'm getting that same strange look from Stuart. Suddenly the penny drops.

'Fleur doesn't know?' I gasp.

'No,' Stuart confirms. 'And I don't think it's our place to tell her.'

I nod slowly. Part of me thinks that Fleur has a right to know, but what impact would it have on her to find out now that she's been lied to all her life? I can feel heat rising in my cheeks. Although this is a much bigger secret and Mari has been keeping it from Fleur for much longer, I'm acutely aware that I'm guilty of not being truthful with my own daughter. Will Jemma be able to forgive me for my lack of honesty? Will our future relationship be affected?

'More to the point,' Stuart continues, 'Mari doesn't know that I know. Mum only told me about it on the drive down from Skye. I think she knew her days were numbered and believed that Fleur had a right to know about her biological father, even though he was a complete and utter piece of shit. He was sent back to prison for the assault on Mari. Once back inside, he beat up and killed a fellow inmate, so he's now serving life in prison.'

'The best place for him,' I say, still coming to terms with the enormity of what my husband has just told me. 'Presumably Todd knows that he's not Fleur's biological dad?' I say eventually.

'According to Mum, it was him who came up with the plan to hide Fleur's true identity so she wouldn't be burdened with it throughout her life. Mari had nowhere to stay once she was released from hospital, and he let her stay at his place because they'd become friendly. As far as Mum could tell, Todd left his job soon after, and the two of them moved to a remote farming community where it was easy for them to lie about Fleur arriving earlier than her due date, just in case anyone ever recognised Mari from the news story.'

'He sounds like a decent guy. It's a shame they didn't have any children of their own.'

'I think there were complications when Fleur was born,' Stuart says. 'I don't think Mari was able to have any more.'

'Would you have told me any of this if Eva hadn't passed away?' I ask.

He looks a bit sheepish.

'Mum asked me not to,' he replies apologetically.

The stab of hurt I feel is real. Eva and I had become close over the years since Donald died, at least I thought we had.

'Then why have you gone against your mum's wishes now?' I manage to ask.

'Because you and I don't do secrets. I never actually agreed that I wouldn't tell you, and if Mum had lived, I would have found a way to explain to her why I felt you should know as much as me about the situation. You're not mad with me for not telling you straight away, are you?'

'Of course not,' I say, resting my head against his T-shirt-covered chest and hoping Stuart will be as understanding with me when I finally share what Callum told me. 'I know now, and that's all that matters.'

'And we keep this to ourselves?' he says.

'Yes. It's not our secret to tell,' I say.

Families are full of secrets and lies, but this one is huge. I think back to what had prompted the confession. If only all we had to worry about with Will is that he sometimes opens his mouth before his brain is fully engaged, then it wouldn't be an issue at all.

But that isn't all we have to worry about. The reality is much worse, and I'm starting to feel really concerned about the possible fallout when the truth eventually rears its ugly head. I don't know how much longer I can keep this from my husband.

TWENTY
TUESDAY 31 OCTOBER

The sound of Stuart closing the boot of the hire car cuts through the early morning quiet like a gunshot. I hear his footsteps walking round from the rear of the car and the opening of the driver's door. He's driving the first part of our journey to Glasgow airport for the flight to Heathrow, and I'll take over when he starts to feel tired after our early start.

My heart is as heavy as the wooden outer door I've just closed and turning the key in the lock feels like the end of an era, which I suppose in some ways it is. We might never come back to this grand old house, Stuart's childhood home, which fills me with sadness, but is not the reason for my low mood.

The past three days have taken their toll on me.

The funeral and the gathering afterwards were not as bad as I'd feared they would be. The day had dawned bright, and it had stayed dry just as the weather forecast had promised. The service itself was held in the chapel of the crematorium and had been a celebration of Eva's life rather than the sombre church service we had endured after Donald died. The photos that Stuart and I had carefully selected ran on a loop throughout, projected onto the pale cream-painted wall of the chapel to one side of the celebrant, Catriona, as she delivered the eulogy.

They tracked every moment of Eva's life. There were only two baby photographs of her being held in her mother's arms in the doorway of a tenement building in the Gorbals of Glasgow, one of the most deprived slum areas in Europe. Her family had the good fortune to be evacuated to the Isle of Skye towards the end of the war and never returned, so there were photographs of her childhood and school days in a much more rural setting. There were pictures of her and Donald when they were courting and, of course, their wedding photo with Eva looking stunning in a white lace gown and Donald resplendent in his kilt. There were plenty of photographs of the young couple both before and after the birth of their first baby, Stuart. There were more baby snaps with Mari when she arrived eight years later.

I have occasionally wondered if the gap in their ages contributed to the lack of a close relationship between Stuart and Mari. He was a moody teenager by the time she was starting infant school. They were never in the same school at the same time, so he was never called upon to protect his little sister if she was being picked on. And unlike Callum and Jemma, with only eighteen months between them, the gap was too vast for Stuart's school friends to become boyfriends for Mari. She must have felt quite isolated at Rowan House once Stuart left to attend university in Stirling. Maybe that was why she got so involved with her pen pal in Canada. She saw an opportunity to do something even more exciting than her older brother, who was by then living in London, and seized the opportunity with both hands.

Mari hadn't shed any tears during the ceremony, unlike Fleur, who was sitting next to her mother. She had tears streaming down her cheeks, and I'd had to pass her some tissues as she'd come completely unprepared. Maybe she was regretting never having met her grandmother whose life we had all gathered to celebrate, and now it was too late.

Callum and Ellie were gripping each other's hands throughout, and I noticed each dabbing at the corner of their eyes with a tissue at certain particularly poignant moments.

Surprisingly, Jemma had not shown much emotion at all. She'd sat very upright rather than leaning into Will as I was leaning into Stuart, and she stared straight ahead throughout, apart from when we all bowed our heads in prayer.

At the end of the service, as Eva's coffin slowly disappeared behind purple velvet curtains, I expected Jemma to reach for Will's hand, but she didn't. It was the same lack of emotion she'd shown since Eva's passing. I know we all grieve differently, but I'd thought it might all come pouring out of her at her grandmother's funeral. I was wrong. Even more concerning is the thought that her uncharacteristic behaviour has nothing at all to do with Eva. What if Jemma has discovered the secret that Callum and I have been keeping from her and has been bottling it up inside until after the funeral? Rather selfishly, I hope that if she has found out about Will's infidelity she will wait until Stuart and I return from the postponed holiday we both so desperately need before confronting him about it. Worse still is the thought that Jemma might have unearthed something else distasteful about her boyfriend and has chosen to try and deal with it herself rather than asking for our help. Our daughter can be her own worst enemy at times.

On Saturday, Callum was keen to show Ellie around the island, and Will expressed an interest in going too. In the end, they all decided to go, so it was fortunate that we'd had the foresight to add Callum's name to our hire car contract. He and Ellie led the way, with Will and Jemma following in his Audi, having suggested to Mari and Fleur that they would be more comfortable in the bigger car. He was right, but it had felt once again that he was showing off his wealth rather than it being a thoughtful gesture.

Stuart and I took the opportunity of no one being around to continue going through Eva's stuff. There were boxes of clothes and trinkets for the charity shop that nobody had expressed a desire to hold onto when we'd asked if anyone would like a keepsake. Obviously, things of more value, like Eva's jewellery, had been allocated in her will. She'd been very even-handed in distributing it amongst female members of the family, and of course Shona. She'd also allocated £20,000 from the final value of her estate to be given to her friend and carer. Mari had tried to question that decision, but Stuart and I weren't having any argument about Eva's last wishes. Before the others got back from their sightseeing, we were sorted, including yet more black bin bags full of shredded paper.

Mari and Fleur left early on the Sunday morning, with Fleur promising to maintain better contact with her family in the UK. I'm glad, especially as I now know that the people she thinks are blood relatives in Canada aren't. In the space of a couple of days, I'd really warmed to Fleur, and I'd increased my effort to be friendly with Mari after discovering what she'd been through.

It's safe to say it wasn't reciprocated. In fact, something she said to me is partly responsible for my low mood.

I didn't mention it to Stuart straight away as I wanted the rowan tree planting and the scattering of Eva's ashes to go off smoothly before we waved the kids off for their long journey home. Last night I almost raised it, but it didn't feel right on Stuart's final night in Rowan House. I really do need to get it off my chest though before it starts gnawing away at me.

I slip the door keys into my handbag, go down the front steps and then turn back for a last look up at the imposing house I'd first seen as a nervous nineteen-year-old all those years ago. So many memories, mostly happy ones, I'm thinking, as I fasten the seatbelt around me with a firm click and close the passenger door.

'There's something a bit déjà vu about our journey today,' Stuart says, stopping in front of the iron gate for the sensor to pick up our presence.

I turn to look at my husband, wondering what emotion he is currently experiencing and what his reaction will be when I tell him what Mari said to me on Saturday night.

'Déjà vu?' I question over the sound of metal on metal as the gate trundles along the runner.

'Yes. After we got married, we travelled to London before flying off on our honeymoon to Barbados two days later. History is repeating itself,' he says, pulling the car forwards and waiting for the gate to start closing behind us.

'Almost repeating itself,' I say. 'Have you forgotten that I've got a night shift to squeeze in tomorrow before we fly on Thursday?' I pull the corners of my mouth down into a grumpy expression.

'I'm sorry you're having to do that, but at least you'll be able to sleep on the plane,' he says.

'You must be confusing me with someone. You know I rarely sleep when I'm flying.'

'Shame you're not more like Mari in that respect. She was telling me that her eyelids feel heavy as soon as the plane's undercarriage is tucked safely away for the flight, and she always asks the flight attendants not to wake her for meals and drinks.'

'Lucky her,' I say, immediately wondering why she hadn't made more of an effort to visit her ailing mother. Before I allow myself to wander down that path of negativity, I say, 'Thank you for organising it, Stuart. I wasn't sure it was the right thing to do when you first mentioned it. I kept thinking of all the stuff that needed doing and how little time we would have if we were rushing straight off, but it's all worked out okay in the end.'

'You definitely need some time away,' he responds. 'You've seemed down since the funeral. Mum wouldn't have wanted that. She was so very fond of you.'

We've turned right at the end of the lane onto the coast road that is hidden from view from the vantage point of Eva's kitchen. I glance up at Rowan House, its outline imposing against the backdrop of the sky still tinged with pink from the sunrise.

'Was she though? Or did she just pretend to be for your benefit?' I say, trying to keep the hurt from my voice.

'What on earth are you talking about?' Stuart says, clearly bemused about what I've just inferred. 'She loved you like a daughter; in fact, I sometimes thought she was closer to you than her own flesh and blood. And by that, I don't mean my sister,' he adds quickly as though aware of my inner wince. 'Mari and Mum's fractured relationship had nothing to do with you, or me for that matter. No one could ever accuse you of trying to steal Mari's place in Mum's affections. She just really appreciated all the kind things you did for her.'

I shrug, but don't reply, and Stuart obviously believes that I need a bit more convincing, so he continues.

'Think of all the good times we've spent with her here on Skye and at our house. She didn't pretend to enjoy herself, Lexi; she genuinely did. Mum loved being at the heart of our family and the way we all made her feel special. I don't know why on earth you would ever think otherwise,' he concludes.

Should I tell him now? The moment has certainly presented itself, but I'm not sure what would be gained that can't wait for a couple of weeks. I don't want anything to spoil our rebooked holiday which we both so desperately need.

'Fleur has turned into a lovely young woman,' he says, a genuine warmth in his voice. 'I do hope she keeps her promise to stay in closer contact with us.'

'Me too, especially as she seemed to get on with our two so

well,' I say, emulating his warmth and reflecting that Mari's decision to distance herself from her family hasn't only affected Eva. We'd all been denied the opportunity to get to know them better. Knowing what I do now about Fleur's natural father, I wonder if that was the reason she chose to stay away. Maybe she was fearful that someone would discover her secret and tell Fleur.

Whatever her reasons, there is no need for Mari to be so unpleasant to me, but the moment to share what she told me is gone... for now.

PART TWO

TWENTY-ONE

16 NOVEMBER – THURSDAY MORNING

The front door slams shut, and Stuart calls out, 'Where are my two favourite girls?'

Looking across at Jemma's tear-streaked face, the flat of her hand raised to me to prevent me going any closer, I feel my heart contract. Her words, 'I don't know if I'll ever be able to forgive you,' are still ringing in my ears. I'm definitely not her favourite person at the moment, and I'm not sure how Stuart will react when he finds out I've been keeping a pretty big secret from him. I can feel the benefit of the relaxing two weeks we have just enjoyed in Barbados ebbing away. Talk about back to earth with a bang.

'In here,' I reply, flinching at the sound of my husband dropping our heavy suitcases on the tiled floor of the hallway. The tiles are a discontinued design, so if there is any damage they can't be replaced, but right now that's the least of my worries.

I see a question forming on Stuart's lips as he appears in the doorway and takes in the scene. Jemma's eyes are red and puffy from crying. I'm still standing to one side of the kitchen door where she had prevented me from going over to comfort her moments earlier.

It seems unfair that she's placing the blame on my shoulders for not telling her about Will when I'd been sworn to secrecy by Callum. He'd done it with her best interests at heart because he wanted to find out more about the situation, but I'm not sure Jemma will ever see it like that. From her perspective, Callum and I have ganged up against her, but nothing could be further from the truth. He feels guilty for the part he played in introducing his sister to Will. My guilt is for not telling my daughter what he had done for fear that she might not believe me and it would destroy our close relationship.

'What the hell is going on?' Stuart demands.

I shake my head slightly to stop Stuart saying anything else. The last thing Jemma needs right now is the third degree. Her dad can be very sensitive in certain situations, but he can also be like a bull in a china shop. I'm not prepared to gamble on which Stuart we'll get after a long flight and the hold-up on the motorway.

'Ask her!' Jemma shrieks, pointing an accusatory finger at me.

Normally, Stuart would rebuke Jemma for speaking to me in that way, but he can clearly sense the gravity of the situation.

'Lexi?' he asks.

His expression is one of concern, but I'm not sure who he is more concerned for. My priority is to separate the two of them. I need to find out what Jemma knows and who she heard it from, or indeed if she found out about it herself. The last thing I want though is for Stuart to find out from Jemma that I've also been keeping a secret from him.

'Stuart, can you put the kettle on?' I say, pleading with my eyes. 'I think we could all do with a cup of tea.'

His eyes flick from me to Jemma and then back to me.

'Sure,' he says. 'Why don't you two go into the lounge, and I'll bring it through when it's ready.'

For a minute, I think Jemma might refuse. She looks as

angry as she is upset. But as her dad brushes past her and lightly squeezes her shoulder, all resistance seems to evaporate, and she obediently gets to her feet to follow me.

I sit in one of the armchairs and Jemma perches on the edge of the sofa. The atmosphere is frosty, and that's putting it mildly.

'Does Dad know?' she almost spits. 'Or is it just you and Callum keeping cosy little secrets?'

There's my confirmation that it's not an unrelated argument with Will that has brought Jemma to our house when she should be at work. So the question is, did she find out or did Callum or Will tell her?

'Jemma, it's not like that at all—' I start to say.

'Really? Cos that's what it looks like from where I'm sitting,' she interrupts. 'Will told me that Callum called him two nights ago and said that if he didn't tell me how he got his job at HvC, you and he would. That makes me think that you kept Dad in the dark too. Were you ever going to tell him? Or did you just take it upon yourself to deal with the situation because you always know best?' she sneers.

Her words sting, but they do have an element of truth to them. I am usually the problem solver in our family, but only because I care, not because I think I know best. Normally I would try to defend myself, but it's pointless while Jemma is so angry and upset. I bite the corner of my lip as a physical reminder that she is hurting. Nothing will be achieved by me getting angry too.

'I didn't tell your dad because Callum asked me not to until he knew whether the rumour he'd heard was true,' I explain patiently. 'I had no idea that he'd spoken to Will. I haven't been in contact with your brother apart from the Drummond family WhatsApp message I sent from the airport three hours ago, because I knew he'd be getting ready for work,' I say, making a big show of looking at my watch.

I don't usually tell the time with my watch, to be honest. It's one of those fitness watches that tracks activity and things like heart rate and blood oxygen levels. It's as well that it doesn't flag up blood pressure readings because I'm fairly sure mine is through the roof right now.

'Really?' Jemma repeats, disbelief in her voice. 'Only he messaged me this morning to say he emailed you yesterday, to warn you that he'd confronted Will and to expect me to be upset, which is an understatement by the way.'

Damn it. I was wondering why Callum hadn't warned me of this latest development, but it sounds like he'd tried. My kids both know I always take my iPad with me when we go away, so I can check work emails that I can't access on my phone. Stuart had suggested I didn't take it on this trip to Barbados because we both needed a complete break from reality. For once, I'd totally agreed and left the tablet at home, never imagining that Callum would email me rather than WhatsApp if there was a problem. Maybe he thought his dad would be less likely to see an email than a message on my phone. I certainly could have done with the heads-up.

'I'm not lying, Jem. I didn't take the iPad with me on this trip. It was your dad's suggestion,' I say.

'What was my suggestion?' Stuart asks, coming into the lounge carrying our tray of hot drinks. Rather optimistically he's brought the biscuit tin too. When she was a little girl, a biscuit could usually make things right for Jemma, but something tells me that this is going to take more than a custard cream to sort out.

'Leaving my iPad at home so that we could both have a proper holiday from everything,' I reply.

Stuart looks confused, probably wondering what not having my tablet on holiday has to do with his daughter's obvious distress.

'Would you rather me leave you two to it?' he asks as he

places the tray down on the oversized Chesterfield-style footstool which I'd persuaded him to buy as our joint anniversary present to each other. It's in a beautiful pearl-grey velvet fabric and is a lot more useful than a piece of pearl jewellery, a gemstone I'm not particularly fond of but is the stone of the thirtieth wedding anniversary.

'No, stay,' Jemma says, her voice calmer.

I hope that by now Stuart has realised the gravity of the situation and will treat it with kid gloves, and I pray that Jemma will be considerate in the way she reveals to her dad that I've been keeping a secret from him.

He sits on the sofa at the side of Jemma and squeezes her forearm gently.

'So, what's brought all this on then, love?' he says.

'Nana dying,' Jemma replies in a voice so small it's barely audible.

'Oh, sweetheart,' he says. 'That was an awful thing for you and your brother to have to deal with. I'm just sorry that your mum and me couldn't get back in time.'

'I didn't mean her actual dying, Dad,' Jemma responds. 'She'd told me the day before, when I found her on the kitchen floor, that if it was her time then she was ready. She wouldn't have done anything to hasten it,' she adds quickly, 'but I think she was saying don't keep her alive at any cost. I won't lie, it was awful when she cried out in pain, but it was really quick right at the end.'

Stuart exhales. Despite enjoying our holiday, there were times when he clearly felt guilty for being there rather than around for either of our kids if they needed us. Maybe that needs to change. Perhaps they are too dependent on us in some respects.

'I'm very proud of you and Cal for handling it all so calmly. Your nana would have been proud too.' He lets that sink in for a moment before saying, 'So come on then, what's this all about?'

I feel like a deer caught in the headlights.

'I've spent the past three years trying to convince myself and everyone else that Will and I are the perfect couple, but since we moved in together I've been having doubts,' she says, a slight wobble in her voice. 'He loves the gym, and I can barely tolerate it. To him, cheese is the enemy, whereas feta and halloumi are my favourite foods.'

Stuart and I exchange a glance. Despite the situation, it's tricky for me to suppress a smile because I'm in 'Team Jemma' when it comes to cheese.

'I know these are only a couple of seemingly insignificant examples, but there are hundreds of them,' she says, moving her arms in a wide, expansive gesture. 'I didn't realise how different we are until after Nana died.'

So that was part of the reason for the tears. Not only has Will told her about his infidelity, but Jemma has also already started to question whether Will is the right person for her. By the sound of things, Eva's death acted as something of a catalyst.

'They say that opposites attract,' I venture.

'Maybe they do, but there has to be something deeper than the initial attraction, and I'm no longer sure there is for me and Will.'

Is it wrong that I feel something approaching relief when she says this? Stuart and I haven't wanted to interfere, but thankfully Jemma seems to be reaching a similar conclusion to us about their relationship. We both stay quiet. She needs to get this off her chest.

'I think I really started to ask myself questions at the funeral when everyone who knew Nana and Gramps said they were a match made in heaven and now they would be back there together for eternity.' She sniffs. 'The answers I was getting were all wrong. The fact is, I don't think I love Will the way that Nana and Gramps loved each other, the way you two love each other, and even the way Callum and Ellie love one another.

Sitting in the car with them for hours on end on the drive back from Skye made me question my feelings for Will.'

'You can't compare yourself and your feelings to others,' Stuart says.

'Yes,' I agree, playing devil's advocate while secretly hoping that she will follow her gut. 'We're all different when it comes to personal stuff.'

'I don't know what to do,' Jemma says, lifting her chin to look first at her dad and then at me.

'It's so hard to offer you advice on stuff like this because whatever you decide, there will be pros and cons,' he says, reaching for a custard cream biscuit and taking a bite before continuing. 'It sometimes helps to do a list of positives and negatives, giving each a mark out of ten for importance. If the total of the positives outweighs the total of negatives, then maybe you should stick with it a bit longer and vice versa.'

I make eye contact with Jemma. I'm absolutely certain that Stuart would do a total U-turn if he knew about Will cheating on his daughter. I raise my eyebrows in question, wondering whether she is going to break that piece of news to him now and, in the process, let it be known that Callum and I had chosen not to tell him.

'Thanks for the advice, Dad,' she says, squeezing his arm.

It seems that Jemma has decided not to tell her dad about Will sleeping with his boss to get his job, at least for the time being while she decides whether she is going to give him another chance, which, in my opinion, he doesn't deserve, or whether she is going to call time.

'Sorry girls, but I'm going to have to leave you to it,' Stuart says, suppressing a yawn. 'This old man needs a nap.'

He gets to his feet, and Jemma does too. The two of them hug, which warms my heart, before Stuart heads for the door. It felt good for my husband to take the lead in offering advice rather than it always falling to me.

'Do you actually think making a list like Dad suggested is a good idea?' Jemma asks once we've heard the door to the bedroom close.

'I do,' I reply. 'You could also maybe talk to Grandma Joan, but perhaps tell her the whole story rather than leaving out the bit your dad doesn't know about.'

'I will,' she says. 'I only didn't tell Dad because I didn't want to put you in an awkward position.'

I smile gratefully.

'You will tell him though?' she adds.

'If you're okay with it.'

She nods. 'I'd rather he knows. It's going to start my list with a huge negative. It's going to take a lot of positives for me to get past what Will did, but at least he had the courage in the end to tell me about it, even if it was after some arm-twisting from Cal.'

'Are we forgiven for not telling you when we first had our suspicions?' I ask.

'I'll think about it,' she replies. 'It was horrible finding out from Will that you and Cal knew about it and didn't tell me. Maybe a girly spa day would go some way towards putting it right?'

There's humour in both her voice and her suggestion, but something tells me she's not entirely joking. It will be a while before I'm back in Jemma's good books, whatever she decides to do about Will.

TWENTY-TWO

THURSDAY AFTERNOON

The light is already starting to fade on the day by the time I open my eyes later that afternoon. The clocks had 'fallen back' on the Sunday before we went to Barbados, so the evenings are setting in noticeably earlier.

Some people love the autumn, a time to cosy up around the fire in the evenings with a book or to watch a bit of television. All it means to me is that if I'm on the early shift at work, I get up in the dark, go into the studio building in the dark, and it's dark once again by the time I finish work for the day. Occasionally, there is enough time for me to nip out to the local Pret A Manger for a coffee and a toasted sandwich, more for the change of scenery and to see daylight than anything else. Usually though, it's a sandwich at my desk while prepping for my shift, so my working days are operated in a kind of twilight zone.

I feel Stuart move at my side. He's been in bed for over four hours which won't help with the jet lag if I don't wake him up now. It's not such an issue for him now that he's retired, but if he wakes up in the night, it will disturb me, and I'm back in at work tomorrow.

'Stuart,' I say, gently shaking his shoulder. 'We should probably get up.'

At the sound of my voice, there is a gentle thud on the bed, and Wilfie strolls up the duvet and plonks himself squarely on my chest, his velvety black nose inches from mine. He's not allowed to sleep in our room at night. I've never been a fan of pets in bedrooms, but he does always come up in the mornings for a cuddle if I've been working late and Stuart is up first.

'Hello, beautiful boy,' I say, stroking his sleek black fur that shows a hint of red when the sun shines on him. He responds by kneading the bedding perilously close to the skin on my jawline, his purrs vibrating through the 13-tog duvet and connecting with my chest. 'I've missed you.'

'Blimey,' Stuart says, rolling onto his back. 'I wish you still spoke to me with that amount of love in your voice.'

I dig him in the ribs, an action which causes Wilfie to jump down off the bed, giving me a disgusted backwards glance as he does.

'Now look what you've done,' I say.

'You and that bloody cat,' Stuart says. 'There are three of us in this marriage, and one of them isn't human,' he adds, misquoting the famous revelation from the people's princess.

We both giggle.

'At least *he* gets up with me on an early shift in the depths of winter,' I respond accusingly. 'Some might say he's earned my adoration.'

'Touché,' he concedes. 'What happened with Jemma? Is she still here? I'm sorry I had to leave you to it, but I just suddenly hit a wall of tiredness.'

'You're forgiven,' I say. 'And to answer your other question, Jemma's not here. Will has been at work today and doesn't know anything about the wobble she was having, so I managed to persuade her to go home and cook the dinner they've planned for tonight as if nothing is wrong. Then when she's on her own, to implement your list of positives and negatives to give herself a better idea of whether it's worth devoting more time to her boyfriend or not.'

'It's kind of sad, isn't it,' Stuart observes. 'Not that either of us are Will's biggest fans, but I feel we were at last getting to know him a bit better. He's been part of some unforgettable family moments, both happy and sad and, for what it's worth, I thought his sharp edges were beginning to smooth out.'

'There's something you need to know about Will before you start feeling too sorry for him,' I say, deciding to take the bull by the horns. 'He... he had sex with his new boss to secure the job,' I blurt out.

'Bloody hell, Lexi! Don't pull any punches whatever you do,' Stuart says, sitting bolt upright in bed. 'Has Jemma only just found out? Is that why she was so upset? I'll bloody kill him. Did she tell you after I'd come to bed?'

'Actually, darling, I already knew, and so did Cal. At least, Cal had heard rumours and wanted to check them out before confronting Will. We thought it would be best to keep it between the two of us until we knew for sure. I'm sorry I didn't tell you,' I say, reacting to his hurt expression. 'I wanted to, but with Eva dying, it didn't seem right.'

'I wish I'd known before I gave her the suggestion of doing a list of positive and negatives. I'd have told her to dump the cheating git.'

'Then maybe it's better you didn't know,' I say, trying to placate him. 'Not that it makes it any more acceptable, but apparently it was a one-off rather than an ongoing affair.'

Stuart still looks thunderous.

'It's not about us, Stuart. People make mistakes, and this one was a biggie, but if Jemma can forgive him and get past it, then we have to support her decision,' I say. 'Our priority is, and always has been, for our kids to be happy.'

Stuart seems to be taking a moment to process my words.

His body language softens, and he lies back on the pillows, staring up at the ceiling.

'You're absolutely right, my darling wife, as you always are,' Stuart concedes. 'Just assure me you're not keeping any other secrets from me,' he adds with a trace of humour in his voice.

I guess there's no time like the present. I might as well unburden myself.

'Well actually, there is one other thing,' I say.

Stuart turns onto his side to face me.

'Do you remember when we were leaving Rowan House and you said about your mum being really fond of me and I said, "Was she though?"'

'Yes,' he says. 'I remember it clearly because I was amazed that you would ever doubt it. What of it?'

'Well, I said what I did because of something Mari told me while we were making hot drinks for everyone on Saturday evening.'

'What did she say?' Stuart demands, his voice sharp.

'Just that Eva had told her a couple of years ago that she didn't really want to be bothered travelling all the way to our house for Christmas and acting all jolly. And that she'd been relieved the year that lockdown had prevented it, so she didn't have to think of an excuse or seem ungrateful,' I say, the words pouring out of me in a gushing torrent. Now I've started, I can't seem to stop. 'She said that your mum never really liked me and only made out that she did to make your sister jealous. Mari claimed that us getting married prevented you from seeing the light and returning to live on Skye. She said Eva believed that I stole you away from her,' I say, finally running out of steam.

'My sister told you that the day after Mum's funeral?' he says, barely concealing the anger in his voice.

'Yes,' I reply, relieved to have finally told Stuart.

'Wow,' he says, drawing the word out to twice its normal length.

'I know. At first, I was shocked and then incredibly hurt. We never forced Eva to come to us, well, apart from the year your dad died. I genuinely thought she enjoyed spending Christmas with us, but apparently not.'

'You misunderstood me. The wow was one of incredulity that you would believe that spiteful, jealous bitch. I had no idea that my sister could be that cruel. Think about it, Lexi. What purpose would be served by telling you that after Mum had died?'

I shake my head.

'Exactly. No purpose at all. If it had been true, wouldn't Mari have told us the year after lockdown when Mum had allegedly confided in her? There would have been a reason for it then. We could have asked her if she felt up to making the journey, or even volunteered to shift our Christmas celebrations to Skye and let your sister look after your mum for once instead of us having them both.'

I flinch. Put like that, it makes it sound as though Stuart resented always having our mums for Christmas, which I know is not true. He loved entertaining them, cracking his corny jokes and chipping in with odd answers to crossword clues, even though he'd be the first to admit that he is no wordsmith.

'I'm sorry,' he says, lacing his fingers through mine. 'I didn't mean for it to come out like that. You know I love playing host, just like I do for the local kids when they come trick or treating on Halloween.'

'I know,' I reply, bringing our interlaced hands up to my mouth and kissing them. 'You love your moment in the spotlight.'

Stuart had been the guitarist in a semi-pro band playing a few pub gigs in the West End of London. He never had any ambition to take it up full time but maintained it was his release from his boring everyday job in the world of finance. When

Callum came along, he gave up gigging to be around his family more.

He sighs heavily, and when he speaks, he ignores my last remark.

'The truth is, Mum never truly forgave my sister for going to live in Canada, and Mari knew it. This was just a cruel attempt to make you think that Eva didn't love you as much as she did. I just can't believe you fell for it.'

'Do you really think that, Stuart?' I ask. 'I've kept going over and over in my head the last few Christmases, and your mum always seemed to be enjoying herself. But Mari was so convincing that I began to wonder...' My words trail away.

'I don't care what happened in my sister's life to make her this bitter and twisted,' Stuart says, his jaw set firm. 'As far as I'm concerned, once the house sale has gone through, I won't care if I never speak to my sister again. End of subject,' he adds, throwing back the bed covers. 'I'm going to have a shower.'

I watch Stuart's tanned body cross our bedroom and firmly close the door to our en suite bathroom. Did I do the right thing in telling him what Mari said? Especially as we're hoping to forge a closer bond with Fleur.

Perhaps I should have realised that Mari fabricated the whole story to get at me because she was jealous of the relationship I had with her mother. At times over the past few years, I've felt more supported and loved by Eva than I have by my own mother.

'Shit!' I mutter under my breath.

I fling back my side of the bed covers, snatch my dressing gown off the back of the bedroom door and head downstairs. With Jemma turning up unannounced and then jet lag kicking in, I haven't let Mum know that we're back safe and sound. If only she used the mobile phone I bought her for Christmas a few years ago, she could have been part of the Drummond family group on WhatsApp and received the notification along with Callum and Jemma.

I snatch up my phone from the kitchen counter and type in *Mum* in the search bar of my contacts. I tap the screen and prepare myself for the tirade of abuse and accusations of thoughtlessness that I didn't let her know earlier. While I'm waiting for her to pick up, which will be several rings just to prove a point, I reflect on the other offering under the word *Mum*. I haven't been able to delete *Mum Eva* as a contact yet, even though I know I'll never hear her voice again. I suspect it will be months, if not years, before I feel brave enough.

TWENTY-THREE
THURSDAY EVENING

As expected, Mum was quite cross with me when she first answered the phone, saying she'd been imagining all sorts of awful accidents when she hadn't heard from me by midday to say that we were home safely. I decide not to make the excuse of Jemma being there as the reason for my oversight, even though it's true.

She'd mentioned that Veronica, her neighbour across the road, who sometimes did a bit of shopping for her if she was feeling under the weather, had gone to visit her daughter in Benidorm for a couple of weeks. She said she was hoping that I would be able to pop over with a few groceries for her. It was her way of reminding me of her age and suggesting that she wasn't feeling too good without actually saying as much. I offered to get her some things and drop them over, which is why I'm currently standing on her doorstep, shivering from the unaccustomed cold having spent the past two weeks in balmy tropical temperatures. I'm about to delve into my pocket for my bunch of keys, including one for Mum's front door, when it finally opens.

Any irritation I may have felt that Mum was trying it on,

suggesting that she wasn't well, disappears at the sight of her. It's only two weeks since I last saw her, but she seems to have aged by two years.

'I'll follow you in, Mum,' I say, pushing the door further open with my shoulder as my hands are occupied with the two Waitrose bags for life. 'You get yourself in the warm.'

'You could have just let yourself in,' Mum grumbles. 'Why do you think I gave you a key?'

I could argue the point as Mum didn't give me the key. I had two extra ones cut for me and Juliet after the time I'd had to call the police when Mum wouldn't answer. They were on the point of breaking in before Mum, drowsy from just having woken up, appeared at the window. Apparently, her neighbour had kept her up half the night because their baby was crying. She'd finally succumbed to trying the earplugs I'd suggested when she first told me of the issue. They'd obviously done the trick as she'd fallen into a sleep that no amount of knocking and calling her name would wake her from. I had the spare keys cut that afternoon.

'It doesn't feel very warm in here, Mum,' I say, closing the front door with my foot and following her into her living room. 'Have you got the heating on?'

'You're always telling me I've got the heating up too high,' she says, sounding exasperated. 'It's probably because you've just come back from somewhere so hot that it feels cold to you. It's on the same setting as always.'

I make a mental note to check the heating thermostat on the wall near the door to the kitchen on my way through to unpack the groceries.

'Have you got anything planned for your dinner?' I ask.

She'd given me a list of stuff over the phone earlier, but nothing that constituted an obvious meal for tonight.

'I've not really been eating much,' she says. 'I haven't felt hungry.'

'You haven't got your tummy problem back again, have you?' I ask, crossing the room towards the kitchen and glancing at the thermostat dial as I pass. As suspected, it's on the overnight setting of sixteen degrees rather than the daytime one I've recommended for her of twenty-two degrees. I'll turn it up when I've dumped the bags.

'No. I'm just an old lady, and sometimes I go off my food a bit.'

'Fair enough,' I reply, relieved that she hasn't had a relapse. At times earlier in the year, I really thought she might not have the strength to fight the Campylobacter she was diagnosed with. The emergency doctor I'd spoken to on her behalf suggested that it might have been caused by eating takeaway Chinese or Indian food, which either hadn't been cooked properly or had reheated rice. Despite the seriousness of the situation, Stuart and I had both thought it hilarious. The idea of my mum getting a takeaway of any description apart from the occasional fish and chips was laughable. As for eating 'foreign muck' as she calls it, that's never going to happen, with the notable exception of the mushroom risotto I sometimes make when she comes over, which for some reason she doesn't seem to regard as foreign.

'How about I do you some scrambled eggs and a bit of bacon?' I say, thinking of the supplies available to me in the shopping bags.

Mum ignores my question about her prospective dinner. She didn't ask about our holiday in the phone call earlier and hasn't mentioned it since I arrived with her shopping. She is now regarding me with a critical eye.

'I do wish you wouldn't sit in the sun so much, Alexis.'

Her use of my full name reminds me of what Mari said about Eva always referring to me as Alexis when the two of them talked. Despite his reassurance of his mum's fondness for me, that's something else I'll have to check with Stuart. The thought of Eva only pretending to be close to me all these years twists my gut. Our relationship meant so much to me. It hurts to think that Eva didn't feel the same.

'Did you hear what I said?' Mum demands loudly.

'About sitting in the sun? Yes, I did,' I reply.

'Not that bit. I said you'll end up with skin like leather or worse still, skin cancer,' she says at her louder volume. 'Nobody died of skin cancer back in my day, because we didn't go exposing ourselves on faraway beach holidays.'

She's right about faraway holidays. They weren't really the norm in the mid-1950s when my mum hit her twenties.

'But you did used to slather on the olive oil and coconut oil, with no suggestion of an SPF factor, to fry during British heatwaves,' I counter. 'I use a factor 50 on my face to protect me from the rays that I don't think even scientists knew about back in the day.'

We have this discussion after most of mine and Stuart's foreign holidays so it's a well-practised response. Mum gives a sort of grunt. This is one argument she can't win factually, but it still doesn't stop her from trying. She changes the subject.

'Did you get me the chicken breasts?' she asks.

'Yes,' I say, holding the cling-wrapped polystyrene tray aloft. 'One for the fridge and one for the freezer as instructed.'

'Or you could stay and have dinner with me,' she says. There is a plaintive note to her suggestion.

'I'm sorry, Mum. I can't tonight. I'm back in at work tomorrow, and Stuart is making us gnocchi for dinner, so I've promised to be home by 7.30 p.m. at the latest. You could join us, but I know you're not a fan of foreign food.'

She wrinkles her nose in disgust.

'I'll cook your chicken for you though,' I continue. 'And I can do some boiled potatoes and broccoli. How does that sound?'

'Well, I'd have rather you stayed for a chat, but it will have to do,' she says, somewhat ungraciously.

'Anything particular you wanted to chat about?' I ask, taking the second piece of chicken out of the polystyrene and placing it in one of those containers with lockable lids before putting it in the freezer.

'Jemma of course.'

I spin around from fiddling with the dials on Mum's oven.

'She's called you already?' I manage to say through my surprise.

'Yes, as soon as she got home from yours,' Mum replies.

So, Mum knew all along that Stuart and I were home safely from holiday because she'd spoken to Jemma. All the rubbish about being frantic not knowing if we'd been in an accident was just to make me feel bad. Or was it? An awful thought suddenly occurs to me. What if Mum had genuinely forgotten that she'd spoken to Jemma until a couple of minutes ago? I get a sick feeling in the pit of my stomach. To my mind, there is only one thing worse than being physically debilitated in later life, and that's a diagnosis of Alzheimer's disease or some other type of dementia. Please, I silently pray, don't let this be the start of a decline in her mental health.

'Well, we can talk while I'm cooking,' I say. 'This is going to take at least forty-five minutes. What did she tell you?'

'Well, obviously she's upset that you and Callum didn't tell her about Will sleeping with his prospective new boss to get his fancy new job,' Mum says.

My heart sinks. I guess I was hoping for a softening in Jemma's attitude towards us for keeping her in the dark, but maybe it's too soon for that.

'To be honest, Alexis, Jemma seemed more upset about you two keeping the truth from her than she did about Will being unfaithful. She told me that she'd already been having a few doubts about whether he was her one, especially at Eva's funeral when she realised that she didn't love Will in the way that Stuart's parents loved each other,' Mum reveals, sitting down on one of the chairs at the two-seater table in her cramped kitchen. 'Now she knows what he did, she's not sure she wants to spend her life with him and wanted another opinion after speaking to you and Stuart.'

'What did you say?' I ask, brushing oil onto the skinned chicken breast, seasoning it with salt and pepper and popping it in the oven in a glass dish, before reaching for the bag of new potatoes.

'Just that I've always believed honesty is the best policy in any relationship,' Mum says, clearly having a dig at me for not being honest with my daughter.

'I was only trying to protect her, Mum,' I say defensively. 'Jemma has this idea that everything in a relationship should be perfect all the time, which, as you know better than most, is unrealistic. Recovering from a rocky patch can sometimes bring two people closer together, assuming Will has now been totally honest with her,' I add, wondering if there are further revelations to come.

I notice Mum's eyes narrow as I'm talking. She knows where I'm going with this, and now that I've started, I might as well continue.

'The thing is, Mum, I didn't expect Jemma to contact you so quickly. I... I was going to ask you whether maybe you might consider telling her what happened between you and Dad before Juliet was born? It could help her understand that relationships are not always smooth sailing, maybe soften the blow a bit?'

I only know about my parents' trial separation because I was a savvy four-year-old when it happened. Dad came back to us after things didn't work out with his 'piece of skirt', which I recall was Mum's favourite description of his girlfriend. I was witness to some awful rows that no small child should ever see. And then suddenly, they stopped, and a little while later Juliet was born.

'Oh, I get it now,' Mum says, her lips set in a thin, hard line. 'You must think I'm stupid.'

I can feel the colour rising in my cheeks.

'You've only brought me this bit of shopping and offered to make my dinner so that you could pressure me into breaking a promise I made to your father. You want me to tell Jemma that mine and your dad's marriage wasn't perfect. What sort of mother are you, Alexis?' she demands. 'You'd spoil the memory your daughter has of her grandfather forever simply because she's hit a bump in the road with Will. Shame on you,' she almost spits.

I'm not shocked, but I am angry that my mum is, as usual, only seeing things through her eyes. How can one person be so self-centred? I wonder. I've finished preparing the potatoes, so they are ready to drop into boiling water when the chicken has twenty minutes left to cook. I'm tempted to storm out. Then I remember my concerns from a few moments ago. I bite my lip and remind myself that she is eighty-seven years old and has earned the right to have her own opinion on things.

'You're right, Mum. It's not fair to expect you to ruin Jemma's memory of her granddad to try and save her relationship with Will when they might be better off apart,' I say apologetically.

She's surprised. It wasn't the reaction she was expecting. A younger version of me might have snapped back, but along with my concerns for Mum's mental health, I also considered Stuart's words from earlier when we were talking about Mari. Yes, I want to help my daughter, but at what cost? It's not nice to speak ill of the dead, whether or not it's true.

'Do you want broccoli, or would you rather have peas?' I continue.

Mum blinks at me rapidly, probably trying to reach a decision which has nothing to do with choosing a vegetable to have with her chicken.

'You choose,' she says, getting to her feet. 'Like I said earlier, I'm not really that hungry, so don't do me too much, please, or it will get wasted.'

With that she leaves me alone in the kitchen to carry on preparing a meal that she has already indicated she is unlikely to eat. It's her call. I'm heading home as soon as it's plated up.

There was another question I wanted to ask her. I want to know if she had any knowledge of Eva's apparent reluctance to spend Christmas with us now that Mari has planted the seed of doubt. It will have to wait. In this mood, Mum will probably claim that they've both simply endured it for years.

TWENTY-FOUR
17 NOVEMBER – FRIDAY MORNING

Our plan to stay up late last night so that we had a chance of a decent night's sleep following our lengthy afternoon nap worked almost too well. When the alarm went off at 7.30 a.m., I reached over and, in my groggy state, hit what I thought was the snooze button to give me an extra ten minutes in bed. I woke with a start almost two hours later, which means I'm now in a rush if I'm to get anything done at home this morning before I head into News 24/7 for my shift. I'm supposed to be in at 1 p.m., which normally means leaving our house in Holyport village forty-five minutes beforehand, but I was planning to go in an hour earlier and catch up on a fortnight's worth of emails to get myself up to speed on all the ongoing news stories.

Stuart had been adamant that I shouldn't check on work emails while I was away. 'Put your "out of office" on and leave work behind like the big bosses do,' he'd said. I knew I couldn't trust myself not to have a sneaky peek from time to time, so to remove the temptation, I didn't take my work iPad with me, and I can't access work emails from my phone. My intention was to go through emails yesterday evening, deleting anything that was no longer relevant, but after crossing swords with Mum, when all I was trying to do was the best thing for my daughter, I didn't feel in the mood. Instead, I enjoyed a glass of Pinot Grigio with the gnocchi Stuart had cooked from scratch. He's done even more of the cooking since he retired and has become more experimental.

I'm downstairs within five minutes, the first job on my list being to clear the poop out of the cat's litter tray. It will need changing this morning as it's a bit smelly after us being away for two weeks. Wilfie is rubbing himself affectionately against my legs while I reach his food down from the cupboard over the sink when Stuart pops his head around the utility room door.

'I'll do breakfast while you have a shower if that will help time-wise,' he says.

'Thanks, it would. My hair looks like I've stuck it in a deep fat fryer, so it'll need a wash,' I say, adding some hard food to the other half of Wilfie's double feeding bowl, next to the chicken and beans in jelly our fussy cat is so fond of.

'Fancy anything in particular?' Stuart asks as I put the bowl on the floor. It's received with a happy chirruping sound.

'Poached eggs if you can be bothered, or just toast is fine. We've had a bit of an egg overload with all the morning omelettes at Crystal Waters,' I add, rinsing the fork I've just used to dish out Wilfie's food and putting it back in the cupboard so that it doesn't accidentally get mixed in with our regular cutlery.

'How long?' Stuart asks.

In response to my raised eyebrows, he continues, 'Until you want your breakfast. I know how long our holiday was. I'm not senile yet.'

I shudder. I didn't mention my fears about Mum's state of mental health when I got home last night because I was still annoyed at her, but it is something I might have to raise with her doctor when I get a minute.

'Erm, about twenty minutes?' I suggest, hurrying up the stairs.

It's a little after ten when I step out of the shower with my hair wrapped in one towel and a larger bath sheet around my body. I look a lot healthier than I did before we went away, I think, catching my reflection in the bathroom mirror, but a golden tan will do that for you, contrary to what Mum said last night. I'm about to free my hair from its towel to comb through some leave-in conditioner when my mobile phone starts to ring. As I'm picking it up from the chest of drawers, I can see that it's Jenny from work, and I hit the speaker button rather than trying to have a conversation through towelling.

'Hi,' I say brightly.

'Where are you?' she asks in a tone that can best be described as brusque.

'I'm just out of the shower,' I reply. 'It's okay. I'm not talking to you naked.' I laugh. 'I've got a towel around me.'

There's a brief pause before she says, 'Haven't you been reading your emails?'

Damn! If they've changed my shift today and I didn't know about it, no wonder she sounds a bit shitty. Then I remind myself, I was on annual leave. If there was a last-minute change, she has my number. She could have rung or WhatsApp'd me.

'No,' I reply. 'For the first time ever, I didn't take my work iPad with me on holiday so I wouldn't be tempted to look at work stuff. I just needed a complete break after the stress of the past few weeks.'

That's when I notice the sound of papers being shuffled, and I realise that Jenny has me on speakerphone too.

'So, are you going to tell me what's in my emails or do you want me to read them and give you a call back? Or I could just stick my head into your office when I get in,' I suggest.

'The thing is, Alexis,' Jenny says after clearing her throat. 'You're not actually on shift today.'

'Oh, right. Is that why you're ringing? To make sure I don't come in unnecessarily?' I ask. I'm starting to get the feeling that something is a bit off. 'Have you moved me to cover the whole of the weekend?' I groan inwardly. I was looking forward to Sunday off before dropping back into my regular shift pattern.

'Not exactly.' There's another brief pause. 'You've been taken off the roster for the time being.'

I'm struggling to follow the conversation. A chill runs down my spine, and not just from standing around in a bath towel in November. What is she saying?

'What? But why?' I manage to ask, panic gripping my insides.

'I can't say too much at this stage, but you were due in a meeting at ten o'clock this morning with me and Roxanne from Human Resources. You were sent an email and the appointment was put on your calendar. A reminder email was sent first thing this morning. I'm only calling because you were a no-show,' Jenny concludes.

I'm now starting to feel a little light-headed. A lot of people have been let go from News 24/7 over the past nine months due to budget cuts, but nothing at all has been mentioned to me about my job security.

'Is this to do with the restructuring programme? Am I in trouble?' I ask quietly.

'No, nothing like that. I can't tell you much because it's an ongoing investigation, but this part is in the email about today's meeting – the one you haven't read. Do you have any recollection of a conversation you had with Lucy in the staff cafeteria during which you made derisory remarks about a colleague?'

'N – no, I don't think so,' I stammer, wracking my brain to try and dredge up the memory. Lucy and I often have a private gossip about some of the less effective members of staff, but nothing springs immediately to mind.

'Well, you were overheard, and the member of staff concerned reported it directly to HR rather than the usual channels of going to their team leader first. HR then did a bit of investigating, and it seems an email was sent potentially commenting on the same person at around the same time.'

Gradually a memory starts to form: Summer Palmer, the bane of my life. A wannabee presenter who was inexplicably given a floor manager's role in preference to other, much more suitable candidates and has messed up repeatedly since.

'It's not acceptable behaviour from anyone, Alexis, but particularly not from someone with your experience,' Jenny concludes.

My legs feel as wobbly as a Jenga tower before someone extracts the last precariously positioned brick and the whole thing topples over.

'So, what happens now?' I ask, almost fearful of the response.

'I'll reschedule the initial meeting with you for 10 a.m. Monday. Is that okay, Roxanne?' I hear her say to the HR representative, whose faint 'yes' I just catch. 'Please be on time. And Alexis—'

'Yes,' I reply.

'You must not contact any of your work colleagues at all until the investigation into this matter is finished. Is that clear?'

I nod mutely before realising that she can't see a nod.

'Yes. I've got it,' I say.

'Right. See you Monday,' Jenny says before terminating the call.

I'm now clinging onto the chest of drawers for dear life. There is a whooshing sound in my ears and my heart is thundering in my chest. Am I having a heart attack?

'What the hell was all that about?'

I spin around to see Stuart standing in the doorway of our

bedroom. He must have come upstairs looking for me when I didn't appear for my breakfast, and judging by his question and the angry look on his face, he heard some of the latter end of the call.

'Help me,' I say before my legs finally give way and I black out.

TWENTY-FIVE

FRIDAY MORNING

When I come to, I'm lying face down on our bedroom carpet next to the chest of drawers. My heartbeat still seems fast and pronounced, but nothing else hurts so I'm assuming I fell without hitting any obstruction. The reason that I passed out comes back to me in a flash when Stuart speaks.

'So, what did you do?' he demands.

Right now, I need the soft and gentle Stuart who always supports me and fights my corner. Not this aggressive imposter.

'Can you help me up, please?' I say, my voice sounding as wobbly as my legs were feeling moments earlier.

Silently, he bends down, loops his arms under my shoulders and twists me round into a sitting position with my back propped against the foot of the bed. His expression is now less angry but more worried.

'I thought I was having a heart attack,' I say a little breathlessly.

'More likely a panic attack,' he says. 'What's going on, Lexi? I only heard the last bit of the call, but it sounds as though you're under an internal investigation for something. How bad is it?'

'I don't know, Stuart, but it doesn't sound good,' I say wearily. 'I'll know more when I check my emails, but apparently, I was supposed to be at a meeting with HR and Jenny this morning and she called when I didn't attend. I've been suspended from the editor roster for now,' I add.

'Bloody hell, Lexi. This is bad. If you're okay there for a minute, I'll fetch your iPad,' Stuart says.

I hear him running down the stairs into the kitchen to retrieve the iPad from the corner unit where all the chargers are for our various electrical gadgets. A couple of minutes later I can hear his feet back on the stairs. I don't know why he's in such a rush to confirm that I'm currently suspended pending investigation. I'm desperate to ring Lucy, but I'm under strict instructions not to speak to any work colleagues. I have a feeling that if I ignore that directive, it could give them grounds for instant dismissal.

'Here,' Stuart says, handing me the iPad. 'I brought the lead in case it's not charged.'

'Thanks,' I say. 'It should be alright. It was fully charged before we left to go on holiday, and nobody's been using it.'

I don't look Stuart in the eye while I'm waiting for the tablet to fire up. I simply can't believe this is happening. Just when I thought things couldn't get any worse, they have. I key in my security code and select my work email. There are hundreds, as I knew there would be, but I scroll past all of them until I find the one I'm looking for. It's from HR and is dated eight days previously. I feel a sudden burst of anger that it was sent while I was on annual leave. How dare they? If I had opened it while I was in Barbados, as I normally would have had Stuart not been so firm with me, it would have completely ruined my thirtieth anniversary holiday for the second time.

The email is short and to the point:

Dear Alexis Drummond,

After some preliminary investigations following a complaint received from a junior colleague of yours regarding derogatory language, both spoken and also written in an email, you are requested to attend a meeting at 10 a.m. on Friday, 17th November with your line manager, Jenny Forest, and a member of the Human Resources team.

Until this matter has been thoroughly investigated you have been removed from the editor roster indefinitely.

You are not permitted to have legal representation at this stage of our inquiry, but you can ask for a member of our 'people' team to accompany you should you wish.

You may not communicate with any member of staff at News 24/7 while this is an active investigation.

It is assumed that the date and time are acceptable, but if not, you are required to give us 48 hours' notice to rearrange.

Roxanne Stannard

(Head of Human Resources)

I read it through twice before handing the iPad to Stuart.

'What did you say, Lexi?' he demands. 'Please tell me it wasn't racist or sexist.'

I shake my head. I'm quite upset that Stuart would consider it might be. I don't have a racist bone in my body and have worked alongside members of the LGBTQ community since before they had a collective name.

'Do you even know who has reported you?' he adds.

'I've got a good idea, although I can't remember either incident clearly. I wish I could speak to Lucy. She's the only one I ever discuss other members of the team with. They will probably have questioned her about it I would think.'

'Well, you can't. You're already in enough trouble, don't

make it any worse. Did I overhear them say that you made these derisory comments in an email too? We should probably try to find it so that you know who you are up against and what you actually said. Honestly, Lexi, what were you thinking? How many times have I said to you, watch your back, be careful what you say and be nice to everybody. Is it that bloody hard?'

His tone has become aggressive again and something inside me just snaps.

'And you're so bloody perfect!' I snarl at him. 'You've caused this by putting me under so much pressure.'

He looks shocked, but he's opened Pandora's box now.

'You wanted this bloody house, not me! At a time when most people are sensibly downsizing because they're approaching retirement and their kids are moving out, you decide you want to live in a rambling detached four-bedroom house in an expensive part of Berkshire. So, we buy it, and what happens with years to run on the mortgage? You're given early retirement, leaving me to make the astronomical mortgage payments each month.'

Stuart is blinking rapidly, but I'm in no mood to stop.

'But it doesn't end there. Oh no. You want us to celebrate our pearl wedding anniversary with a swanky holiday in the Caribbean. A holiday we can't really afford, so I've had to work overtime and syphon off part of my monthly salary over the past two years to make it happen.'

Stuart is now looking aghast.

'Don't get me wrong, Stuart,' I say, continuing with my rant. 'It's a lovely idea but someone had to pay for it and that someone is me! And then there's our mums. Neither of us is an only child and yet we are the ones who've had to look after them. And before you say it, I know you did the driving to and from Skye most of the time, but that was because I was working, and who did most of the looking after when Eva was here? Yes, me again. And according to your absent sister, it turns out she didn't even want to be here, so that was a wasted effort.'

'I told you that's not true...' Stuart starts to say, but I waft my hand at him to stop speaking.

'Then there's *my* mother, who seems to think the sun shines out of your arse. Stuart this, Stuart that,' I say in a simpering tone, 'while all the time being positively vile to her own daughter. It's great that she loves you and that you know how to handle her, but how do you think that makes me feel?' I demand. 'Like a pile of unloved shit!'

'Stop it now, Lexi,' Stuart pleads. 'You'll give yourself another panic attack.'

'I don't bloody care,' I screech. 'I've had it with everything and everyone. I love both of our kids dearly, but they always park their problems at my door. Who was there when Cal and Ellie had the miscarriage? ME! Who does Jemma come running to when her latest relationship is in danger of going tits up? ME! And now, because I was forced to go into work because we needed the money and my heartless company wouldn't give me paid compassionate leave, I've been suspended for calling a spiteful, useless bitch a snowflake.'

'You didn't use the word bitch did you, Lexi?'

'I don't know! And what's more, I don't care. I've made the mistake of being overheard criticising someone who is crap at their job, and now it looks as though I might lose mine. Everyone treats me as though I'm some kind of superwoman, but I'm not. I'm just Lexi, and I've royally fucked up,' I say, finally dissolving into floods of tears.

Stuart starts to move towards me, but I hold my hand up to keep him at arm's length.

'Don't come anywhere near me, Stuart,' I say between my huge gulping sobs. 'Everything has been chipping away at me like a thousand tiny cuts. Snip, snip, snip until finally the last tenuous strand that has been keeping me hanging on to my sanity by my fingernails is severed. And now I'm in free fall, and when I land at the bottom of the abyss in a crumpled heap, everything will come crashing down on top of me.'

Stuart is looking down at me, his eyes full of concern, an expression of hopelessness on his face.

'At least let me help you up onto the bed,' he says, starting to bend down towards me.

'Just get out of here and give me some space,' I shriek at him.

As though he has finally got the message, he straightens himself up and walks out of the room without a backward glance, slamming the door behind him.

It's what I told him I wanted, but I didn't really. I wanted him to force his strong arms around me and tell me it was all going to be alright. I push myself up onto my feet and fling myself dramatically onto the bed and start howling like a wounded animal.

TWENTY-SIX

FRIDAY LUNCHTIME

I must have eventually cried myself to sleep, because the next thing I'm aware of is the squeaking sound of our bedroom doorknob turning followed by the door opening an inch or two.

'Go away, Stuart,' I sniff, all trace of my former fury gone. 'I told you I don't want you around me at the moment.'

There's no reply, so I assume he's taken the hint. A couple of moments later, there is a gentle thud, and Wilfie strolls up the bed. He touches my nose with his, and then when I don't start to stroke him as I normally would, he headbutts my hand until I lift it up from the grey, patterned duvet cover and fondle his ears. He responds by turning on his purr machine, and I roll onto my back so that he can climb onto my chest, allowing me to feel the resonance of the vibrations.

Wilfie is an incredibly intuitive cat. He seems to have a second sense that tells him when I'm upset, although the howling cries that I'm now so embarrassed I made might have given him a clue on this occasion. I stroke him along the length of his body from his head to his tail for a few minutes, sometimes extending the stroke to incorporate his tail right to the very tip. I've always found this action to be extremely calming and today is no different.

'What have I done, Wilf?' I whisper while continuing to fondle his ears. 'I've screwed everything up.'

I hear the sound of a teaspoon against a china mug and look up from Wilfie's perfect cat features to see my husband standing in the doorway.

'Is it safe to come in?' he asks. 'I sent Wilfie in as my advance scouting party to get the lay of the land.'

'I'm sorry I went off on one,' I say, beckoning him into the bedroom with my free hand. 'I guess I've been bottling stuff up for a while and this stupid situation at work just tipped me over the edge.'

'I wish you'd told me how you were feeling before it mounted up so much,' Stuart says, coming around the bed to my side and setting the cup he's carrying down on the bedside table. 'Chamomile and honey,' he adds, responding to my eyebrows arching in question. 'I thought it might help.'

'Where did you find that?' I ask. 'I haven't been having those on a regular basis for ages. Did you check the date?'

'End of November 2023, so it should be okay,' he says, crossing his fingers. 'Last one in the box, almost like it was waiting for a situation like today.'

I smile weakly and wriggle myself into a sitting position, reaching across for Stuart's pillow to prop me up.

'I think it's going to take more than a chamomile and honey tea to sort this mess out.'

'So, I've been thinking,' Stuart says. 'I reread the email a few times and it doesn't actually say anywhere on it that you are suspended from work, just that you are not on the roster for the foreseeable future.'

'It amounts to the same thing, doesn't it?' I say glumly, taking a sip of the tea which Stuart has thoughtfully allowed to cool slightly before bringing it up.

'No, it doesn't. If you were suspended, my idea wouldn't work. We're going to have to act quickly mind, but if we can get you signed off work with stress before your meeting on Monday with HR, you won't have to attend. It will also help build a case that you said what you did because you were under extreme pressure after my mum died.'

'I was,' I say.

'I know that,' he says, reaching for my hand. 'You were trying to be strong for me and the kids, as per usual. Anyway, we can talk about that later. The most important thing is for you to book a private GP appointment on the app, preferably to talk to them today, so that they can issue you a fit to work note giving you time off due to stress.'

'Can they do that without seeing me, or referring me to someone who is better placed to give that kind of diagnosis?' I ask.

'I think so,' Stuart replies. 'I was doing a bit of internet research while you were sleeping. You'll probably have to ask to be referred to a therapist, but to be honest, it might not be a bad idea,' he adds, giving the hand he is still holding a gentle squeeze.

'Are you saying you think I'm going crazy?' I joke, having another sip of tea. 'I suppose it's a fair assumption after my earlier outburst.'

'Not going crazy, darling, you are completely batshit bonkers, which is precisely why we all love you so much... including your mum, by the way.' He holds his hand up to stop me speaking. 'Like I said, we can talk about everything once we've set the ball rolling with the private GP appointment. Thank God News 24/7 have the private health scheme, or we really would be up shit creek without a paddle. Do you know your login details?' he continues, going to fetch my phone from the top of the chest of drawers.

'I think so,' I say, putting my mug down on the bedside table and taking my phone from him. 'I think I was in a sarcastic mood and chose NEWS247cares!'

I tap on the app and enter my email and password where indicated and hold my crossed fingers up for a few moments while it does a bit of whirligigging.

'Yay, I'm in,' I say, selecting *Book GP Appointment*. 'Blimey, how easy is this? Why have I never used it before?'

'Because you're one of the few News 24/7 employees who goes to work unless you're actually dying. And then, for some inexplicable reason, you put yourself through the hell of trying to get an NHS appointment with our local surgery. Like I said, batshit bonkers. Have they got any today?' he asks.

'Loads,' I reply, the surprise in my voice genuine.

'Just book the earliest one, whoever the listed doctor is and whatever their speciality. We just need you signed off from today.'

I choose 3.15 p.m. with Dr Amirah Singh, and my phone pings to confirm it is booked.

'How come you are such an expert on all this?' I ask, logging out of the app.

'I told you; I was doing some research while you were sleeping. Your outburst, as you describe it, made me realise that I expect you to do and know everything, and that's not fair. Things are going to change, Lexi. I'm going to start pulling my weight more.'

We've not long finished having our lunch of cheesy scrambled eggs on toast, which more than made up for missing the poached eggs Stuart had made for breakfast, when I get a text message to say the private GP will be calling me in ten minutes. I've got a list of things that Stuart wrote out while I was sleeping to cite as reasons for feeling depressed. He really has been busy with his research, as one of the main things that employers are nervous about arguing over is menopause.

To be honest, I more or less sailed through menopause unscathed. I didn't suffer many of the associated problems apart from the raging hot sweats in the early days, and more recently the loss of libido, although Stuart and I are now working on that together. I did sometimes find it difficult to focus and remember things, which was tricky in my line of work. But stress is common during menopause, feeling out of control, so Stuart told me to play dumb and ask the doctor if it could be menopause-related even though I was almost through that journey.

Stuart also pointed out that stress can be a cause of panic attacks like the one I had earlier. Although we both know what triggered it, it's not something I have to share with the doctor, just that I experienced one which I'd found very frightening and that I'd blacked out for a couple of minutes.

Obviously, I needed to mention the recent bereavement and the effect that has had on me and that my workplace hasn't been particularly understanding in giving me time off to grieve properly.

He told me I was to ask for a sick note starting from this morning and a referral to see a therapist, and request that a list of therapists be emailed over to me as soon as possible as I was feeling completely overwhelmed with everything.

When my mobile rings, he gives me a thumbs up from where he's sitting across the kitchen table from me and continues to do so throughout the phone consultation, where I put forward all the things on our list. At the end of the call, Dr Singh tells me she will email me a sick note for a week and that I'm to call back if I need it extending for a further week without physically seeing a doctor. I'm to forward it to News 24/7. She'll also email a referral to see a therapist. When I receive that, I'm to ring News 24/7's private health provider directly for a list of approved therapists in my area. The entire call lasts precisely seven and a half minutes.

'Well done you,' Stuart says after I've pressed the red *end call* button. 'I particularly liked the way you delivered the line about feeling completely overwhelmed. How you didn't make it as an actress, I'll never know.'

My aspirations to become the next Helen Mirren were short-lived once Stuart and I had become an item. I'd never been particularly fond of the whole casting process, which back in the day was always in person rather than the preferred method of self-videoing these days. I hated sitting in the casting director's office along with a dozen or so other hopefuls and learning a few lines of dialogue which would determine whether I would get the role I was up for. If it had just been the delivery of the lines, it wouldn't have been so soul-destroying, but sometimes I'd walk into the audition room and know instantly that I didn't have the right look. I persevered for a couple of years, but a six-month tour of rundown regional theatres with a repertory company, which involved stage management duties as well as performing, was the final nail in the coffin. The only upside of that job was that the stage management experience I gained helped me secure a role as floor manager at News 24/7 when they were starting out, so I guess I owe them.

'It wasn't an act, Stuart. Talking about it even for a few minutes made me realise that I genuinely am overwhelmed with almost every aspect of my life at the moment. I've honestly never considered going to see a therapist. I always thought I could handle whatever came my way. That if I needed to reach out to a total stranger and air all my innermost secrets, it made me weak. But maybe that's exactly what I need. Someone who'll listen without judgement and then guide me towards the best way to cope, because I never want what happened this morning between you and me to happen again.

Stuart comes around to my side of the table and envelopes me in one of his infamous bear hugs, almost squeezing the life out of me.

'Me neither,' he says, kissing the top of my hair which is only just dry after I fell asleep on the bed with the towel wrapped around it. 'I honestly haven't given enough consideration to how bogged down you must be feeling, but now that I know, I promise we'll work it out together. Deal?'

For a weird moment I picture a big red box with a member of the public sitting behind it enjoying their fifteen minutes of fame, with the presenter saying, 'Deal or no deal?'

'Thanks for helping me with this,' I say, lifting my head up so that I can look into his eyes. 'When I got that call this morning, I couldn't see how on earth I was going to keep my job, particularly because they've been actively looking for people to make mistakes so that they could get rid of them without paying compensation. What an idiot I was to take my eye off the ball.'

'You've had a huge amount of stuff going on, which we're going to list as mitigating circumstances. We're going to fight this, Lexi, and we're going to win!'

TWENTY-SEVEN
FRIDAY EVENING

No one is more surprised than me to be standing outside 43 Lavender Close, the home and workplace of Beverley Laing, the therapist I selected from the shortlist that was emailed from my medical insurance company. It's been three hours since receiving the list and a little over four hours from the initial call with the private GP. It's all happened so quickly that I haven't really had much time to think about what's expected of me, and I must admit to feeling a tad nervous. I hate not feeling in control.

True to her word, Dr Singh had sent me both the sick note and the referral letter within ten minutes from the termination of our call. I'd sent the sick note to Lydia, the scheduler at News 24/7, and also sent a copy to Jenny accompanied by a very brief email stating that as I'd been signed off sick with stress, I wouldn't be able to attend the meeting on Monday morning and that I'd given her in excess of forty-eight hours' notice as requested. I haven't had a reply from Jenny as I expect she will have to speak to HR to decide on their next course of action. However, Lydia very sweetly replied with, *get well soon, lovely,* which I strongly suspect is not correct company language for acknowledging a sick note.

I'd then rung the medical insurance company and managed to speak to one of the nurses straight away having described my case as urgent. Stephanie was very understanding when I briefly ran through the points I'd raised with Dr Singh, and she emailed me a list of therapists while I was still on the phone to her. 'Good luck with it all,' had been Stephanie's sign-off.

I didn't have time to research any of the therapists, and anyway, the purpose wasn't for me to actually seek help, it was for me to be seen to be seeking help. I did say to Stuart while he was looking through the list that I would probably find it easier speaking to a woman than a man, although in light of my recent experience at work, I'll need to be careful who I express that opinion to.

'It looks like Beverley Laing is the nearest to us,' Stuart said after checking the postcodes. 'Why don't you try her first?'

Beverley didn't answer her phone, and I didn't really know what to say in a voicemail message, so I just hung up. Thirty minutes later my phone rang, and it was from an unknown number.

'Hello?' I'd said a little sharply, fully expecting it to be someone pretending to be my internet provider, trying to sell me a better deal.

'Oh, hi,' a female voice had said, sounding a little taken aback. 'This is Beverley Laing. Did you try to call me half an hour ago? I'm sorry, I was with a client. How can I help you?'

I immediately liked the gentle tone of her voice and the fact that she had bothered to ring me back.

Initially, she said she couldn't see me until next week, but she must have detected the disappointment in my voice, because she then said, 'Unless you can do 7.30 p.m. tonight? I've had a cancellation so was simply going to finish early, but you're welcome to the appointment if you can make it?'

So that's how come I'm standing outside a therapist's home on a frosty Friday evening waiting for the door to be opened. I hear a dog bark from within the house and a female voice shushing it, followed by the sound of a door closing. Moments later, the door swings open allowing light and warmth to wash over me.

'Alexis?' asks a slim, dark-haired woman who I would imagine is a similar age to me.

'Yes,' I reply. 'Thanks for seeing me at such short notice.'

'No worries. I never want to be that therapist who turns away a client when they've reached out. It takes courage to pick up the phone and make that first call. Come in out of the cold,' she says, standing to one side of the doorway and indicating the direction I should move towards with her extended right arm. 'You look like you've recently been away somewhere warm, so it must feel even colder to you.'

'Yes. We only got back from Barbados...' I pause for a second. How can so much have happened in thirty-six hours? 'Sorry, we got home yesterday, but it seems a lot longer.'

'I know what you mean,' she says, ushering me into a small room with two chairs set facing each other in opposite corners, a small desk, a standard lamp, an occasional table and an electric heater, which thankfully is on. 'Funny how holidays always pass by in the blink of an eye and the rest of the year drags on. Please take a seat.'

'Thank you,' I mutter, which is half drowned out by the dog barking again.

'Oh, don't mind Carlton,' Beverley says, waving her hand vaguely in the direction of where the barks are coming from. 'He's a softie, but I'm never sure with a new client if they're comfortable around dogs. He'll settle down in a few minutes when he realises he's not going to be allowed out to meet the new arrival.'

'I'm more of a cat person, to be honest,' I say, conjuring up

Wilfie's adorable face. And then, without warning, tears start to roll down my cheeks before I've even taken my coat off. 'I'm so sorry,' I sniff, taking a tissue from the box Beverley is offering.

'You keep them over there. I've a feeling you're going to need them,' she says. 'And please don't apologise. You're here to let it all out whatever form that takes.'

She sits quietly, making no attempt to fill the space with small talk until I manage to bring my tears under control.

'Well, it was good to get that out of the way,' she says in her soft voice, which I can now detect has a hint of the northeast in her almost non-existent accent. 'Shall we start at what you think is the beginning of your problem? That will give us a chance to work out what the real beginning is.'

I start talking, uncertainly at first as I'm pouring my heart out to a complete stranger, but gradually I gain confidence and, with it, speed. Beverley interjects occasionally with questions and makes notes. I start with Eva dying while we were away on holiday, and my guilt that the kids had to deal with it.

'How old are your children?' Beverley asks.

'Callum's twenty-eight and Jemma's twenty-six,' I reply.

There is a slight raise of her eyebrows.

'So not teenagers then.' It's a statement not a question.

I move on to work not allowing me to have time off for the funeral because I'm not a blood relative, despite Eva being in my life for thirty-five years, and how difficult I'd found it going into work as though I was completely fine and having to deal with people not doing their jobs properly. I notice Beverley making another note here, but she doesn't say anything, so I carry on telling her how distressed I was just after the funeral to find out that Eva hadn't really enjoyed coming to our house every Christmas.

'Who did you find that out from? Someone reliable, or someone with their own agenda?' Beverley asks.

'Stuart's... he's my husband, so Eva's son. It was his sister,

Mari, who told me. She's lived in Canada since she was eighteen, and Eva never really forgave her for going, so I suppose you could say she had an agenda.

I can't believe I'm giving out all this information so freely.

'Does Stuart know his sister told you this?' she asks, scribbling furiously.

'I didn't tell him straight away, but he knows now and says there's no truth in it,' I say.

'But judging by the doubt in your voice, you're not so sure?'

I nod. Maybe it had all been too much to expect a lady in her eighties to travel for a whole day by road and rail to spend a few days with her son and his family, no matter how welcome we made her.

'So, Stuart rebooked our holiday that we'd had to return from when... when Eva died,' I stammer, 'and we had a really great time, but arrived home yesterday to find our daughter in floods of tears because she doesn't think she loves her boyfriend any more after discovering something about him that me and her brother had been keeping from her.'

Beverley is nodding and writing but doesn't speak.

'And then this morning, I had a call from work to say I should have been in a meeting with HR today because a junior member of staff had made a complaint about me.'

'What job do you do?' she asks.

'I'm an editor for a twenty-four-hour television news channel,' I reply.

'So quite a pressurised job, I'd imagine, even when you're feeling at the top of your game?'

'I guess so. I've been in the role for eighteen years after working my way up through the ranks, so although it is pretty full-on, I've always just taken it in my stride,' I say.

'Until now? Do you mind me asking what the nature of the complaint is?' she asks, her pen poised over her notepad to jot it down. 'You don't have to tell me, of course, but anything you talk about within these four walls is completely confidential.'

I hesitate. I've been instructed not to talk about the investigation with anybody at work, but Beverley doesn't work for News 24/7, although there is a certain irony that they are paying for her time through their insurance company.

'I was overheard in a private conversation making some comments about a member of our team who doesn't pull her weight.'

'Did she actually overhear you, do you think? Or was it second-hand hearsay?'

'I don't know. That was what I was supposed to find out in the HR meeting today, which they rescheduled for Monday, but Stuart came up with a plan for me to get myself signed off sick with stress so that I wouldn't have to attend. It's probably a temporary stay of execution, but it gives me some breathing space to look for mitigating circumstances,' I say.

'Smart man, your husband. No big company is going to want to terminate someone who might claim unfair dismissal due to mental health issues. I'm no lawyer, but I'd say unless they've got some really damning physical evidence against you, there is no real case to answer. They just need to be seen to be doing the right thing. It will probably end up with a rap across the knuckles and a don't do it again.'

I sigh.

'That doesn't sound good,' she says.

'There was an email to a colleague too. They've found it, and apparently that's part of their case.'

'Do you remember what you said in the email and could the person you sent it to have reported it?'

'No, Lucy's my best friend at work. We sometimes send WhatsApp messages to each other on our personal numbers that are critical of members of the team who don't pull their weight, but I'd just received an email from my boss telling me that the company wouldn't give me any compassionate leave. I forwarded that email to Lucy along with a comment about a younger work colleague, but I didn't use her real name because Lucy and I have a nickname for her. I'm assuming that's the email they are talking about,' I reply. 'I'm not making excuses, but I was tired and emotionally overwrought and just didn't think.'

'Did Lucy reply to your email?' Beverley asks, looking up from the notes she is making.

'No,' I say, shaking my head. 'She appeared at my desk a few minutes after I pressed send, and we went to the cafeteria for a coffee and to talk it through. To be honest, I was so upset and angry that Lucy had to stop me from going and handing my notice in there and then,' I add, recalling the animated conversation.

'Do you think that's where your conversation may have been overheard?'

'Most probably. Lucy and I usually grab a coffee or a drink away from the News 24/7 building if either of us feels a need to unload after a particularly stressful day. It was just a set of extraordinary circumstances. I'm usually so careful about stuff like this, but...' My voice trails off and the tears threaten again.

'Have you spoken to Lucy about all this?' Beverley asks.

'I'm not allowed to speak to anyone at work and I've been taken off the roster indefinitely, although Stuart spotted that they haven't actually used the word suspended.'

'He sounds like a keeper, your husband,' Beverley says.

I've been mostly calm while I've been relaying everything to Beverley, but tears suddenly spring into my eyes again.

'He'll probably divorce me after all the dreadful things I screamed at him this morning,' I say, reaching for another tissue.

'Not likely,' Beverley says. 'Maybe you needed the shout up for him to realise just how much pressure you've been under outside of work, which has unfortunately spilled over into the workplace. The fact that he's devised this "plan" would suggest he intends to support you rather than leave you. Well, we've got through a lot in this first session, but it's clearly only the tip of the iceberg,' she adds.

I glance at my watch. How can it be quarter past eight already? I've been talking virtually non-stop for forty-five minutes of my fifty-minute session.

'It's pretty clear that Eva's death is the catalyst that has brought a lot of things to a head, and not just for you by the sound of things,' she says, clearly referring to Jemma's issue with Will. 'Now we need to unpick and separate the issues so that we can deal with each one. Next session, I'd like to delve into your childhood and your family growing up, if that's alright with you?'

I nod.

'Just to give me a quick picture, are both your parents still alive, and do you have any siblings?' she asks.

'My dad's dead, my mum is still living, and I have a sister, Juliet,' I reply.

'Good relationship with Mum and sister?' she asks.

'I guess,' I reply, giving a light shrug of my shoulders. She must know I'm lying.

'Okay. Well, like I said, that's for next time. The most pressing issue for you right now is work. How long are you signed off for?'

'A week initially,' I reply.

'And what was the reason given on the fit to work note?'

'Stress,' I reply. 'I... I had a panic attack this morning after the phone call, and when I told the GP that, she didn't hesitate in issuing it.'

Beverley makes a note in her book and then closes it, laying the pen down next to it on the small desk at her side.

'That really is all we have time for tonight, but I'll have a think about the best way to approach the situation at work before your next appointment. Can you do Monday at 12 noon,' she asks.

'Yes,' I reply. 'I'm unexpectedly free,' I add with a small smile.

'Make the most of your free time, particularly as News 24/7 are paying for it,' she says, getting to her feet.

I follow suit and slip my arms into my quilted coat, which I'm going to need if the temperatures of an hour ago are any indication.

'Thank you for listening to me, Beverley,' I say as I follow her out of the room and along the hallway.

'It's my job to be a good listener,' she says, opening the front door to a blast of icy air, at which point Carlton, who has been as quiet as a mouse for the duration of our appointment since announcing his presence in the first couple of minutes, starts barking again almost as though he is saying goodbye.

I walk back to my car feeling as though a giant weight has lifted from my shoulders even though we've only scratched the surface. There's a saying about a problem shared being a problem halved, but I would never have imagined that this could be the case when sharing your feelings with a stranger, albeit one who is trained to listen.

As I press the button on the dashboard to start the engine, I experience a pang of guilt. I'd used the time with Beverley to talk exclusively about me and the way I was feeling. Should I have gone into more detail about Jemma and her current predicament? I indicate and pull out onto the deserted street, the light dusting of frost covering the tarmac unscarred by tyre tracks. No, I reprimand myself. Until I'm functioning properly, I'm unable to help anyone else. For once, I must put myself first.

TWENTY-EIGHT
FRIDAY EVENING

There was hardly any traffic on the roads on the drive back from Beverley's, so less than fifteen minutes later I'm opening our front door to be greeted by the spicy aroma of penne arrabbiata. I smile. I'd told Stuart not to bother cooking anything from scratch when I'd left the house earlier as I wasn't feeling very hungry. I'm so glad he ignored me as my stomach has been grumbling like crazy all the way home. I hang my coat up and drop my bag onto the console table in the hall before heading through to the kitchen.

'Perfect timing,' Stuart says, tipping the pan of pasta tubes into the colander in the sink. 'Sit yourself down and tell me all about it. What was she like?'

'It was like talking to an old school friend,' I say, reaching for the bottle of red wine in the middle of the table that Stuart has been allowing to breathe. 'It's quite dangerous when you think about it,' I add, pouring myself a generous glass of wine and taking a deep slug of it. I would have poured some for Stuart too, but his glass is on the work surface next to the cooker, so he's obviously been indulging whilst he's been cooking.

'Dangerous in what way?' he asks, dishing out the brownish-coloured penne into two pasta bowls. Despite it not looking so appetising, I prefer the taste of wholegrain pasta.

'I opened up and told her everything, both family and work, even though we hadn't done any research into her to make sure she was legit.'

'This work business really has given you trust issues,' Stuart says, spooning the chilli-laden sauce onto the pasta and lightly forking it through. 'I'm pretty sure News 24/7's insurance company will have thoroughly checked her out before adding her name to their approved list.'

He's right. I am feeling edgy. Even if I manage to hold onto my job, it's going to be difficult going back in to work. Nothing like this ever stays completely confidential, so people will know I've been the subject of an HR investigation and that will make life more difficult with me having to watch everything I say to my work colleagues and even the tone of voice in which I say it.

'True,' I say, accepting the pasta bowl that Stuart is handing me. 'This smells so good. Maybe you should stop being a gentleman of leisure and open an Italian restaurant,' I add, helping myself to a generous spoonful of Parmesan cheese.

'What are you smirking at?' Stuart asks, refilling his empty wine glass before topping up mine.

'I was just thinking that Will would be horrified with the amount of Parmesan I've just sprinkled onto my dinner,' I reply.

'I wonder how all that's going,' Stuart says. 'I take it Jemma hasn't messaged today?'

'No, nothing,' I reply, shaking my head. 'I wanted to let the dust settle on the conversation she had with Mum, but I was planning to ring her today before all this work stuff kicked off,' I say, wafting my fork in the air before plunging it into the vibrant bowl of pasta. 'I think I'll leave it until tomorrow. I'm shattered,' I add, taking my first mouthful of dinner.

I focus on the explosion of taste on my tongue. Just the right blend of heat from the chilli and fruitiness from the tomatoes. I am shattered, both physically and mentally. Right now, I don't have the capacity to even start thinking about how I repair my relationship with Jemma.

'I might have to give your suggestion some thought,' Stuart says. At my puzzled expression, he adds, 'Opening an Italian restaurant? This really is damn good.'

I'm just putting the last piece of olive ciabatta bread into my mouth, having wiped my bowl with it so as not to miss any of the rich sauce, when my mobile rings. I look across to the area of the work surface where our phones usually live when we're charging them, but it's not there. Of course, I was so distracted by the appetising food smell when I walked in the front door that I forgot to take it out of my handbag. I push my chair back from the table to go and retrieve it, already knowing that it will be a lost cause because after six rings the voicemail will kick in. Sure enough, it stops ringing before I get to my bag, and there is no voice message, just a missed call from Callum.

The feeling of panic is immediate. My heart starts pumping hard in my chest. Please God, don't let it be the baby. It would be absolutely devastating for them to go through another miscarriage. They both want children so badly. It seems unfair that they are having such a battle when other people end up with children they don't want.

'Jesus, what's wrong?' Stuart says. 'You look like you've seen a ghost.'

'It was Callum,' I manage to say.

'Everything okay?' Stuart asks without adding the obvious. He was as upset as me when our son had rung us with the awful news. We'd just got used to the idea of being grandparents for the first time, discussing with Ellie's parents what big item we would treat the newborn to. We'd settled on a car seat that converted into a pram, and they'd gone for a swanky cot with a drop side and height adjustments for the mattress, which would last until the baby was old enough for its first bed. Then the call came, and it was snatched away from us all.

'I didn't get to my phone in time, and he didn't leave a message,' I say.

'Get a grip, Lexi,' Stuart says uncharacteristically sharply. 'I thought something bad had happened with the baby. Look,' he adds in a gentler tone, 'ring him back and find out what he wanted. There's no point imagining the worst when it might be nothing.'

I lay my phone on the kitchen table and press *call*, having selected speaker so that Stuart can hear too. If it is bad news, I don't want to hear it on my own.

Callum picks up on the second ring.

'Well, hello stranger,' he says in a cheerful voice.

My shoulders relax and the panic melts away.

'I'm assuming you two had a good holiday?' he continues. 'We got your group WhatsApp message to say you were back yesterday morning and then nothing. You haven't been sleeping off the jet lag, have you?'

'Sorry, love,' I say. 'We did have a snooze, as it happens. We're not as young as we were, you know. And then I popped over to check in on your grandma and drop off some groceries while Dad made my dinner.'

'How is she?' Callum asks.

'Actually, I thought she looked a bit pale, and she said she'd been off her food for a few days, but she was still well enough to tell me that I was too tanned.'

'Sounds par for the course,' Callum says, using the golfing analogy. Our son hadn't played prior to meeting Ellie, but her dad is a keen golfer and offered to take him to the course where he is a member. It's become a regular Saturday morning treat for the two of them, and Stuart goes occasionally too now that he's retired.

Stuart hasn't spoken up until now and decides to join the conversation.

'So, to answer your other question, we had a fabulous time. We got up early to watch the racehorses training on the beach...' he starts to say.

'Hold your horses, Dad,' Callum says. 'See what I did there?' he adds, pointing out his own joke.

'Remember what I always tell you, son. If you have to explain a joke, it probably wasn't worth telling in the first place.'

'You're right, but it wasn't really a joke. I just stopped you launching into telling us about your holiday because we wondered if you'd like to come over for dinner tomorrow night and you can tell us all about it then,' Callum says.

'Oh, that would be lovely,' I reply on behalf of us both. 'If you're sure it's not too much trouble?'

'No trouble at all. We've been practising your famous lasagne recipe on the quiet and we think we've perfected it sufficiently to try it out on other people,' he says. 'I'm so glad you can make it. We thought you might have been working, Mum.'

I lock eyes with Stuart who shakes his head at me. As recent experience has shown, keeping secrets from our kids is not the best idea, but in this instance, I think it's the right thing to do.

'I've got some more time off,' I say, careful to not actually lie. 'That should help with the jet lag. What time would you like us to come over?'

'We've told Jemma and Will 6.30 p.m. if that works for you?'

'Oh, are they coming too?' I say, trying to keep the surprise from my voice.

'It's okay, Mum. Jemma rang me earlier and told me what happened at yours yesterday. She was still mad at us for not warning her that we thought something might have gone on between Will and his new boss, but by the end of our conversation I think she was part way to understanding that we'd done it to protect her if there was no truth in the rumours. In fact, it was her that suggested inviting you guys too after I'd asked if she and Will wanted to try out the lasagne.'

Relief floods through me. While I'm not sure how I feel about sitting face to face at a dinner table with Will after the things my daughter said about him yesterday, I guess it will have to be done sooner or later if she decides to stay with him. And it's good that she and Callum are at least talking. It was heartbreaking to think that Will could have come between Jemma and her family when he was the one in the wrong.

'Should we feel offended that we were an afterthought?' Stuart says, clearly trying to relieve the tension.

'I could have said no to her suggestion,' Callum counters. 'So, is 6.30 p.m. okay for you guys?'

'Yes, fine,' I say.

'Great. See you tomorrow,' Callum says, ending the call.

'Well, that's not going to be awkward at all,' I say.

'It won't be if we don't make it awkward,' Stuart replies, placing his hand over mine while it is still resting on the phone in the middle of the table. 'I take it as a good sign that Jemma made the call to speak to her brother and their chat has gone some way to clear the air. After what you told me yesterday, I had serious doubts whether she would ever be able to forgive your and Cal's well-meaning actions. Maybe our son said something that convinced Jemma to give Will another chance. After all, they were good mates until he heard the rumours at work. I thought they'd seemed a bit less friendly lately but wondered if it was because Will had been flashing his cash around.'

I'm sure Stuart's comment wasn't intended to make me feel guilty about not sharing the secret with him, but it does. I put forward a different suggestion for Jemma's change of heart rather than drawing attention to it though.

'Or maybe Mum said something to change Jemma's mind.

Sorry,' I say reacting to Stuart's surprised expression, 'I forgot to tell you that she'd spoken to Mum too.'

'What words of wisdom did Joan offer to her granddaughter?' he asks.

'To be honest, I don't really know,' I say without adding that we didn't talk about it because our conversation had descended into an argument. I also realise that I haven't voiced my concerns about Mum's mental health. Now is not the time. It's been a hell of a day. All I want to do this evening is help my husband clear the table and load the dishwasher, before snuggling up on the sofa for a couple of hours of British TV, which is the only thing, apart from my family and my cat, that I missed about the UK while we were away in Barbados.

'Well, whatever she said, maybe it helped,' Stuart says, getting up from the table and carrying our pasta bowls over to the sink next to the dishwasher to give them a rinse before loading them in. 'Perhaps that's what prompted Jemma's call to her brother. Crikey,' he says before I have time to respond. 'I'm not sure your bowl needs to go through the dishwasher. You're worse than Wilfie.'

Right on cue, Wilfie strolls into the kitchen. It's 9.45 p.m., the time we feed him dinner and put him to bed in the utility room for the night, but without a watch or a mobile phone, how does he know that?

'Hello, boy,' I say, reaching down to fondle the cat's ears before responding to my husband. 'Are you okay doing the dishwasher while I feed Wilfie and then we can settle down with a hot drink in front of the telly?'

'Hot chocolate?' he asks.

'Mmmm, lovely. The diet restarts tomorrow.'

'Have you already forgotten we've agreed to go out for dinner and it's pasta again?' he says. 'Maybe that Italian restaurant idea isn't so far-fetched after all. We could start a family business with the number of recipes we cook between us.'

'It's certainly food for thought,' I say as I start to head past him going towards the utility room with Wilfie in tow.

'Oh God, that's who Callum gets the dodgy jokes from! But it's good to hear a bit of the old you after the day we've had,' he says, grabbing my arm and spinning me round to face him.

'Love you,' I say, planting a kiss firmly on his lips.

Eventually he pulls away and says, 'Love you more.'

TWENTY-NINE

18 NOVEMBER – SATURDAY MORNING

I'm in the kitchen, humming along to Smooth Radio while I make a start on preparing breakfast. We've decided on a full English today, although I draw the line at black pudding, which must be a throwback to Stuart's Scottish heritage. I can't even claim that I don't like the taste of it, it's the thought of what it is that makes me gag. The coffee is brewing, and the bread is in the toaster ready for the lever to be pressed the moment Stuart makes an appearance. We were intimate again last night, and his closeness afterwards, holding me in an embrace and stroking the hair back off my face, rather than rolling over and going straight to sleep, made me feel loved and special.

I sometimes wonder if I deserve Stuart. I can be very short-tempered with him, especially if he has misheard something or forgets an instruction and asks me to repeat it. When that happens, I speak very slowly and loudly. I don't think I would tolerate him speaking to me in that way, but we are totally different personalities, and that's probably why we get along so well.

Maybe it's because of the lovemaking, or perhaps it's down to the fifty minutes I spent with Beverley, the therapist, yesterday, but I feel remarkably calm considering what is going on in my life at the moment.

Therapists must have to go through a lot of training before they qualify to help people with some of the most challenging times in their lives. I think I've struck lucky with Beverley though, as I'm pretty sure not all would be as empathetic as she is, not to mention practical. I just know she will help me to weather this storm, and maybe by unlocking suppressed feelings from my past, I will be better able to face future tempests.

I've just cracked the second egg into the frying pan, accompanied by much hissing and spitting, from the hot oil rather than me, when Stuart walks into the kitchen carrying a fistful of post. Considering most people don't bother with 'snail mail' as I call it, preferring the immediacy of email, he seems to have quite a few letters in his hand.

'I forgot all about these with everything that's gone on over the past couple of days,' he says, looping his arm around my waist and nibbling the back of my neck. 'With the cost of stamps these days, I'm surprised people still post letters.'

'Pop them on the table,' I say. 'I'm just about to dish up if you want to pour the coffees.'

'Yes, boss,' he says, saluting with his free hand and putting the pile of post next to my place setting.

Sadly, I'm pretty sure it will all be junk mail and bills.

As we sit down to eat, Wilfie saunters out of the utility room and jumps up on the chair next to mine, waiting for his dairy treat, which he's obviously been missing while we were away. I put a tiny amount of butter on the tip of my finger, and he licks at it appreciatively with his sandpaper-like tongue. I repeat the process three times and then say, 'All gone.'

Wilfie obediently jumps down and wanders out into the hallway to find himself a sunny spot to lie in and lick the greasy substance all over his fur.

'You spoil that cat,' my husband remarks through a

mouthful of bacon and grilled tomato. 'Are they even supposed to have butter?'

'I'm not sure,' I say, taking a sip of my coffee. 'But without life's little pleasures, what's the point of it all?'

Stuart raises his eyebrows and positively smirks, clearly remembering our antics in the bedroom the previous evening. It doesn't annoy me quite as much as it sometimes does, so clearly I'm not feeling as stressed as I have been lately.

'We're lucky boys, me and Wilfie, to be on the receiving end of your favours.'

I need to change the subject before my bonhomie disappears. I lay my knife and fork together and pick up the pile of post, feigning interest in the flyers for gutter clearing and house cleaning. Also in the mix are my credit card bill and the bank statements for both my personal account and the joint account from which we pay the mortgage. I choose not to open any of them now; after all, why spoil the prospect of a good day? They keep trying to slyly stop sending me paper bills unless I ask them to continue by logging on to online banking. I do most of my banking online these days, but I still like to keep paper copies of everything and don't see why I should print it up rather than them sending it out to me. People of my mum's generation though, some of whom still write cheques out for things rather than tapping bank cards, can easily miss payments if they don't realise they were due. I've had many an angry conversation with customer services representatives who simply don't get that some older people find the world of computers and online everything too confusing. I don't really know why I bother though, as I never get a word of thanks from her.

Right at the bottom of the pile is a largish envelope, which, when I turn it over, I can see is from the funeral directors in Portree.

'That's odd,' I say. 'This one is from Campbell's. I thought I settled the final bill before we went away.'

'It's probably just the receipt,' Stuart says, mopping the last of the yolk from his plate with the extra piece of bread I always cut for him. It really is infuriating how he stays so slim when I have to work so hard at it.

'It's addressed to you,' I say.

'You open it. After all, you oversaw all the dealings with them. It's bloody annoying how they always write to the man in a marriage.'

I raise my eyebrows. I think Stuart's reluctance to open the letter is twofold. He doesn't want to be reminded of the cost of transporting Eva's body back to her beloved Skye for the funeral, even though it will eventually be reimbursed from her estate. The other reason is quite simply he hasn't finished the final chunk of his extra slice of bread which he is currently slathering in butter.

I slip my finger under the flap and tear the envelope open leaving a jagged edge and tip the contents onto the table at the side of my plate. There is a single piece of headed notepaper folded around a white envelope addressed to Stuart c/o the funeral directors, which I put to one side while I read the few typed lines.

Dear Stuart,

This letter arrived at our offices a few days after the funeral, but Shona informed us that you had already headed down south, so we are forwarding it to you in one of our envelopes as letters with forwarding addresses have a tendency to go astray in our experience.

Kind Regards,

Donald Campbell

'There's a letter addressed to you, care of the funeral directors,' I say in response to Stuart's raised eyebrows. 'Do you want me to open it?'

Stuart makes a 'give it to me' sign with his free hand, reminding me of the 'muffin me' line in a television advertisement for a building society, the name of which escapes me, but it always makes the pair of us laugh. He repeats the action I did a few moments earlier, running his finger along the long edge of the envelope.

He starts to read and then says, 'Who's Andy?'

I shrug.

'A friend of your mum's, maybe?' I suggest.

'No,' he says, handing the letter over to me. 'It's not really for me. It's from someone you were talking to at the airport petrol station the day Mum died.'

To say I'm surprised is an understatement. How on earth had the policeman who was so kind to me at Gatwick managed to find out where to send a letter of condolence, which is what I'm assuming this is.

18 Bentley Avenue
Bagshot
GU19 5LN
ABPlod93@gmail.com

Dear Stuart,

You don't know me, but I spoke to your wife in the shop at the BP garage at Gatwick Airport on the day your mother died.

I hope you don't think I'm invading your privacy, but your wife was clearly upset, and I just wanted to check that she is okay, and you too, of course. During our brief conversation, she let slip a few names and locations from which I managed to piece together enough information to be able to send a letter of condolence.

I'm so sorry for your loss. I lost my own mum five years ago to an aggressive form of cancer, and I just wanted to reassure you that the pain does lessen eventually.

I hope you don't mind me writing to you.

Kind regards,

DS Andy Broadmead

'Oh, wow,' I say. 'What an incredibly kind and thoughtful thing to do. I was in a right old state having just found out from Jemma that your mum had died, and not knowing whether to tell you or not. And he said would finding out before getting to the hospital change anything?'

'Hold on a minute. So you knew that my mum had died before we got to the hospital?' Stuart asks, frowning.

'Yes,' I reply, realising that this is yet another secret I had kept from my husband. 'I'm sorry. I had to make a snap decision, and I could see the sense in what Andy said. I think he was worried about either of us driving having just heard such devastating news.'

'It was sensible advice,' Stuart says after a moment's consideration. 'Is he a traffic officer then?'

'I have no idea, but if he is, his detective abilities are clearly being wasted. How amazing that he could track us down like this.'

'Not really. If you mentioned Skye, there wouldn't have been many deaths recorded on that date, and presumably in the upset state you were in, you mentioned Eva's name too?'

'I guess I must have done. And, of course, we put the obituary in the West Highland Free Press so that all the locals would know the date and time of the funeral. Even so,' I say, 'what a kind gesture. Do you think we should reply? He's given his address and email, and it feels rude to just ignore him,' I add.

'You do what feels right for you,' Stuart says, pushing his chair back from the table and reaching across to take my plate with his spare hand. 'You need to be surrounded by nice people with all the shit your work are putting you through at the moment.'

'I'll give it some thought,' I say, tucking the letter into my dressing gown pocket.

Even as I say the words, I think I already know I'll reply. This small act of kindness has gone some way to restore my faith in human nature. And Stuart might be right. If I surround myself with nice people maybe, just maybe, things will start to work out for me and my family.

THIRTY

SATURDAY NIGHT

'Verdict?' Callum asks, glancing around the table expectantly.

'A-maz-ing, to quote Craig Revel Horwood,' replies Jemma. 'Almost as good as Mum's.'

'Actually, I think it's better,' I say. 'The tomato sauce on mine is sometimes a bit thick, and it makes the whole thing cloying. You've got this spot on, Cal.'

He does a slight bend from the waist as though accepting applause at the end of a theatre performance. Ellie clears her throat.

'How about some credit for the sous-chef here?' she teases.

'I must admit that Ellie did all the chopping, and she made the cheese sauce.' Callum laughs.

'So, in other words, Ellie did all the hard bits, and you did the assembly, but you were prepared to take all the credit,' Jemma says.

'Teamwork makes the dream work, sis,' Callum says, winking.

I've always loved this banter between our kids, and it's a relief that Jemma has clearly forgiven her brother for not letting on what he knew about Will and for forbidding me from saying anything too. There was a moment on Thursday when I thought it might have irrevocably destroyed their sibling relationship, not to mention hers and mine.

They've been this way since they were little and they're also fiercely protective of each other, which must have made it more difficult for Jemma to understand why her brother had insisted we keep her in the dark when he involved me. A little shiver runs through me.

Earlier, while Stuart was turning the car around and parking it in one of the designated guest parking bays, Callum and I stood waiting for him on the doorstep while Ellie kept an eye on the dinner.

'I don't think we're out of the woods yet,' he'd whispered in my ear. 'I'm not sure that Will's job is entirely legit.'

'What do you mean?' I'd asked.

'No time now, Mum, but you know I was doing a bit of digging?'

I nod.

'Well, something concerning flagged up. When I know more, I'll tell you, and this time we include Dad,' he added, before turning his attention to Stuart who was striding towards us.

I'm relieved Callum wants to include his dad. I'm not prepared to keep another secret from my husband after the hurt I saw in his eyes on Thursday when I told him about Will. But now I'm worried as to what Callum has discovered. Will has clearly smoothed things over with Jemma because the two of them have seemed more at ease in each other's company tonight than I've seen them in a while. But has he told her everything? And would this latest discovery put Cal and Jemma's sibling relationship in jeopardy again?

I'm not going to pretend that there has never been any jealousy between my children, especially if it was perceived by one that the other was getting preferential treatment. There have been minor arguments too, but nothing like the issues between Stuart and Mari, and Juliet and me for that matter. Maybe it's to do with the age difference. There are five years between me and my sister, and eight years between Stuart and Mari. Fleur never had that problem because she's an only child.

As though he's reading my mind, Callum says, 'I had an email yesterday from Fleur with photos of Carter and Bradley. They look like a pair of terrors, to be honest. I'll show you the pics after dinner,' he adds, spooning another forkful of lasagne into his mouth.

I'm relieved for the change of topic even though I can't respond because my mouth is full. Instead, I nod and give him a thumbs up with my free hand.

The recipe is one I stumbled on a few years ago when Stuart and I had a trial period as vegetarians. I'm not fond of lasagne made with a mix of only vegetables. It tastes too much like ratatouille to me. This recipe replaces the meat with a mixture consisting of chopped spinach, walnuts and cottage cheese, topped with a tomato and basil sauce. Instead of béchamel, which in my opinion is quite tasteless, I use a cheese sauce made with strong cheddar. Come to think of it, it's a very cheesy dish as it's also topped with a generous layer of grated Parmesan. I steal a glance at Will's plate. It's almost empty. I can't resist.

'Not too cheesy for you, Will? I ask.

'I'm not going to lie,' he says, wiping a chunk of French bread around his plate to mop up the last of the sauce, 'I was dreading the cheese overload when Jem told me what was in it, but it's actually really nice.'

'Thanks, mate,' Callum says, raising his glass of red wine in a toasting action. The warmth of his words doesn't reach his eyes.

I notice Callum's wife take a sip of her orange squash,

which prompts me to ask, 'Are you over your morning sickness now, Ellie?'

'Yes, thank goodness,' she replies. 'I'm well into the second trimester now, the best phase, according to the midwife, before I get really big and uncomfortable. Not that I'm moaning,' she adds, shooting a look at Callum. 'Any discomfort will be worth it to carry to full-term.'

The table falls quiet for a moment, and then Jemma breaks the silence by saying, 'So, we have some news.'

My fork of food doesn't reach my mouth, and I grip Stuart's thigh hard with my other hand, so hard that he will probably have a few little bruises later tonight where my fingertips dig in. Surely Jemma can't mean what I think she does. After all the doubts she expressed about her feelings for Will on Thursday, this would be a disaster of epic proportions because she would probably feel duty-bound to stick their relationship out for the sake of the child. Maybe that's why they've been so tactile tonight. I hold my breath waiting for the announcement that I now feel pretty sure is coming.

'Will and I are going engagement ring shopping next weekend,' Jemma says, beaming up at her boyfriend.

I feel enormous relief, followed swiftly by guilt, before the reality of what she has just said sinks in. Did Will propose to win his way back into her affections after his forced confession? Or maybe the proposal wasn't his idea. Did Jemma give him a push with some kind of ultimatum? Either way, I can't help feeling that this might not end well. Realising that no one has spoken, I say, 'Oh, that's lovely news, darling. It's just a bit out of the blue.'

Ellie gets up from her side of the table and goes round to give Jemma a hug.

'This is just the best news,' she says. 'We'll be proper sisters-in-law once you're married.'

I don't bother to point out that they already are as Ellie is married to Jemma's brother. She seems genuinely excited at the prospect, which suggests to me that whatever was said between Jemma and her brother to smooth things over, nothing has been shared with Ellie. Cal is determined to protect his wife and unborn child from any kind of unnecessary stress.

'I don't remember you asking for my daughter's hand in marriage, Will,' Stuart says, seeming to have recovered from the shock.

'I – I haven't actually asked her yet. We thought we'd check out the sort of thing she's after first, and I'll work out if I can afford it,' he stammers, a flush of embarrassment creeping up his neck and staining his cheeks.

'The old man's teasing you,' Callum says. 'That's something you'll have to get used to if you're going to be part of our family.'

It could be my imagination, but Callum seemed to put a lot of emphasis on the word 'if'. I wonder what he has now discovered about our potential future son-in-law. I sneak a glance at Jemma. Although she sounded very sure while making the announcement, she now seems less so. Part of me wonders if my daughter is accepting Will with all his shortcomings because she feels like she is lagging behind her older brother in the marriage and children stakes.

'I'll give you a few tips,' Ellie says, smiling reassuringly at Will. 'Now, who would like dessert? I've made tiramisu from scratch without the help of a sous-chef, and I hope no one minds, but it's an alcohol-free version.'

The dessert is every bit as good as the main course, so there isn't much chat around the table until we've all finished eating.

'So,' Stuart says, 'I haven't mentioned it to your mum yet, but I've invited Grandma Joan over to ours for Sunday roast tomorrow as we haven't had the chance for a few weeks. You're welcome to come over if you fancy it,' he says magnanimously before adding, 'You know I always get carried away and make too much of everything.'

'I would have thought you would have been working this weekend, Mum,' Jemma says. 'I was surprised when Cal said you could make it tonight after all the time you've had off lately.'

Stuart and I had discussed it in the car on the way over as it was bound to crop up during the evening, so I have my response prepared.

'Actually, I've taken a bit of sick leave. Being away made me aware of how stressed I've been lately with everything that has happened, and I didn't think it was sensible to carry that stress into work with me,' I say. It's all true of course; I've just left out the bit about the complaint and the HR meeting.

Jemma shoots me a guilty look. I'll have to reassure her next time we speak in private that her outburst in our kitchen the moment I walked in from our holiday played no part in my decision to get signed off from work. In truth, it was one of the straws that contributed to the camel's back finally breaking, but nothing will be gained by telling her that. I can almost hear Beverley's voice admonishing me for putting my daughter's feelings before my own.

'I bet you're popular with the rest of the production team,' Callum chips in. 'Just back from a swanky holiday and then pulling a sickie.'

Stuart must have felt me tense up.

'That's harsh, Cal,' he says, a sharp edge to his voice. 'You know your mum is too professional to "pull a sickie" as you put it. She's only ever off for a valid reason.'

The conversation I had with Lucy flashes into my mind. I don't remember a lot of what was said, but I'm pretty sure taking sick leave when not actually sick was part of it.

'Lighten up, Dad. I was joking. I know Mum would never take time off without a good reason, unlike some of her younger colleagues,' Callum says, glancing in my direction and winking. 'Take as long as you need, Mum. No one there fully appreciates how much you've done to keep the broadcast standards so high.'

I smile indulgently at my son. Little does he know how near the mark he is.

'Perhaps we should give you a quieter Sunday lunch then?' Jemma says.

'Nonsense,' I reply. 'It would be nice for you to see your grandma, and her you. And anyway, if I'm perfectly honest, it will be less stressful for me with you guys there to keep her busy, so she won't be picking holes in me.'

'We can't, Jemma,' Will says. 'We've already committed to going round to Zoe and Adam's.'

'Oh God, yes. I forgot. Sorry, we'll have to pass,' she says.

'We'd love to come though, wouldn't we, Cal?' Ellie says immediately.

If I'd made a wish for the perfect daughter-in-law, Ellie would have been it.

'Yes, we'd love to,' he agrees. 'The thought of missing out on your roast potatoes doesn't sit well with me. Do you need us to pick Grandma Joan up on our way?'

'No, that's alright, mate, I'll fetch her, but you can drop her off if you wouldn't mind.'

'That's a plan,' Callum says, smiling at his near use of his dad's favourite phrase, *we have a plan*. 'Ellie's not drinking anyway, for obvious reasons, so she can drive, and you and I will be able to enjoy a couple of glasses.'

Normally, I wouldn't let a sexist comment like that go, but I resist the urge to rise to the bait. I have something much more important on my mind.

'Why don't you guys go through to the front room while Jemma and I clear the table and load the dishwasher?' I say. 'No arguments, Ellie,' I add as she starts to protest. 'It's the very least we can do after such a delicious meal.'

The kitchen door closes behind them, and I start to gather up the dessert dishes.

'Nice move, Mum,' Jemma says.

I could pretend that I hadn't engineered this time alone with my daughter, but what would be the point? She would dismiss my protestations, and it would get this conversation off on the wrong foot.

'I just wanted to reiterate that I really am sorry for not telling you sooner, Jem,' I say. 'Cal and I thought we were doing the right thing, but with the benefit of hindsight, we should have trusted you to make your own decisions.'

'It's me who should be apologising, Mum. Yes, I was furious with Will for being weak enough to sleep his way into a fancy new job, but I wasn't overly upset by it when he told me how it went down,' she says, giving a slight shoulder shrug. 'He said he'd felt pressured by Heidi von Clattenburg in a role reversal of the old Hollywood casting couch scenario. It happened only the one time and didn't mean anything to him. He knows he behaved like a total idiot and begged me to forgive him. Believe it or not, that paled into insignificance when he then said that you and Cal had known for a while and had eventually forced him to confess. That's what really upset me. Two people I've known all my life, and who I love and trust, had betrayed me. I was devastated.'

'Oh, Jemma,' I say, putting the dishes on the draining board to free up my arms and pull her into a hug. 'We thought we were protecting you from pain if the rumours turned out to be false. But you're right, we should have trusted you to deal with Will in your own way.'

She moves her head away from my shoulder where it had been resting, so she can look into my eyes.

'The trouble is you both know me too well. I might not have given Will the opportunity to explain the circumstances if Cal hadn't forced him to tell me. In case you've forgotten, I have been known to have a knee-jerk reaction to things,' she adds with a rueful smile. 'But it's water under the bridge, and we're all friends again now,' she says, giving me another quick hug before returning to her task of loading the dishwasher.

Callum's whispered words from earlier fill my mind. What if all the water hasn't flowed under the bridge yet? I can't bear to think of my girl being hurt by Will again.

'So, this engagement. It isn't one of your knee-jerk reactions, is it?' I probe gently.

'Don't, Mum,' she says turning back to face me. 'Don't spoil it. I've forgiven Will and you and Cal. Let's just leave it at that, shall we?'

I bite my lip. Even if Cal uncovers something else unsavoury about Will, nothing will be gained by upsetting Jemma now.

I'm quiet in the car on the drive home, and Stuart obviously notices.

'Are you cross with me for speaking to your mum and inviting her over for Sunday lunch tomorrow?' he asks.

'Were you going to tell me or were you just going to arrive with her as a surprise?' I ask wearily. I'm not in the mood for an argument after my exchange in the kitchen with Jemma. She made a showy display of snuggling into Will when we'd gone into the lounge after we finished tidying up the kitchen in virtual silence. I made our excuses to leave about fifteen minutes later, citing jet lag.

'I was trying to find the right moment,' he replies. 'You didn't really leave her house on the best of terms on Thursday, so I thought this would be a good opportunity to smooth things over, especially with one or other of the kids as a distraction.'

'And you thought mentioning it at Cal's was safer than

when we were alone so that I didn't throw my toys out of the pram,' I say, managing a hint of amusement in my voice.

'Something like that,' he admits. 'Listen, I know she's annoying and not very nice to you sometimes, but she's old, Lexi. We may not have her for much longer, and I'd hate for something to happen to her following an argument between the two of you.'

He has a point. I've often fretted over exactly that when we've had an exchange of words.

'You're not mad, are you?' he persists.

'Not really. But I'm relieved that Jemma and Will declined the invitation. I don't know what Mum might have said if Jemma had mentioned going shopping for engagement rings after their conversation on Thursday when she was all for breaking things off with Will.'

'To be honest, I'm with your mum on that. I want to be happy for Jemma, but is she doing it for the right reasons?' Stuart says. 'The trouble is, we can't interfere. We must let our kids make their own mistakes. It's the only way they'll learn.'

He's right. The mother in me hates taking a back seat when either of them has issues, but Jemma made it quite clear that I wasn't to question her decision. I need to change the subject.

'Do you think they bought the whole "time off work because I'm stressed" story?' I ask. 'It felt a little disingenuous if I'm honest.'

'I think it was the right thing not to tell them about the investigation at work just yet, particularly Cal and Ellie. The last thing any of us want is for anything to have a detrimental effect on this pregnancy.'

I nod.

'If it does go badly,' he continues, 'we'll have to tell them, of course, but for now we keep it to ourselves. Agreed?'

'Agreed,' I say.

I always want to tell the kids everything because I'm all about honesty and trust, but every so often, honesty isn't necessarily the best policy.

THIRTY-ONE

19 NOVEMBER – SUNDAY MIDDAY

The potatoes are peeled, the carrots and parsnips are scrubbed and quartered, and I'm just rinsing the broccoli in the colander after dividing it into florets when I hear Stuart's key in the front door. I did question why he was picking Mum up so early, but he quite rightly pointed out that the chicken needed to go in the oven at midday if lunch was going to be ready for 1.30 p.m., the time we'd arranged with Callum and Ellie.

'All the prep is done, and the oven is up to temperature, chef,' I say as Stuart comes into the kitchen with Mum following him.

'Good work,' Stuart says. 'Why don't you two go through to the lounge and I'll bring you both a nice cup of tea? The maestro needs space to work,' he adds with a flourish.

'You're so funny,' Mum says, a hint of flirtation in her voice.

'I'm glad you appreciate my wit, Joan.'

I roll my eyes.

'Come on, Mum,' I say. 'I can take a hint. I know where I'm not wanted.'

I'm not quite sure what expression flickers across Mum's face as I take her elbow and direct her back out into the hallway.

It might be disappointment, as I'm sure she would have preferred to sit and have a natter with my husband than be banished to the lounge with me. Or it may be trepidation after we'd parted on bad terms on Thursday evening. If Mum is aware that her behaviour towards me is sometimes unkind, she's not one to admit it, much less apologise. The first move to smooth things over will have to come from me as always.

'Did you manage to eat most of your dinner the other night?' I ask, starting the conversation with something neutral. I don't want to be sitting in silence when Stuart brings our tea through. I sit on the sofa so that she can take one of the two chairs that she finds it easier to get up out of.

'Yes,' she replies, lowering herself into the chair using the arms. 'I hadn't realised how hungry I was. I finished every bit, and it was very tasty.'

I'm now feeling slightly off balance. Mum is being overly nice to me. Either she's had a bout of conscience or Stuart has said something to her in the car.

'So, what were you and my husband talking about on the way over?' I enquire, trying to keep my voice casual. We've agreed that, like the kids, Mum doesn't need to know anything just yet about my issue at work.

'Oh, this and that,' she says vaguely. 'Stuart was telling me that you were over at Callum's last night and that Jemma and Will seem "back on",' she says, using her fingers as speech marks. 'He told me about them going engagement ring shopping, probably to prepare me in case Callum or Ellie let something slip over lunch. A shock like that could kill an old lady,' she adds with a chuckle.

Mum's clearly on good form today, but then she usually is when she's been in Stuart's company.

'We were all quite surprised when she announced it last night,' I admit. 'Thursday must have been a storm in a teacup.

I'm sorry I got you involved, but she seemed so upset, and I wasn't sure I could handle it on my own.'

'To be honest, Alexis, it was nice to feel needed. You always seem to have everything under control, no matter how many balls you're juggling, without asking for anyone else's help. It was good to see that you're not infallible,' she says as the door edges open, courtesy of Stuart's foot, and he comes into the room carrying a tray with our hot drinks and a plate of biscuits.

'Here you go, girls,' he says, laying the tray down on the grey buttoned footstool. 'Don't go eating too many biscuits or you won't want your lunch.'

'Thank you, Stuart,' Mum twinkles, accepting the proffered bone china cup and saucer that is reserved for her exclusive use. 'You always remember that I prefer my tea in a proper cup and saucer rather than a mug. Just the one,' she adds, taking a digestive biscuit and balancing it on her saucer.

'Are you sure?' Stuart asks. 'I've only just put the chicken in, so lunch will be an hour and a half.'

'Leave the plate then, just in case I get peckish.' She smiles.

'I'd love to stay and chat, but some of us have got work to do,' Stuart says, giving me a surreptitious wink before retreating to the kitchen.

'You struck gold with that one, Alexis,' Mum says, settling herself back in her chair and nibbling the edge of her biscuit.

'I know,' I say, taking a sip of my tea, 'Although he's not perfect...'

'Nobody's perfect, as I know better than most,' she says, a wistful look in her eyes.

I think of my dad and his moment of madness that almost destroyed our little family. I've often wondered how Mum found the strength to take him back, knowing that he'd been intimate with another woman. I also wonder if she ever truly forgave him, something Eva had been unable to do when her daughter had chosen to leave her home and family and move to

Canada. I find myself wondering if I would have been able to forgive Stuart if I found out that he'd been unfaithful.

'You do understand why I wasn't willing to tell Jemma about her Grandad's indiscretion, don't you?' she asks. 'I promised him that no one would ever hear about it from me, and I've kept my word all these years because it was mine and your dad's business, no one else's.'

'But surely people must have known about it at the time? I know I was only little, but he was away from home for ages,' I say, memories of Mum crying a lot and using harsh words to me flooding my mind.

'I just said he'd had to go away for work, and as far as anyone knew, that's all there was to it. Neither of us had any idea that you were aware of the truth until you told me otherwise after he died. I'm glad he went to his grave not knowing that you knew. You were his firstborn, his favourite, the apple of his eye.'

'Mum, we both know that's not true. He was completely besotted with Juliet from the moment he first held her in his arms. Nothing was ever the same for me after she was born, and you know it,' I say, the heaviness I always experience when I think about how my life changed after my sister was born settling on my heart.

'It's always going to feel different for the firstborn when the second child comes along,' Mum says, taking another bite of her biscuit. 'The dynamic of the relationship changes to include the new arrival. It's true that he lavished attention on Juliet because she saved our marriage, but you always held the biggest piece of his heart.'

I'm surprised to hear Mum say this. It certainly didn't feel that way from my perspective.

'If Juliet hadn't come along when she did,' Mum continues, 'I don't think your dad and I would have stayed together. It would have been a tragedy because we were made for each other, just like you and Stuart. He succumbed to flattery from a younger woman at a moment in his life that we all face at some point, where we question if we've chosen the right path when there are so many alternatives.'

She's right. I've sometimes wondered what my life might have looked like if I hadn't met Stuart in that bar in Soho and had instead taken a chance on my dream to become an actress. My agent at the time said I had the right 'look' for the American market. He claimed he had contacts in the film industry. If I was prepared to chance it and go over to California to wait tables, he was sure my big break would come. I'd been giving it some serious consideration before I met and fell head over heels in love with Stuart. We all have life-defining moments.

'It must have been hard for you to forgive him though, and take him back after what he'd done,' I say. 'I'm not sure I would have been able to do that if Stuart had cheated on me.'

'It's different these days. Couples split up all the time and end up with second and even third families. It's considered normal. But back in the 1960s, things were bleak for single mothers. Your childhood would have been very different. I had to swallow my pride and put you first,' she says, reaching across the arm of the chair for my hand. 'I took him back because of you, Alexis.'

There is a lump in my throat that is making it difficult for me to breathe. I've always believed that my parents favoured Juliet, and I didn't question it because she was the baby, and I loved her too. But as we grew into adulthood and the balance of affection still seemed to be tipped in her favour, I'd found it harder to accept. It now appears that she overcompensated for Dad, and in doing so, she unwittingly made me feel less loved. If what Mum has just claimed is to be believed, that truly is a mother's love.

'Oh, Mum,' I say, grasping her hand tightly in mine. 'Why are you only telling me this now?'

She takes a moment before responding.

'I suppose the whole situation with Eva has shaken us all up. I was caught a bit off guard when Jemma said you'd told her to ring me for advice. You've never done that before. You always seem to have the right answer for everything, so I've never tried to compete. Then Stuart rang me on Friday night and told me that you'd had some kind of minor breakdown and that you'd been screaming and shouting about me not loving you. It's not true, but it made me realise that perhaps I don't show it in the way I should.'

I'm off the sofa now and have taken the cup and saucer from Mum so that I can pull her into a hug. I can't trust myself to speak without bursting into tears. I've spent years believing that my own mum didn't really like me, much less love me, and it now seems that couldn't be further from the truth. We stay in a tight embrace for several minutes, and then she pushes me to arm's length so that she can look me in the eye.

'During Stuart's call, I began to wonder if I'd missed seeing the vulnerability in my older daughter because I was so focussed on making sure my younger one didn't feel second best. All I could think was, what if I was to die suddenly, like Eva did, and you never knew how truly loved you were by your dad and me? Well,' she ends simply, 'now you know.'

'You're not going to die, Mum,' I say, reaching for her hands again.

'Hopefully not for a while, but it comes to us all in the end, and it will come to me sooner rather than later. And that's okay,' she says, clearly reacting to my devastated expression.

I can't imagine a time when I can't just pick up the phone to my mum or pop round to see her, even if she hasn't always been that welcoming. The thought of all the wasted years believing that I was less loved than other members of my family is a little overwhelming. I'm determined not to waste another minute.

'Eva and I have been so lucky,' she resumes, releasing one of my hands and pushing the strand of hair which has fallen across my face back off my forehead. 'We had it so good up until a couple of years ago when the niggles of old age caught up with us. You and Stuart have looked after us wonderfully well, but things will be different now that she's gone, and different again when I go.'

The tears I've been holding back now start to fall freely.

'Please stop talking about dying, Mum,' I beg. 'I'm not ready to lose you.'

She reaches into her pocket for a cotton handkerchief and dabs at my cheeks with it before relinquishing possession of it for me to blow my nose on.

'I'll do my best to hang on for a while,' she says, smiling. 'After all, I wouldn't want to be accused of being selfish. But when my time does come, you and Stuart will get a chance to enjoy the next stage of your life without feeling sandwiched between caring for your parents and your kids. You deserve it, Alexis. You've worked so hard for everything you have, but soon it will be your turn to retire and spend some well-earned time with your husband.'

For a moment I wonder if Stuart might have mentioned something about my issue at work to Mum, but then I dismiss the thought. Even this more empathetic version of my mother wouldn't have been able to not mention it.

'Which reminds me,' Mum is saying. 'That's what Heather's parents are doing. You know she and Juliet always go to Wales for Christmas?' I nod. 'Well, apparently this year Bethan and Stan have booked to go away on a Caribbean cruise while they're still young enough to enjoy it.'

'Did you want to go to Juliet's for Christmas then?' I ask, dreading the thought of a very empty Christmas table, missing both my mum and Eva.

'Actually, I was going to suggest you could invite them here,' Mum replies.

'That's a lovely idea,' I say. 'I'll get on to them about it after lunch. It will be nice to have everyone together.'

'And maybe we can lay a place for Eva and raise a glass to her,' Mum says.

My heart warms. It's one of the most unselfish things I have ever heard my mother say.

THIRTY-TWO

20 NOVEMBER – MONDAY MIDDAY

Beverley answers the door today wearing fitness leggings and a sports top, with her hair tied back in a ponytail. I get the feeling that, like Friday evening, she hasn't really got an appointment free for me but has squeezed me into her lunch break. I follow her into her small consulting room where, once again, the heater is on, and today there is a box of tissues already alongside the glass of water on the small table at the side of the chair I'll be sitting in, presumably pre-empting waterworks after what happened at our last meeting.

'So,' she says taking her place in the chair opposite me. 'How was your weekend?'

'Much better than it would have been if I hadn't been able to see you on Friday. Thank you, I feel so much calmer about everything already, even though nothing has been resolved yet,' I reply.

It's true, I do. Before I left for my appointment, I checked my work email to find one from Jenny asking me if I would consider coming in for my meeting with her and HR during my sick leave as they were anxious to get the matter resolved and have me back on the roster. It feels as though there has been a shift in their attitude towards me since I forwarded the sick note from the private GP on Friday. Perhaps they've realised that they are in some part responsible for my words after the highly stressful situation they had placed me in by not granting me compassionate leave. I'm glad to be able to ask Beverley's opinion as to whether I should agree or not to the requested meeting during a period of sickness absence.

'Where would you like to start today?' Beverley asks, pouring herself a glass of water. 'Do you want me to share my thoughts on the best way to handle your work issue, or shall we start with a deep dive into your family background?'

'Bearing in mind how quickly the fifty minutes seem to go in this room, I think we should probably talk about work first, especially as I received an email from them this morning,' I say.

A look of concern briefly flashes across Beverley's normally neutral expression.

'No, it's nothing bad,' I say. 'At least I don't think it is. They've asked me if I would mind attending the HR meeting during my sickness leave as they want to get the matter resolved as quickly as possible. What do you think I should reply?'

After a moment or two of consideration, Beverley says, 'It seems somewhat unethical to me. If you are signed off with stress, surely attending a meeting to deal with a complaint that has been levelled at you is going to add to your stress levels, wouldn't you say?'

She has a point.

'I hadn't thought about it like that,' I say.

'Obviously, it's entirely your decision,' she continues. 'But I would be inclined to reiterate that you have sickness leave because you are feeling stressed, and as such, you are not sure you're able to properly represent yourself in a meeting which could determine your long-term future with the company.'

It makes sense. It could leave me open to the suggestion that I only contacted the private GP to be signed off from work to avoid the meeting with HR that they had rescheduled for this morning, which in fairness is true.

'Why do you think they are trying to rush this meeting?' she asks.

'I thought it was probably due to them being short-staffed. There's always loads of bugs doing the rounds at this time of year, so people are on sick leave. But after what you've just said, I'm now not so sure.'

'Well, let's assume you are right and that they just want this whole thing over asap. I don't think you should go in during your sick leave, and like I said, I'm very surprised that they asked you to. You could agree to Friday morning, if you feel up to it, and that way, if things don't go as well as we hope they will, you can call the private GP and get a week-long extension to your sick note. You won't have been back at work per se, so I think it would be extremely difficult for them to terminate your contract. That said, I'm not a lawyer.'

'They said I'm not permitted to take a lawyer into the meeting with me,' I say. 'But do you think I need to seek legal advice?'

'You've suggested that money is tight for you at the moment, so that's probably an unnecessary expense until after the initial meeting,' she says. Her eyes are scanning my face, and I flush slightly. 'I think you'll get a better feel for how the land lies when you've been face to face with them and know precisely what evidence they have. Do you think you can manage Friday?'

'Yes,' I reply, nodding my head. 'I'll email Jenny when I get home.'

'Good,' Beverley says. 'Whatever happens, having stuff like this hanging over us for long periods of time is never advisable, in my opinion. So, shall we talk about your family? Maybe the relationships you have with your mum and your sister would be a good place to start.'

For the next twenty minutes, I offer information and answer questions mostly about mine and Mum's relationship and how it all changed after my sister arrived on the scene. Despite really liking Beverley, I decide not to tell her the reason that Dad left us when I was young, just that he did, and it was a difficult time for me and Mum. I do share how aware I was of the dynamic changing within our family after Juliet's birth.

Beverley lets me talk, only interrupting occasionally if there is something she specifically wants to ask, but she makes lots of notes and mostly avoids eye contact, almost as though that might bring me back into the room and inhibit what I divulge. Eventually, I pause for a sip of water, and she seizes the opportunity to speak.

'Would you say you felt guilty about the temporary split between your parents?' she probes. 'As in, did you think it was your fault?'

I give a light shrug.

'The point is, that it's as common for children to come between parents as it is for them to bring them together. A couple becomes three, and each parent is syphoning off some of their love for each other. It does change things, and usually it doesn't need a trial separation to sort things out, but it sounds as though in your parents' case it did. Once your dad came back, did he ever leave again, or was that his one and done?'

It's a strange turn of phrase and has me wondering if Beverley suspects that there was another woman involved, even though I haven't mentioned it. I suppose in her line of work, dealing with relationships on a day-to-day basis, it must be quite commonplace.

'He never left us again,' I confirm. 'Mum and Dad were together until he died after suffering a stroke when he was only seventy-one. They were two years short of their golden wedding anniversary,' I add.

'And throughout the part of their marriage after your sister was born, did you always feel as though they loved her more than you?'

I'd noticed Beverley raising her eyebrows and underlining something when I'd been telling her how I'd felt pushed into second place in my parents' affections after Juliet was born.

'Yes,' I admit. 'Dad wasn't too bad. He tried to be fair, but it always seemed as though I could do nothing right in Mum's eyes. She was always more critical of everything I did than she ever was of Juliet. In fact, I've often felt that the only thing I did right in her eyes was to marry Stuart, who she absolutely adores.'

Beverley is about to speak, but I hold my hand up to stop her.

'The thing is, since I saw you on Friday, Mum and I have had a proper heart-to-heart about all this and she maintains that she only favoured Juliet because it always appeared to her that I was the apple of my dad's eye, and she didn't want my sister to feel second best.'

'That's a pretty big admission to make,' Beverley says. 'What brought that on?'

'Stuart. While I was here on Friday evening, he rang Mum and told her about my hysterical rant on Friday morning. I don't think she realised how unfairly she'd always treated me until my husband told her how it was affecting me. I know,' I say, managing a smile. 'He's a keeper.'

There is another momentary slip of Beverley's impassive mask. This time, she looks wistful.

'So, it seems your rant, as you put it, did some good,' she says, regaining her composure. 'Are you able to accept your mum's explanation and move forward to a better relationship?'

'Yes, definitely. I just wish it hadn't taken all these years for the truth to be aired when she may not have that many left,' I say.

'It's not about the time you have; it's about the use you make of it,' she says. 'Speaking of time, ours has run away with us again.'

I'm surprised to see that she is right when I glance at my watch.

'Shall we wait until after your meeting on Friday before your next session?' she asks.

I nod in agreement while slipping into my puffa jacket and pulling up the zip to protect me from the cold.

'I could pencil you in for Friday afternoon or next Monday if you prefer,' she says, her pen poised over her diary.

'Can I message you once I've got a time for the meeting?' I ask.

'Of course,' she replies, putting the pen and diary down. 'Don't leave it too long though as I do get quite booked up.'

'Oh, and there was one other thing,' I say, suddenly remembering the letter from Andy, the policeman.

I briefly explain and then ask, 'Do you think I should respond? It just feels rude not to when he was so kind to me.'

I follow her out into the hallway, and over her shoulder, she says, 'I would if it was me, but it really is your call. I'm a big believer in things happening for a reason. In this business, we often talk about people coming into your life for a reason, a season or a lifetime. Maybe that accidental meeting on the day Eva died was meant to happen.'

The door is open, and I say goodbye, promising to message about our next appointment as soon as I have confirmed details about the HR meeting. It's only as I'm walking down the driveway back to my car that I realise Carlton didn't bark today.

THIRTY-THREE
24 NOVEMBER – FRIDAY MORNING

I feel ridiculously nervous sitting in one of the purple velvet seats in the reception area of News 24/7, but maybe that's because I was told to come in the front entrance and wait to be collected rather than signing in at the staff entrance as I've done for the past twenty-plus years.

I must admit, it's an impressive reception area for visitors, with modern chandeliers suspended from double-height ceilings and a wall of television screens showing the current live output. It bears little resemblance to the rest of the building, which is very functional.

When I arrived home from my appointment with Beverley Laing on Monday, I'd immediately emailed a response to Jenny suggesting a meeting for today, as technically I would be past the period I had been signed off for. She'd messaged back within ten minutes suggesting 11 a.m., as she had strategy meetings prior to that time. 'It's in the diary,' I'd replied, trying to appear more confident than I felt.

I'd taken slightly longer over the email I'd written to Andy.

Dear Andy,

> Thank you so much for your letter of condolence which we have only just received from the funeral director on Skye. We went away shortly after Eva's funeral to have a second attempt at the holiday that we had cut short when she was taken ill.
>
> Both Stuart and I appreciate your kind words. As you can imagine, neither of us can foresee a time when this feels less raw and painful, but having experienced something similar yourself, we are hopeful that time will indeed be a great healer, as you suggest.
>
> As you may surmise, we don't live far from the hospital, and you said you are in this vicinity also, so if you are ever passing, please let me know as I would love you to meet Stuart.
>
> Thank you again for your kindness,
>
> Alexis

Before I could change my mind about the invitation to drop in on us and meet Stuart, I pressed send. Although not as speedy as the response from Jenny, there was an email from Andy in my inbox the following morning. It had been sent at 5.57 a.m., so I presumed he must still be working night shifts.

> Dear Alexis,
>
> I was wondering if I'd overstepped the mark by writing to you and Stuart via the funeral directors and had started to think that maybe they had not forwarded my letter on, so it was lovely to find your email in my inbox when I clocked off this morning.
>
> I'd love to take you up on your offer to meet Stuart and to bring you both the flowers I would have sent for Eva had I

known whether the family wanted flowers or, as is the modern way, donations to a favourite charity.

Without being too presumptuous, are you both around this Saturday morning? It's not my weekend to have my daughter, and it always feels a little flat unless I organise something nice to do.

I won't be offended if it's a no.

Andy

I didn't say much in the reply, just that Saturday morning would be fine, followed by our address. It has given me something pleasant to look forward to after all the tension in preparing for today's meeting.

I hear the beep of the card reader prior to the almost silent swoosh of the heavy glass doors opening, and I see a small middle-aged woman in a smart navy work dress and loafers heading in my direction. I stay seated. I'll get to my feet when she introduces herself.

'Alexis?' the woman asks.

She must know it's me. She works in HR, and we're required to update our photos, which are kept on file every five years. I get to my feet slowly, just as I intend to do everything surrounding this meeting. Stuart had said to take my time and not be rushed, and that's exactly what I'm going to do. Once standing, it's pleasing that I'm a couple of inches taller than her, so I don't feel intimidated by her. I don't speak.

'I'm Roxanne Stannard, Head of HR. Thank you for coming in today,' she says. 'We're in S4 meeting room. I've only booked it for an hour as I don't envisage this taking too long.'

I'm not sure whether it's a good or a bad sign that Roxanne doesn't think the meeting will last long, but to be honest, throughout the course of the week, I've adopted the attitude that what will be will be.

'Jenny will be joining us shortly,' she continues, leading the way back through the frosted glass doors from which she emerged a couple of minutes ago. 'Her previous meeting is over-running a little.'

I follow her along the rabbit warren of corridors and into a small bland room which I'm assuming is S4. I still haven't spoken.

'Can I get you a coffee or a water while we're waiting for Jenny?' she asks.

'A water would be great, thanks,' I say.

'Okay, I'll be back shortly,' she responds, heading back out into the corridor.

I don't really want a water, nor do I need one as I have my trusty reusable Chilly bottle in my handbag, but I didn't fancy making small talk with Roxanne from HR while we waited for Jenny to arrive. I reach into my bag and pull out a notebook and pen. I will ask if I'm allowed to record the conversation, but I'm pretty sure they will say no, so I intend to make a big deal out of taking notes. I've barely written the date at the top of the lined page when Roxanne appears in the doorway with not only my water but also Jenny.

'You're looking well, Alexis,' she says, taking a seat on the opposite side of the table from me, next to Roxanne, who is sliding a glass of water in my direction.

'Thanks,' I say to Roxanne, before raising the glass to my lips and taking a sip of the cool liquid. I lower it back to the table and redirect my gaze to Jenny. 'It's amazing what a tan can do, although my holiday feels like a distant memory now.'

A flush colours her cheeks. At least she has the good grace to be embarrassed by this circus. Stuart has kept saying to me that Jenny's hands have been tied because Summer went above her head. He thinks Jenny will be furious with Summer for doing that and will actively look for ways of getting rid of her whatever the outcome of the investigation. I have to hope he's right.

'So, like I said, we only have the room for an hour,' Roxanne says, clearly aware of the frosty atmosphere and anxious to get down to business. 'Shall we make a start?'

'Yes, let's,' I say. 'Are you okay for me to record the meeting or would you rather I didn't?'

'I'm sorry, but that's not permitted. However, you are of course free to take notes,' Roxanne says, gesturing towards my notebook and pen. 'Have you now read the original email we sent you regarding the complaint we received about you from one of your colleagues?'

'Yes,' I say.

'Do you have any idea who might have made this complaint?' she continues.

'Yes,' I say.

At my lack of identifying the person who reported me, Roxanne continues.

'So, you are aware that the complaint was made by Summer Palmer after she overheard a conversation between you and Lucy Castleton in the News 24/7 cafeteria in which you referred to Miss Palmer in a derogatory fashion?' When I make no attempt to respond, she asks, 'Do you remember what you said about Ms Palmer?'

I glance up from my note-taking to make eye contact with Jenny. Prior to the whole compassionate leave incident, Jenny and I had always had a fantastic working relationship. I've dug her out of many a hole when she couldn't get anyone to cover shifts for holiday or sickness. Whatever the outcome of this enquiry, our relationship will never be the same again.

'To be honest, no.' I'm not lying. While I've got a good idea that I was less than complimentary about my younger co-workers skiving off for the slightest thing, I have no recollection of whether I named Summer or not. 'I was very upset, having just been told that I was not entitled to any compassionate leave following the sudden death of my mother-in-law, who had been a constant in my life for over thirty-five years.'

Jenny shifts uncomfortably in her chair, and the two women exchange a glance.

'Ah, yes,' Roxanne says, retrieving a sheet of A4 paper from a folder which must already have been on the table in S4. She wasn't carrying it when she came out to fetch me from reception.

I make a note of the fact that the folder had been left unattended in an unlocked room which anyone could have accessed while Roxanne was away collecting me. This was exactly the sort of thing that both Stuart and Beverley had told me to watch out for: mistakes.

'This was the email from Jenny informing you of that, which you then forwarded to Lucy Castleton with a message in which you call into question the commitment of some younger members of our team.'

I glance down at the sheet as though I'm studying it. I'm not. I know what it says word for word because we printed it up at home and went through it with a fine-tooth comb to make sure that there is nothing in writing that names Summer or anyone else. Thankfully, as wound up and upset as I'd been, I'd used mine and Lucy's nickname for Summer Palmer, *Snowflake Personified*.

'Like I said. I was very upset at the lack of empathy and consideration shown to me after being a loyal and hardworking employee for over twenty years. With the benefit of hindsight, and had I not been so emotionally overwrought, I probably wouldn't have emailed Lucy, but it was in the heat of the moment.'

Judging by Jenny and Roxanne's facial expressions, I think they preferred it when I was giving monosyllabic answers.

'Moving on to the overheard conversation,' Roxanne says. 'Can you remember any of it?'

I give her a withering look but manage to avoid rolling my eyes.

'I can't remember what my husband and I talked about over breakfast this morning, so the chances of me recalling a private, emotionally fuelled tirade from several weeks ago, since which I've had to bury my mother-in-law, are virtually zero.' I let that point sink in before I go for the jugular. 'I don't know where you're at with your menopause journey, but memory lapses and stress feature heavily in mine.'

And that is the moment I know that their hands are tied. Even if Summer had recorded the conversation on her phone, which she might have done for all I know, it's inadmissible as evidence as it was a private conversation.

'Well, I think that's all for now,' Roxanne says. 'Jenny and I will go through everything and let you know what the next steps will be. Did you have any further questions, Alexis?'

'No,' I reply, going back to my monosyllabic answering.

'How are you feeling stress-wise now, Alexis?' Jenny asks.

'Better than I was,' I reply truthfully.

'I just wondered if you would be well enough to work next week if I roster you, depending on the outcome of the investigation, of course,' Jenny says, glancing in Roxanne's direction.

'Possibly,' I say, tucking my notebook and pen into my handbag and getting to my feet. 'I'll take the advice of my therapist and let you know. She's been unbelievably helpful so far.'

Once I'm out of the building, I feel like punching the air. Whatever the outcome of their investigation, I feel as though I did myself proud.

THIRTY-FOUR

25 NOVEMBER – SATURDAY MORNING

Stuart was up and out early this morning. I'd organised for Andy to come to our house to meet my husband without asking Stuart if he was available. I should have checked. He'd already accepted a round of golf with Ellie's dad and Callum. He normally stays for a bite of lunch and a drink with them at the nineteenth hole, but he has agreed to come home straight after he has potted at the eighteenth, albeit reluctantly.

Rather than stay in bed, I got up shortly after Stuart left and set about cleaning the house. It's doubtful that Andy will go beyond the kitchen, the lounge and possibly the downstairs loo, but you never know, and I do like to create a good impression.

I've just finished vacuuming the upstairs landing and am about to do the stairs when I glance down them and can't stop myself from emitting a small scream. Jemma is standing in the hallway.

'Sorry, Mum. I didn't mean to scare you,' she says. 'I did knock, but you obviously couldn't hear it with the vacuum on.'

It's a huge relief that she is sounding upbeat. For one awful moment I thought I was in for a repeat performance of the previous week when she'd been at our house unannounced.

'This is a nice surprise,' I say. 'Pop through to the kitchen and put the kettle on for a coffee while I finish the stairs. I'll just be a couple of minutes.'

I do a less thorough job on the stairs than I normally would, but that's probably because I'm keen to know what has brought Jemma round to our house on Saturday morning without ringing ahead first to make sure we'll be in. When I've finished, I hang the vacuum back up on its charging point in the understairs cupboard, wash my hands in the downstairs loo and head into the kitchen.

'No Dad?' Jemma asks.

There is an extra mug next to the kettle on the work surface, but Jemma must have realised before making him a hot drink that his car was not on the driveway.

'No. He's playing golf with Callum, and Ellie's dad,' I say, sitting opposite Jemma at the kitchen table and taking a sip of my coffee. 'I use the term "playing golf" loosely. Fingers crossed he has a better round than the last time he went out with them.'

'Yes, Callum told me about that.' She laughs. 'Will and I are wondering about getting him some lessons with the club pro for Christmas. What do you think?'

'Not to be unkind, but it might be a waste of money if your brother's assessment of your dad's game is anything to go by. He's just not a natural sportsman, although he really enjoys all the walking between the holes,' I reply. 'Maybe a subscription to a rambler's club might be better value for money?'

'Mum!' she says in mock horror. 'That is so cruel.'

'Sometimes you have to be cruel to be kind,' I say. 'Anyway, to what do I owe the honour of a visit from my daughter, and on a weekend too?' I add, changing the subject quickly.

Although everything is on a jokey footing at the moment, Jemma could easily slip into one of her lectures about how unhealthy it is for me to constantly criticise her dad. I don't, at least I don't think I do, but it is a perception of our relationship that she has voiced previously. Today it seems she has a different agenda.

'I wanted to ask your opinion on engagement rings. I'm meeting Will for lunch, and then we're going window shopping this afternoon, and I thought you might have some advice on what to look for as neither of us has a clue.'

My heart sinks. I'm still not convinced that Jemma's reasons for getting engaged so soon after tearfully voicing her doubts about the whole relationship are the right ones. It feels to me as though she thinks that putting a sparkly diamond on the third finger of her left hand is going to change the way she feels. Of course, I can't say any of this.

'It's really down to personal preference,' I say. 'You can either go for smaller stones with fewer inclusions or bigger stones which are of slightly lesser quality in terms of flaws, but still with a good blue-white colour, if I remember rightly from when we chose mine. Are you after a solitaire, which is the classic engagement ring,' I say glancing down at the simple one-carat round brilliant cut stone mounted in platinum, which was unusual in the late 1980s, 'or do you want more than one stone?'

'I like yours, Mum, but I think I'd prefer one of those square-shaped stones and maybe a little bit bigger, because I've got bigger hands than you. But deffo just the one stone.'

She's making a good point. Both she and Callum are tall like Stuart's side of the family and consequently have bigger hands and feet than me. There was a short period of time when Jemma was in her early teens when she was the same shoe size as me, and it was a nightmare as she was always borrowing my shoes. Thankfully, she can no longer squeeze her size seven feet into my size fives.

She's right about the stone size. To achieve a similar display to mine, she's going to need a carat and a half, or even two carats, and they don't come cheap for good quality stones. It's lucky that Will has plenty of cash to splash since he started his IT role at HvC.

Jemma had called around on Tuesday evening while Will was at the gym. It could have been our conversation in Callum's kitchen on Saturday, or maybe she wanted to satisfy her own curiosity, but something prompted her to quiz her future husband about what his high-paying job actually entailed. According to Jemma, he'd been reluctant to discuss it at first, but had eventually revealed that some of the financial transactions he dealt with were to do with sales on the dark web.

Although I couldn't say as much to Jemma, for fear of being accused of interfering, it seems that the concerns Callum voiced to me in a whisper might carry weight. He and Will had both been surprised at the level of salary being offered for a job in IT that Will had been asked to supply candidates for. Along with various other CVs, he had submitted his own to Heidi von Clattenburg, the CEO of HvC, intrigued to find out what would bring such a high level of remuneration. To his surprise, he'd got through the initial interview stage, as had two of his other candidates, but they both declined a second interview after discovering that the role involved some work on the dark web.

Jemma emphasised that Will had assured her that it was all perfectly legitimate trading, but Stuart and I had exchanged a doubtful glance which she'd obviously noticed. 'It's not illegal, so what does it matter?' she'd said defiantly.

We'd swiftly changed the subject but had voiced our concerns to each other after Jemma had left. 'If it was me, I'd want to know more, but maybe that's just me after working in television news for years,' I'd said, and Stuart had agreed that he would too and that it was nothing to do with my news background. We both went to bed on Tuesday feeling slightly uneasy about the whole Will situation.

'Earth to Mum,' Jemma says, dragging me back to the present.

'Sorry Jem, I was just reminiscing about going engagement ring shopping with your dad,' I lie, hoping she won't question the flush of colour that I can feel heating my cheeks. 'I think there's something called a cushion cut, which is less angular at the corners than some of the square shapes,' I'm saying when I'm interrupted by the doorbell.

'I thought you said Callum was playing golf,' Jemma remarks.

'We do get other visitors apart from you and your brother, you know,' I say, smiling at my daughter as I get up from my chair. 'I hadn't realised it was that time already.'

'Sorry. I didn't know you were expecting company. I should have guessed with the house cleaning. You could eat your dinner off the tiles in the hall,' she remarks. 'Shall I leave you in peace?'

'No, of course not. I'd like you to meet my visitor. He was incredibly kind to me on the morning your nana died.'

Jemma looks suitably intrigued as I head out into the hallway, but her expression is quite different when I return a minute or so later carrying a huge bunch of flowers and with Andy in tow. She has the startled look of a rabbit caught in headlights.

'Jemma, this is DS Andy Broadmead and Andy, this is my daughter Jemma,' I say, glancing from one to the other.

My introductions are met with a moment of total silence before Jemma demands, 'What the hell are you doing here?'

'Jemma, that's uncalled for,' I say, shocked at the venom in her voice.

'Your mum invited me,' Andy says simply. He looks surprised rather than shocked to see Jemma.

'So, clearly you two know each other,' I say, stating the obvious in my confusion. 'I had no idea.'

I also have no idea why my daughter has literally sprung to

her feet and is tipping the remainder of her coffee down the sink.

'I'm out of here, Mum,' she says, pushing past me into the hallway and retrieving her faux fur jacket from one of the pegs near the front door. 'Like I said, I'm meeting Will for lunch before we go engagement ring shopping!'

The front door slams so hard that the whole house shakes.

After a moment, Andy says, 'Would you like me to leave?'

'No,' I say in a measured tone. 'I'd like you to explain to me what all that was about.'

By the time Stuart is due home twenty minutes later, I've had the whole story from Andy. It seems that he and Jemma had come across each other on an online dating site after both had gone through horrible break-ups. There was an instant connection when they'd met up in a pub for a lunchtime drink, so much so that they'd decided to extend the meeting to include a mac 'n' cheese lunch. The second and third dates had gone just as well apparently, but then Andy had messaged my daughter to say he couldn't see her any more. Jemma, being Jemma, had demanded a reason, and he'd replied, telling her that his former girlfriend had been in touch to say she was pregnant and that they were going to try and give their relationship another go for the sake of the baby.

Apparently, Jemma hadn't believed him, which doesn't surprise me knowing how my daughter can overreact and jump to conclusions. She was already in a fragile state, so a further rejection wouldn't have gone down well with her. Unlike Jemma, I suspect he was telling her the truth. I remember the expression on his face when he talked about his daughter, whose mum he was estranged from.

'So is the daughter you were seeing on the morning you

were so kind to me the baby that your ex was pregnant with?' I ask.

'Yes. I went back to her because it didn't feel right for her to go through the pregnancy and birth of our baby on her own,' he says.

'That was a brave decision to make, putting other people before yourself,' I say.

He shakes his head.

'It wasn't brave. It was entirely the wrong reason to go back to Laura. We argued all through the pregnancy, even though I tried not to because I was worried it might have a negative effect on our unborn child. If anything, it was cowardly, allowing myself to be bullied by a not very nice person.' He sighs. 'After Mabel was born, Laura became even more unreasonable, barely allowing me to touch the baby and then screaming at me that I did nothing to help. I stuck it for six months, and then I couldn't take any more, so I moved out. After that, she refused to let me see Mabel at all. I've had to go through the family court to get access.'

'Oh, Andy, that's awful,' I say. 'How selfish and cruel to weaponise your little girl to punish you. At least you're seeing her now though, so silver linings and all that.'

'I'm very thankful that attitudes towards absent fathers have changed and that magistrates now seem more aware that a couple splitting up isn't always the fault of the man. But I don't think they've reached the point of awarding full custody to the dad unless there's a very good reason,' he says, sounding resigned to the situation.

'I'm sorry you've had this to deal with, especially while you were still coming to terms with losing your mum,' I say.

'It sounds an awful thing to say, but in a way I'm glad Mum died before all this happened,' Andy admits. 'Laura was fine in the early days of our relationship, and that's all Mum ever knew. She would have been heartbroken by all this.'

The mum in me wants to act as a surrogate and fling my arms around him to comfort him, but I must remember that I'm Jemma's mum, and she was hurt in the fallout of all this. A sudden thought occurs to me.

'Did you know that I was Jemma's mum when you were so kind to me that day? I ask.

'No, it wasn't until I was paying for my coffee that I realised why some of the names and places you mentioned seemed familiar,' he replies. 'You were obviously shocked and distressed, and I just wanted to help, but thinking back over our conversation, I began to wonder if fate had given me a second chance. I really liked Jemma and hated the way I'd ended things. I knew her dad was called Stuart and that he was from the Isle of Skye, which was where his mum still lived, because Jemma and I had got on so well that we'd told each other a potted history of our life stories by the end of the second date. I started to think that maybe yours and my paths had crossed for a reason.'

Beverley's words, *People come into your life for a reason, a season or a lifetime,* flash into my mind.

'I'm in the right line of work to pull a few favours from colleagues, and after some preliminary investigations, I knew that my suspicions had been right, so I wrote the letter. You probably hate me for manipulating the situation in the hope that it might lead me back to Jemma,' he says, looking crestfallen.

He couldn't be further from the mark. Andy had made an immediate impression on me in those few minutes at the service station at Gatwick Airport, and while I'd been surprised to hear from him courtesy of the letter from the funeral director, it had been a happy surprise. It's not that I don't like Will, it's just that I'm not convinced he will make Jemma happy in the long term, and I'm still not sure that what he does on the dark web is morally sound, even if it's not illegal. Something tells me there is a bit more shit to hit the fan surrounding Will's job.

The trouble is, Jemma is stubborn and hates changing her mind once she's arrived at a decision. If Andy's letter had arrived sooner there might have been a slim possibility that she would have given him a chance to explain his actions, but at this moment she is out shopping for an engagement ring with someone else.

'Of course I don't hate you, Andy, but I can't say the same for my daughter. I think that boat has now sailed. A case of unfortunate timing, I'm afraid,' I add.

'Should I leave before your husband gets home?' Andy asks.

'It's too late for that,' I say, hearing the crunch of tyres on our gravel drive. 'But I think we'll keep the fact that you dated and dumped his daughter to ourselves.'

He flinches at my words but doesn't attempt to contradict me. However you dress it up, and whatever his motive, he ended things with our daughter knowing she was in a fragile state following a previous break-up. She'd told me at the time that she thought she'd finally found her 'one', not even telling me his name because she didn't want to jinx it, and then he ended things abruptly, causing her further heartbreak.

I should hate this man for what he did to Jemma, but he thought he was doing the right thing by his daughter, exactly as I'd believed when I'd kept Will's suspected infidelity from *my* daughter.

'In the kitchen, darling,' I call out as the front door closes.

The sound of his golf bag clattering on the hall tiles precedes his appearance at the kitchen door.

'Stuart, this is DS Andy Broadmead, and Andy, this is my husband, Stuart,' I say in almost a carbon copy of my introductions of half an hour ago. It's a relief that this time there is no flicker of recognition in my husband's eyes as he strides across the room, his hand outstretched in greeting.

THIRTY-FIVE

28 NOVEMBER – TUESDAY LUNCHTIME

'Well?' Stuart asks as he hands me my glass of Malbec and sits down in the low armchair across from me next to the roaring log fire in our local pub. 'Are you going to tell me what happened or not?'

I'd rung Stuart the moment I was out of the News 24/7 building and told him to meet me at the pub for lunch. Despite his questions, I hadn't given him any inkling as to what the outcome of my meeting with HR and Jenny was. This one had been even shorter than the meeting last Friday, lasting a total of fifteen minutes. I wanted to tell Stuart about it in person rather than over the phone. He must have realised it was good news from the expression on my face and the spring in my step when I walked into the dimly lit interior from the bright, crisp November day outside.

I raise my glass to chink against his and say, 'Well, the good news is that I still have a job, but with certain provisos.'

It would seem that Stuart either didn't hear or has chosen to ignore the last part of my sentence as relief clearly floods through him and he takes a long drink of his full-bodied red wine. These past ten days have been horrible for me, but it hasn't been a bed of roses for my husband either.

'I'm really pleased for you,' he says. 'They've behaved so badly towards you at a time when you needed their support. If you ask me, they need to take a long hard look at their processes and how they treat loyal members of staff.'

He takes another big swig of wine, making me glad that I told him to walk to the pub. One of us is going to have to moderate our alcohol intake to drive the car home, and there are no prizes for guessing who.

'Hmmm, I don't think they view it like that,' I say. 'Like I said, there are certain provisos. Their priority is to be seen to be doing "the right thing" regardless of the individuals involved.'

'What do you mean?' Stuart asks, lowering his glass.

'Basically, HR had to act on the received complaint because of the email rather than the alleged overheard conversation in the cafeteria. I've had my knuckles firmly rapped for forwarding Jenny's email to Lucy and for the additional comments I made. They've put me on a disciplinary warning, stressing that if anything similar were to happen in the future it could result in dismissal,' I say, raising my eyebrows.

'Are you bloody joking?' Stuart asks.

'Nope, and it gets worse. They want me to write to Summer Palmer, saying that I'm sorry if she thought that anything she'd overheard related to her and to assure her that it didn't.' Stuart goes to comment, but I hold my hand up to stop him. 'They've also asked me to agree to a face-to-face meeting with Summer and someone from HR to discuss how our working relationship can be improved upon moving forward.'

Stuart's jaw has dropped open. He looks totally aghast at what he is hearing.

'Are they having a bloody laugh? Honestly, I'll fully support your decision if you tell them to shove their provisos up their corporate arses,' Stuart says in a raised voice.

'Sshhh,' I say. 'You'll get us thrown out.'

I raise my glass and smile sweetly at the woman behind the bar who is looking nervously over in our direction. She appears very young, nineteen or twenty is my best guess, and is clearly anxious that the raised voices might be some kind of argument that could escalate. I indicate Stuart's glass and hold up one finger, hoping that she's recognised that I'm asking for a refill for my husband. It takes a moment for the penny to drop and then she gives me the thumbs up and turns to take a wine glass down from the shelf behind her.

'How are you taking this so calmly?' Stuart hisses.

I shrug.

'I can write Summer a nice email and even have a face-to-face meeting with her. Words are just words. They mean nothing. At the moment, the priority is to hang on to my job whatever that might take, and besides, there's more,' I say.

'I don't think I can take any more. I bet you wouldn't have handled this so well if you hadn't been having the sessions with Beverley. Maybe you should book some for me.'

'It's unethical for them to see two members of the same family at the same time unless it's couples' counselling, apparently,' I say. 'So, hands off Beverley, my need is greater than yours!'

Stuart raises his hands in a gesture of surrender, almost knocking his fresh glass of wine out of the barmaid's hand as she arrives at our table.

'Sorry,' he says. 'I didn't see you there.'

'No problem, sir,' she replies, picking up the empty glass from the low table and replacing it with the fresh one. 'Shall I add it to your tab?'

'Yes, thanks,' Stuart replies.

Once she's out of earshot, I continue.

'Anyway, the "more" I referred to is the reason I've accepted their proposals. They admitted that their policy surrounding paid time off only for biological family members was flawed. They agreed that they should consider requests on an individual basis rather than have a blanket policy. They also said I should have been treated with more empathy and understanding.'

'No shit Sherlock,' Stuart chimes in.

'Unfortunately, their decision regarding non-familial compassionate leave can't be altered retrospectively, but lessons have been learned if a similar situation were to arise in the future,' I announce.

'So, like always, you've had to go through all this to make things better for other people in the future while not benefitting yourself,' Stuart says.

'But I have benefitted, Stuart, I've won,' I say, smiling broadly. 'They are going to have to pay me for the days when they decided not to roster me, today included. Instead of being stuck in a stuffy gallery for hours on end, I'm out having a boozy lunch with my husband on their time. Not to mention all the sick leave days. It's like a period of extended leave but without losing any money.'

'I suppose,' Stuart grudgingly accepts.

'What time did you book our table for? I couldn't face breakfast this morning and now I'm absolutely starving.'

'Half past twelve, like you said,' Stuart replies.

'Good,' I say, draining my glass and standing up. 'I'm going to make the most of my last day of freedom. I'm certainly not looking forward to a five-thirty alarm in the morning,' I say, shuddering.

'You're working tomorrow?' he asks.

'Yes. Remember I told you that Jenny asked at the meeting on Friday if I was well enough to work if the internal investigation went my way? When I mentioned it to Beverley on Friday evening, she said it would be better for my mental health to return to work asap.'

'She's probably right. You thrive on working hard. Goodness only knows what you'll be like when it's eventually time for you to retire,' he says, draining his second glass of Malbec before following me over to the entrance of the dining area, where we wait to be seated.

'You know, I've never minded the early shift in the summer,' I say. 'Waking up as dawn breaks makes you feel as though you're not missing a moment of the day. But these dark winter mornings are a whole other ball game,' I add, faking a shiver.

My husband slips one arm around my shoulders and, with his free hand, raises my chin to kiss me on the lips.

'What's that for?' I ask.

'Because I love you,' he replies simply.

Lunch is delicious, as it always is at The Three Crowns. I had battered halloumi with chunky chips and peas, and Stuart indulged in a dirty burger, the pub's speciality. We considered a dessert because they do an amazing sticky toffee pudding served with Madagascan vanilla ice cream, but in the end, we were both too stuffed to even share one.

As we're waiting for the bill, Stuart reaches across the table for my hand.

'I need to tell you something, Lexi,' he says. 'Don't worry, it's nothing bad,' he adds, clearly reacting to the look of mild panic on my face. 'It's about what Mari said to you re: Mum not enjoying her Christmases at our house.'

'You're not going to tell me it's true, are you?' I say, getting a sinking feeling.

'Not exactly, but there was an element of truth to it that I didn't want to burden you with while the whole investigation thing was going on at News 24/7. The thing is, Mum had already started to dread the journey down south before the pandemic, and the Christmas she spent on her own during lockdown wasn't as bad as she'd feared it might be. The following year, she asked if I would mind terribly if she didn't come to ours, and I told her I thought it would upset you because you loved our big family Christmas.'

It's funny that Stuart should have said that to his mum. There's no denying that I've loved entertaining everyone at our house since the children were born, but it's exhausting. I've sometimes wished for a year off to enjoy a quiet Christmas with just the two of us. Even during the lockdown year, we had Jemma and Will staying at ours because they weren't living together at that point and couldn't agree on whose flat to stay in. The idea of a lazy morning in bed before sloping downstairs in our dressing gowns and enjoying a leisurely breakfast is quite appealing, especially as I work either Christmas or New Year on alternate years. Fewer people would mean a small turkey crown rather than a whole bird, which in turn would take less time to cook and no hours spent peeling potatoes and prepping four different types of vegetables, just a few carrots and Brussels sprouts.

'You should have asked me, Stuart. You might have been surprised at the answer,' I say quietly.

'Really?' he asks. 'I thought you loved having our mums and the big family get-together.'

'I do. But I guess what I'm saying is that I wouldn't mind having a quieter one at some point.'

'Did you ever say anything to Mum?' he asks.

'Of course not. I never wanted either of our mums to feel like they were a burden, especially once they were widowed.'

'But you were so upset when Mari told you what Eva had said to her,' Stuart recalls.

'I think I was more upset because she told Mari rather than talking it over with us. And then doubly upset because your sister chose to put such a negative spin on it. I can see now that

Mari only told me to assuage her own feelings of guilt for never seeing Eva at Christmas once she'd emigrated to Canada.'

'Beverley?' Stuart asks.

I nod. Beverley is single-handedly the best thing to come out of the whole episode with News 24/7. I would never have considered going to see a therapist if I hadn't felt backed into a corner. I now can't imagine my life without her in it.

'She also said that we shouldn't hold it against Mari and should try and build bridges for Fleur's sake.'

Stuart looks at me intently for a few seconds.

'You told Beverley about Fleur's dad, didn't you?'

There is no accusation, merely a question.

'Yes, I did. I've lost a bit of confidence in my own decision-making, and I just wanted to be sure that we are doing the right thing in not telling her.'

'And?'

'And she thinks the same as we do. It's not our place to tell Fleur. It would have to come from Mari if, or hopefully when, she is ready to tell her daughter the truth. Are you angry with me for telling Beverley?' I ask.

'No,' Stuart says shaking his head as the waiter comes towards us with the bill and the card reader machine. 'Just pleased that you have someone other than me that you can talk to completely openly without fear of judgement.'

THIRTY-SIX
29 NOVEMBER – WEDNESDAY AFTERNOON

There is a small part of me that is regretting agreeing to meet up with Lucy for a coffee after my first day back on shift for almost a month, but she seemed quite insistent, and I felt as though I owed her. They will have interviewed her about the email and the overheard conversation, and Lucy will have fought my corner.

I suppress a yawn. I'd forgotten how exhausting being in the gallery is, which is compounded by my early start. Despite going to bed at 10 p.m. because my alarm was set for 5.30 a.m., I only managed two or three hours' sleep as I was afraid of sleeping through the alarm and being late on my first day back. I'm already on a warning; it wouldn't do to get fired before my feet are back under the editor's desk.

'Here you go,' Lucy says, placing a frothy cappuccino on the stripped pine table.

We've come to Lucca's, which is a fifteen-minute walk from the studios, because it has only ten tables in the whole place, all of which are visible to each other from wherever you are sitting. There is no way that any conversation we may have could be accidentally overheard, and Lucca's English consists mostly of the items and prices on the menu board behind the counter.

'Thanks Lucy,' I say, noting the chocolate heart decoration on top of the froth and flashing a big smile in Lucca's direction.

'So, how did it feel to be back driving the show?' she asks, taking a sip of her frothy mochaccino and in the process giving herself a white moustache.

'Surprisingly enjoyable,' I admit. 'Even the horrific subject matter of some of the news stories couldn't dampen my mood. I guess I'm a closet workaholic, if truth be told. Stuart's right to be concerned about how I'll keep myself busy when I eventually retire.'

'Did anyone ask you why you'd been off?' Lucy asks, taking another sip of her drink and adding to the froth on her top lip before realising it is there and running her tongue over it. 'You wouldn't have let me leave with a moustache, would you?'

'Course not, I've got your back, just as you've had mine throughout this debacle. And to answer your first question, I think people just assumed it was a delayed reaction to Eva dying, which in a way it was,' I say.

'I'm sorry I couldn't warn you about what was going on,' she says, placing her oversized cup down on the saucer and picking up the biscotti. 'Obviously, I knew they were investigating you because they questioned me about the email, but I was forbidden from contacting you or I risked being fired. Honestly, Lexi, what were you thinking sending an email rather than a WhatsApp? Thank God you didn't mention *you know who* by name,' she says, holding up the biscotti she has just taken a bite from and her fingers to create the speech marks. 'If you had, it could have been a very different outcome.'

'I know,' I say, reaching over to put my biscuit in her saucer. 'You can have mine too. Stuart's cooking me gnocchi tonight and I don't want to spoil it.'

'Ooooh. Stuart's cooking me gnocchi,' she mimics. 'While

I'm going home to chicken tikka masala served fresh from the microwave. I hope you're aware of just how lucky you are,' she adds.

'Oh yes.' I smile. 'Do you know who else they interviewed?'

'No one said anything to me, but that could have been because we are sworn to secrecy on stuff like this. Mind you, something usually leaks out, but I didn't hear any whispers, just a few people asking me if you were feeling better, and when you would be back at work. I think the assumption was that you were off sick.'

'It's a wonder that Summer didn't accidentally let it slip to her friends,' I say.

'Well, to be honest, she's not very well-liked among the production crew, and I think I've discovered why,' she says, tapping the side of her nose with her index finger. 'That's why I wanted to catch up with you tonight.'

'What do you mean?' I ask.

'Well, I decided to do some digging when this all kicked off, and I've found out something very interesting about Summer Palmer.'

Lucy has my full attention now.

'You'll never guess who her dad is,' she continues.

I pucker my brow, trying to think of someone with the surname Palmer, but I'm drawing a blank.

'Who?' I eventually concede.

'Barry Laurence,' she announces.

'As in *the* Barry Laurence, our major shareholder?' I say, completely shocked.

'Yep,' she replies. 'No wonder they agreed to take this complaint so seriously. Money talks! Summer must have gone to Daddy with a sob story, and he's backed her up and demanded an investigation.'

'Oh my God,' I eventually say, after momentarily being stunned into silence. 'It's all slotting into place now, including her being promoted ahead of better candidates for the floor manager position. Nepotism is alive and kicking, and none of us knew because she uses a different surname.'

'It's her mum's maiden name apparently. She reverted to it when her parents got divorced, and Summer dropped the second half of the double-barrelled name because she said it was too much of a mouthful.'

'Or because she didn't want people to know that her meteoric rise was less about ability and more about connections after her dad bought the majority shareholding,' I say, unable to keep the scepticism from my voice. 'Come to think of it, she started at News 24/7 shortly after, and she's American. How did none of us put two and two together?'

'A proper case of who you know rather than what you know,' Lucy agrees.

'Part of me wishes I'd known this before my meetings with HR, but I guess if I had, I would probably have ended up getting myself fired by levelling accusations at them caring more about money than people. Wow... just wow! I wonder if he's aware that I'm back at work,' I muse. 'It's going to be interesting doing my first shift with Summer.'

'You don't know, do you?' Lucy says.

'Know what?' I ask.

'Check your emails,' she says.

I reach into my cavernous slouchy handbag for my iPad. There are two new emails which must have landed moments after I sent my shift report and headed out of the building for this catch-up with Lucy. The top one is from Jenny. I click on it, scan through it quickly and then say to Lucy, 'Listen to this.'

Dear Alexis,

By now you might be aware that Barry Laurence is Summer Palmer's father. I knew, but it wasn't common knowledge.

Yesterday, after learning the outcome of our investigation into you, he threatened to sell his shares, which could have destabilised the channel unless we reversed our decision and fired you.

This went to the very top. While you were in the gallery this morning, our CEO was on a conference call with Barry Laurence, who was quite belligerent and simply would not accept the findings of the investigation.

To cut a long story short, our CEO stood her ground and said that she refused to be bullied into making the wrong decision and that if he was unprepared to accept the findings of our internal process, he must do as he saw fit with his shares. He told her to 'f*** off' and exited the call!

For what it's worth, I was never in favour of removing you from the roster or proceeding with this investigation. I tried to talk HR into allowing me to deal with it in my own way, but they said it had gone beyond that because Summer had gone above my head and reported the issue to them directly. My hands have been tied throughout, and I'm so sorry for the additional anguish this must have caused you, on top of the recent loss of your mother-in-law. I hope you will accept my apology.

'Bloody hell,' Lucy says. 'What a turnaround.'
'There's more,' I say.

There will be no need to write a letter of apology to Summer or arrange a suitable time for a face-to-face meeting. I have this afternoon been informed by HR that she has handed in her resignation, which they've accepted without her being required to work the normal notice period.

We do value you, Lexi, and I hope the decisions taken today illustrate that.

Jenny

I'm speechless.

'Could you forward me Jenny's email?' Lucy says.

I'm about to reply when I realise that she's teasing me.

'Only joking,' she says. 'There's also an email from HR informing relevant departments that Summer has left the company with immediate effect.'

I click on the other email, and as Lucy has said, it's just a one-line statement with no reason given.

'Wow,' I say.

'Good riddance to Summer Palmer, the lazy, self-opinionated, entitled snowflake personified,' she says raising her cup to chink against mine.

It's not quite the same as champagne glasses, but it feels right to toast the sentiment, even though it's with the remnants of our frothy drinks.

THIRTY-SEVEN

30 NOVEMBER – THURSDAY EVENING

I was looking forward to my session with Beverley this evening. I could hardly wait to get through the door to tell her all about the latest developments at News 24/7. She sat and listened without comment until I told her that our CEO had refused to give in to a bully.

'We need more company bosses like that,' she observed.

'To be honest, you could have knocked me over with a feather when I read Jenny's email,' I say. 'I thought they were using this whole investigation as a way to get rid of me because of all the cost-cutting measures, but it turns out that it couldn't be further from the truth.'

'I'm really pleased for you, Lexi. You've had one hell of a time over the past couple of years. I hope this marks the start of an easier period for you.'

'I hope so too,' I say. 'We just need to get Eva's house on the market and that will be something else ticked off the list.'

'Can I ask you something?' Beverley says.

'Of course,' I reply.

'Why are you selling Eva's house?'

'Because Eva left it to Stuart and Mari jointly and she's

pressing for her half of the money. We don't have that sort of cash lying around, so we don't have any choice.'

'But would I be right in thinking that both you and Stuart love that house?' she persists.

'Well, yes, but I don't see what that has to do with anything. We can't afford to keep it as a holiday home, if that's what you're suggesting,' I say.

'Actually, that wasn't what I was thinking,' she says. 'You told me that you'd really like to retire from your high-pressure job at News 24/7 and spend some quality time with Stuart, but you can't afford to because you've still got a chunk to pay on your mortgage. Why not sell your house down here, pay off Mari and your mortgage and move into Eva's house on Skye?'

For a moment, I picture myself gazing out of the kitchen window down the fields to the sea beyond, the Scottish mainland in the distance. I've always wanted to live in a house with an uninterrupted sea view, but that would be way beyond anything Stuart and I could afford in somewhere like Devon or Cornwall. Would it be possible to up sticks and move so far away? The dream disappears and I come crashing back to reality.

'Even if I did take early retirement, which I must admit is very appealing after all I've just been through at work, Skye is too far away from my family. Callum and Ellie are expecting their first baby, and I'd hate to be so far away that I had hardly any contact with my grandchild. I want to be around for babysitting duties if asked. It would be the reverse of Eva and Mari's situation but with the same outcome. Then there's Jemma and Will. They're about to get engaged, followed by a wedding and hopefully more grandchildren. And of course there's my mum to consider. Who would look after Mum if Stuart and I just upped sticks and moved. No,' I say, shaking my head. 'There are just too many obstacles in the way to make it viable, however much we love Eva's house.'

I can feel Beverley's steady gaze, but she doesn't speak. It's as though she is waiting for me to reassess the situation through different eyes.

'I know what you're thinking,' I say eventually. 'You think I'm putting other people's needs ahead of my own, but I'm not really.'

'Aren't you?' she gently probes. 'Granted, the Isle of Skye is a long way from Berkshire, but if you and Stuart are both retired, you'd be able to visit frequently, and as you know from your own children, Skye is a lovely, unspoilt place for grandchildren to spend holidays with their grandparents. Yes, it would be different from the relationship you think you want with your grandkids, but it might end up making you feel less taken for granted.'

'Even if that could work, you're forgetting my mum,' I say.

'And you're forgetting that you have a sister who is several years younger than you and who hasn't really done her fair share of caring,' Beverley points out. 'Or another solution would be to have your mum come and live with you. Didn't you say that Eva's house was huge? You could perhaps convert part of it into a granny annexe so that she's living independently but with you a couple of minutes away in an emergency.'

'No, I can't see that working,' I say, shaking my head.

The trouble is, Beverley has planted a seed. Could it work?

'It should be your time now, Lexi. You've put other people first all your life. Isn't it time to start looking after number one?' she says. 'And speaking of time, we've run out again, I'm afraid.'

'Really? I swear the clock goes faster the moment I'm through your front door,' I say, reaching for my faux fur jacket.

'What are your plans now that everything is back on track for you?' Beverley asks.

'As in?'

'Well, do you want to keep seeing me or shall we call today the last session?'

'To be honest, I haven't given it much thought. I just assumed I'd continue coming until the sessions News 24/7's insurers are happy to pay for run out.'

'Well, you've only had four so far, and the allocation is usually ten, which some insurers will extend to a further ten if the therapist recommends it, so we can certainly carry on for the foreseeable future if that's what you'd like,' Beverley says.

'Definitely,' I reply. 'I honestly don't know what I would have done without you in the first couple of sessions. Just being able to talk without inhibition to someone who was non-judgemental lifted an almighty weight from my shoulders. Thank you so much, Beverley,' I say.

We're at her front door, and I realise once again that Carlton didn't bark on my arrival, and he isn't barking now.

'Carlton seems to have got used to me,' I say.

'He's not living with me any more. He's gone to live with my husband now that he and his new girlfriend have got a place together. It was only ever temporary,' she says, smiling as she opens the front door.

And that's when I see the *For Sale* board. I'd been so wrapped up in my own problems that I hadn't noticed it before. I turn back to look at her, and she shrugs.

'A reason, a season or a lifetime. It's just the way it is.'

'I'm sorry,' I say.

'Don't be. I've wanted to move back to Saltburn for a long time, and soon I'll have the opportunity.'

'Is it selfish of me to hope that your house doesn't sell too quickly?' I say, taking her by surprise by flinging my arms around her in a hug.

She allows the moment and then frees herself.

'It's your turn to be selfish now,' she says.

. . .

Walking away from Beverley, down the driveway of her cosy house which won't be her home for much longer, I feel sadness. Even those who appear to have all the answers are deep down just like the rest of us. We're all trying to navigate what life throws at us.

I slip behind the steering wheel and fasten the seatbelt with a firm click. If Beverley can move on from the past, so can I. With a sense of calm I don't think I possessed before my sessions with Beverley, I feel ready to face the next chapter of my life, whatever that might be.

EPILOGUE
23 DECEMBER 2024

I'm standing back admiring my handiwork when I feel Stuart's arms pull me into an embrace, the soft bristles on his chin brushing the back of my neck as he kisses it.

'I think it's the nicest Christmas tree we've ever had,' I say. 'Perfectly proportioned and the most gorgeous natural aroma.'

'Exactly like my beautiful wife,' Stuart says.

'Have you been at the mulled wine?' I tease.

'Someone had to sample it to make sure it was good enough to offer to our guests. Speaking of whom, what time are we expecting the first arrivals?'

'Callum and Ellie said they would probably get here around four so that they can feed and bath Evie at her normal time without upsetting her routine,' I reply.

Our first grandchild, christened Eva, although we all call her Evie, arrived in March weighing a very respectable 8 lbs and 10 ozs. I'm not sure I'll ever truly be able to express the feelings of relief and adoration that collided in my heart as I held her in my arms around four hours after she made her entrance into the world. She had a mass of dark hair, exactly like Callum's, and inky blue eyes. It really was love at first sight, and we've been besotted with her ever since. She isn't quite walking yet, but she does haul herself up by holding onto furniture and taking a few steps sideways before sinking back down onto her nappy-padded bottom. She has slept through most nights from the age of ten weeks without the need for the midnight car journeys that we experienced with both of our children. I don't know why we're all surprised that she is such a contented baby. Research suggests that a baby picks up on the mother's moods, and in that respect, she couldn't have had a better start.

'What about Jemma?' Stuart asks. 'Did she give an ETA, or do we just expect her when we see her with her mystery guest?'

Things hadn't gone to plan for our younger child. She and Will went engagement ring shopping, and she chose an exquisite cushion-cut solitaire set on a platinum band which Will said he would go back and buy later. He'd gone down on one knee to propose to Jemma when everyone was gathered at our house on Christmas Eve last year. We were all standing with our champagne flutes, ready to toast the happy couple, but Jemma stunned us all by turning him down. I've never heard such an awkward silence.

Initially, I felt quite sorry for Will, but as her mum, I think it was the right decision for them both, especially when Jemma told me that the ring he proffered wasn't the one she had chosen. That's when the truth was finally revealed about his job. Along with priceless art, wine and original manuscripts, HvC was also trading in so-called 'blood diamonds' on the dark web. It transpired that he'd had a ring made in a similar design to the one Jemma had chosen but at a fraction of the cost. Unsurprisingly, Jemma broke things off immediately and was back living under our roof for a few months until their house sale went through. She wasn't devastated, merely disappointed that she had invested so much of her time in someone who couldn't be trusted to be honest with her and didn't have the moral compass to recognise that trading blood diamonds was wrong, quite apart from presenting one to his future wife in an engagement ring.

Apparently, Will started seeing someone else within a few weeks of the split, but Jemma was single the whole time she was living with us. It would appear she is now seeing someone though, as she asked if it would be alright for her to bring a guest. We could hardly say no.

I'm fervently hoping that this Christmas will be less dramatic than Christmas 2023. It was our first one without Eva, but we did as Mum had suggested and draped Eva's favourite Christmas jumper over the back of a dining chair and laid a place for her at the table with a lavender-scented candle burning on her place mat. We all raised a toast to her before pulling our crackers. Surprisingly, having Juliet and Heather at ours for the first time lightened the mood considerably. It turns out my sister is an absolute whizz at charades, and Heather makes amazing cocktails. We enjoyed their company so much that we invited them again this year and they accepted. They volunteered to bring Mum too, which is a relief, as we won't have to go and fetch her.

I'm suddenly aware of Wilfie brushing against my legs. He does it sometimes when Stuart and I embrace, almost as though he's jealous of my husband showing me affection.

'Guess who's coming to stay for a few days, Wilfie,' I say bending down to stroke his silky fur. 'Baba. You like baba, don't you?'

'He's so good with Evie,' Stuart says.

'Yes, he is. But to be fair, she seems to know the word gentle when she touches him.'

'I'd better fetch some more logs in,' Stuart says. 'The weather forecast is predicting snow. Are you coming, Wilfie?'

'I'm so glad we decided to start letting him go outside when we moved here,' I say. 'It's given him a whole new lease of life, and we don't have to worry about him being knocked down.'

Wilfie saunters out of the room behind Stuart, and I reach into Eva's box of decorations for another exquisite bauble. It's sad to think that for all the years she came to our house for Christmas, these gorgeous adornments stayed wrapped in tissue paper in a box in the attic. I'm not a hundred per cent sure, but I think I caught Stuart wiping a tear from his eye when I lifted the lid of the box marked *Christmas Baubles* in Eva's distinctive handwriting and inside were two smaller boxes, one marked *Stuart* and the other, *Mari*. He'd opened his box to find the decorations he'd been allowed to choose, one each year from the age of two. They'll be on display every year from now on.

We'd Facetimed Mari to tell her about the discovery, asking if she'd like us to send her box of baubles over to Canada for her to decorate her tree next year. The start of her response had not surprised me. 'No, don't bother,' she'd said. I'd shot Stuart a sideways glance, as if to say, *I told you so,* before she added, 'Fleur and I have been talking, and we wondered if you might extend the invitation to include us for Christmas next year?'

If there had been a feather handy, Stuart would have been able to knock me over with it. By next year we will have been up and running as a bed and breakfast for six months, if all the renovations are finished on time, so there will be plenty of room for Mari and Fleur, their respective partners and Fleur's two boys. Callum did as he said he would and continued to exchange emails with Fleur, along with photographs, especially after Evie was born. He has played a huge part in trying to bring us all closer again as a family.

I'm just storing the decorations box in one of the cavernous cupboards under the stairs, which will be converted to a downstairs loo in the coming months, when the sound of metal on metal indicates that our gate is opening to admit the first of our guests. My heart flutters with excitement.

The drive from Fort William obviously hasn't taken Callum and Ellie as long as it sometimes does. Since selling up and moving from their two-up, two-down in Bracknell in July so that they could be closer to us and Ellie's parents, who live in Glasgow, they've been to visit us several times already.

It's not exactly close to either set of grandparents, but closer than it would have been if they'd stayed in Berkshire, and Callum is enjoying working from home as a recruitment consultant, a business he's been able to set up with some money we gave him following the sale of our house.

It had sold to the first people who had come to view before it had officially gone on the market. They loved it as much as Stuart had when he first laid eyes on it, which makes me happy as it was a lovely family home. I'll miss the house, but the location pales into insignificance. The satisfaction of handing my notice in at work after all they subjected me to at a time when I needed their support will live in my heart forever. Despite Stuart's concerns, I'm enjoying my early retirement from my pressurised job at News 24/7, although a lady of leisure, I'm not. Stuart and I are doing as much of the renovation as we can to keep costs down, and once we have paying guests, it will be pressure of a different kind if we're as busy as Shona has suggested we will be. At least we'll have her to help with the laundry and cleaning rather than having to advertise.

I can hear car doors opening and closing. On my way to the front door, I pop my head into the old library to make sure that the radiator is working effectively in there. We've converted it into a bedroom for Mum to save her having to go up and down the stairs while she's here. The offer is there for us to install an adjoining bathroom for her if she changes her mind about moving up here permanently. In the meantime, she'll have to make do with a flannel wash in the little loo off the scullery. It was a relief to discover that the wall-mounted electric bar heater over the basin was safe to use with its pullcord; otherwise, we'd have had to have a rethink. Her room is toasty warm, and I pull the door closed so as not to allow in the cold air from outside.

I can see two shadowy outlines through the frosted glass as I fling the door open.

'Hello, you two—' I start to say before catching my breath.

It isn't Callum and Ellie. Jemma has beaten her brother to be the first to arrive for our Drummond family gathering in our new home, and at her side is her surprise guest.

'Hello Lexi. Thanks for allowing me to come for Christmas,' Andy says.

Jemma's eyes are sparkling as she looks from me to Andy before reaching for his hand. I have never seen my daughter so happy. Something tells me there could be another Christmas proposal on the cards for Jemma, and this time, I'm pretty sure she'll say yes.

A LETTER FROM JULIA

Dear reader,

Thank you so much for choosing to read *Just Like Her Mother*. If you enjoyed it and want to keep up to date with all my latest releases or check out my back catalogue please sign up at the following link. Your email address will never be shared and you can unsubscribe at any time.

www.bookouture.com/julia-roberts

Like most authors, I'm often asked about the inspiration for my latest book. On this occasion, I can honestly say that Lexi's set of circumstances, caring for elderly parents and being there for her own children while still working herself was very loosely based on my own life experience. Often called the 'sandwich' generation, more and more of us find ourselves in this situation as people are living longer and it's never easy, particularly if geographical distance enters the equation.

In *Just Like Her Mother*, Stuart's mum, Eva lives on the Isle of Skye and that was inspired by my own parents moving there in the 1970s, although they had a crofter's cottage rather than a seven-bedroom house. The view I describe from Eva's kitchen window, over the fields and down to the sea with the Scottish mainland in the distance, was the view from my parents' kitchen window, a kitchen that my dad built and is still standing today. I have in fact considered going back to stay in the cottage as it is now available as a holiday let – Rowan Cottage, near Culnacnoc if anyone is interested.

There are a few 'real life' moments in *Just Like Her Mother*. Eva dying, holding the hands of her grandchildren, Callum and Jemma while Lexi and Stuart were away on holiday is not dissimilar to what happened with my mother-in-law, Audrey whose middle name was Eva. It took me a long time to get past the guilt I felt that our children were placed in that position.

I've also drawn on my own life experience for the many Christmases that Eva and Joan spent with Lexi and Stuart's family. Originally, it was a round trip to Lincolnshire to collect Audrey followed by Nottinghamshire for my mum, Josie, but as they both got older and frailer it became two separate trips from our home in Berkshire. The Christmas after we lost Audrey, my mum did come and it was her suggestion to light a candle and place Audrey's favourite jumper over the back of the chair where we had laid a place for her, as Joan does in *Just Like Her Mother*.

We also have a black cat called Wilfie! If you are a cat parent, I'm sure you will recognise many of the things I've described. Wilfie knows when I'm upset and will sit on my chest with his nose inches from mine. The vibrations created by his purring are very soothing and calming which I've needed recently following my mum's death at the grand old age of ninety-eight. She had been urging me to hurry up and finish *Just Like Her Mother* as she has always read my books. Sadly, I didn't type quick enough.

The other similarity with my own life is being fortunate enough to find your soulmate in the great metropolis of London, as Lexi does. Chris and I met when he was playing in a band in a night-club in Streatham – that was forty-seven years ago. I'm not going to lie and say there is never a cross word between us, and the occasional shout up but, just like Stuart and Lexi, we weather our storms together.

I hope you loved Just Like Her Mother. If you did, I'd be most grateful if you would take a few minutes to write a review. Not only is your feedback important to me, it can make a real difference in helping new readers discover my books for the first time.

I love hearing from my readers – you can get in touch on my Facebook page, through X, Instagram, Goodreads or my website.

Julia Roberts

www.juliarobertsauthor.com

facebook.com/JuliaRobertsTV
x.com/JuliaRobertsTV
instagram.com/juliagroberts

ACKNOWLEDGEMENTS

This is where I say a huge thank you to all the members of 'Team Julia' for their work on *Just Like Her Mother*.

This is my second book with my editor, Ruth Jones and I must say there has been an even greater understanding between us with this one. The relationship with your editor does grows closer with every book so I'm quite sad that Ruth is moving on to pastures new after us only having two books together. But at least we got to work on *Just Like Her Mother* and her input in the early editing stages was invaluable. I have faith in Bookouture that my next partnering with a new editor will be as successful and pleasurable.

My copy editor for *Just Like Her Mother* was Helen Hawkins. It's so interesting when someone other than your editor sees your book for the first time and makes suggestions for small changes or notices something that requires more explanation. The standout for me on this round of edits was Helen querying what I meant by a 'shout up'. Did I mean 'shout out'? It wasn't something she recognised, and she is probably not alone as it might only be something that would be said by a member of the older generation, which both Lexi and her therapist Beverley are. To be honest, I didn't know the origins of the expression, but it was comprehensively explained by Lynne Walker who was my proofreader on this book.

It's the first time I've worked with Lynne Walker and although, just like your children you shouldn't have favourites, she and I were on the same wavelength... most of the time.

There was a question about Wilfie the cat licking his fur after being treated to butter. Lynne commented that it sounded as though Wilfie was spreading it all over his fur rather than licking it off and did I want to change it? No, my experience as a cat mum several times over is that cats groom themselves with the residue left on their tongues. My favourite comment from Lynne though must be this, 'Joan is so well-written and observed.' It gave me a warm fuzzy feeling so thank you Lynne.

Covers and book titles are the hook that draw readers in, and I must say I absolutely LOVE this title which perfectly describes this book. The title was revealed to me on the day my own mum died, 30 January 2025 and it made me catch my breath. I have dedicated this book to Mum and also to my mum-in-law Audrey. I think we all have elements of our mothers in us and in *Just Like Her Mother* it applies to Lexi and her daughter Jemma, Lexi and her mother Joan and even, to a degree, Eva and her daughter Mari. I'm proud to say that I have elements of my mum in me in our love of cats, dancing and gardening.

All of the characters in *Just Like Her Mother* were a joy to write and I might possibly have been influenced by my own daughter for some of Jemma's traits. She always asks before she starts reading my latest book, 'Who am I in this one?' There is often a touch of both my children when I'm writing twenty-or-thirty-somethings although only in character traits rather than plot lines. So, a big thank you to my family not only for their continued belief and support but also for providing me with character inspiration.

There are two more family members to mention. Thank you, Chris, for being the wind beneath my wings and for providing me with hot drinks and snacks when I'm glued to my writing desk. And apologies that once again some of our holiday last October was taken up with me tapping away on the computer keys. The other family member who deserves a fanfare is our cat Wilfie. What would I do without the comfort he brings me? Although I could do without him parading back and forth across my computer keyboard while I'm trying to write!

Everyone in the PR, publicity and marketing team at Bookouture have my eternal thanks as I understand so little of what goes on behind the scenes to help my books to fly. Please know that you are all so appreciated, but a special mention goes to Sarah Hardy for the work she puts in to organising blog tours and making suggestions on how best to spread the word prior to and post publication.

Which leads me to my final thank you, and as ever it is to you for choosing to read *Just Like Her Mother*. I truly hope you've enjoyed reading.

PUBLISHING TEAM

Turning a manuscript into a book requires the efforts of many people. The publishing team at Bookouture would like to acknowledge everyone who contributed to this publication.

Audio
Alba Proko
Melissa Tran
Sinead O'Connor

Commercial
Lauren Morrissette
Hannah Richmond
Imogen Allport

Cover design
Emma Graves

Data and analysis
Mark Alder
Mohamed Bussuri

Editorial
Ruth Jones
Lizzie Brien

Copyeditor
Helen Hawkins

Proofreader
Lynne Walker

Marketing
Alex Crow
Melanie Price
Occy Carr
Cíara Rosney
Martyna Młynarska

Operations and distribution
Marina Valles
Stephanie Straub
Joe Morris

Production
Hannah Snetsinger
Mandy Kullar
Ria Clare
Nadia Michael

Publicity
Kim Nash
Noelle Holten
Jess Readett
Sarah Hardy

Rights and contracts
Peta Nightingale
Richard King
Saidah Graham

Printed in Dunstable, United Kingdom